The Collected Supernatural and Weird Fiction of W. C. Morrow

The Collected Supernatural and Weird Fiction of W. C. Morrow

Eighteen Short Stories of the Strange and Unusual Including 'The Haunted Burglar,' 'The Gloomy Shadow,' 'The Haunted Automaton,' 'The Woman of the Inner Room' and Many Others

W. C. Morrow

LEONAUR

The Collected
Supernatural and Weird
Fiction of
W. C. Morrow
Eighteen Short Stories of the Strange and Unusual Including Eighteen Short Stories of
the Strange and Unusual Including 'The Haunted Burglar,' 'The Gloomy Shadow,' 'The
Haunted Automaton,' 'The Woman of the Inner Room' and Many Others
by W. C. Morrow

FIRST EDITION

Leonaur is an imprint of Oakpast Ltd

ISBN: 978-1-78282-006-2 (hardcover)
ISBN: 978-1-78282-007-9 (softcover)

http://www.leonaur.com

Contents

The Resurrection of Little Wang Tai   7

The Hero of the Plague   16

His Unconquerable Enemy   31

The Permanent Stiletto   42

Over an Absinthe Bottle   56

The Inmate of the Dungeon   67

A Game of Honour   81

Treacherous Velasco   89

An Uncommon View of It   101

A Story Told by the Sea   113

The Monster-Maker   128

An Original Revenge   147

Two Singular Men   153

The Faithful Amulet   164

The Gloomy Shadow   174

The Haunted Automaton   183

The Haunted Burglar   197

The Woman of the Inner Room   203

The Resurrection of Little Wang Tai

(A story from *The Ape, the Idiot & Other People*)

A train of circus-wagons, strung along a dusty road, in the Santa Clara Valley, crept slowly under the beating heat of a July sun. The dust rolled in clouds over the gaudy wagons of the menagerie. The outer doors of the cages had been opened to give access of air to the panting animals, but with the air came the dust, and the dust annoyed Romulus greatly. Never before had he longed for freedom so intensely. Ever since he could remember he had been in a cage like this; it had been so all through his childhood and youth. There was no trace in his memory of days when he of a time had been free. Not the faintest recollection existed of the time when he might have swung in the branches of equatorial forests. To him life was a desolation and a despair, and the poignancy of it all was sharpened by the clouds of dust which rolled through the grated door.

Romulus, thereupon, sought means of escape. Nimble, deft, sharp-sighted, he found a weak place in his prison, worked it open, and leaped forth upon the highway a free anthropoid ape. None of the sleepy, weary drivers noticed his escape, and a proper sense of caution caused him to seek security under a way-side shrub until the procession had safely passed. Then the whole world lay before him.

His freedom was large and sweet, but, for a while, perplexing. An almost instinctive leap to catch the trapeze-bar that had hung in his cage brought his hands in contact with only unresisting air. This confused and somewhat frightened him. The world seemed much broader and brighter since the black bars of his prison no longer striped his vision. And then, to his amazement, in place of the dingy covering of his cage appeared a vast and awful expanse of blue heaven, the tremendous depth and distance of which terrified him.

The scampering of a ground-squirrel seeking its burrow soon caught his notice, and he watched the little animal with great curiosity. Then he ran to the burrow, and hurt his feet on the sharp wheat-stubble. This made him more cautious. Not finding the squirrel, he looked about and discovered two owls sitting on a little mound not far away. Their solemn gaze fastened upon him inspired him with awe, but his curiosity would not permit him to forego a closer view. He cautiously crept towards them; then he stopped, sat down, and made grotesque faces at them. This had no effect. He scratched his head and thought. Then he made a feint as though he would pounce upon them, and they flew. Romulus gazed at them with the greatest amazement, for never before had he seen anything skim through the air. But the world was so wide and freedom so large that surely everything free ought to fly; so Romulus sprang into the air and made motions with his arms like to those the owls had made with their wings; and the first grievous disappointment which his freedom brought came when he found himself sprawling on the field.

His alert mind sought other exercise. Some distance away stood a house, and at the front gate was a man, and Romulus knew man to be the meanest and most cruel of all living things and the conscienceless taskmaster of weaker creatures. So Romulus avoided the house and struck out across the fields. Presently he came upon a very large thing which awed him. It was a live-oak, and the birds were singing in the foliage. But his persistent curiosity put a curb upon his fears, and he crept closer and closer. The kindly aspect of the tree, the sweetness of the shade which it cast, the cool depths of its foliage, the gentle swaying of the boughs in the soft north wind—all invited him to approach. This he did, until he arrived at the gnarled old bole, and then he leaped into the branches and was filled with delight. The little birds took flight. Romulus sat upon a limb, and then stretched himself at full length upon it and enjoyed the peace and comfort of the moment. But he was an ape and had to be employed, and so he ran out upon the smaller branches and shook them after the manner of his parents before him.

These delights all exploited, Romulus dropped to the ground and began to explore the world again; but the world was wide and its loneliness oppressed him. Presently he saw a dog and made quickly for him. The dog, seeing the strange creature approach, sought to frighten it by barking; but Romulus had seen similar animals before and had heard similar sounds; he could not be frightened by them. He went boldly towards the dog by long leaps on all fours. The dog, terrified by the strange-looking creature, ran away yelping and left Romulus with freedom and the world again.

On went Romulus over the fields, crossing a road now and then, and keeping clear of all living things that he found. Presently he came to a high picket-fence, surrounding a great inclosure, in which sat a large house in a grove of eucalyptus-trees. Romulus was thirsty, and the playing of a fountain among the trees tempted him sorely. He might have found courage to venture within had he not at that moment discovered a human being, not ten feet away, on the other side of the fence. Romulus sprang back with a cry of terror, and then stopped, and in a crouching attitude, ready to fly for his life and freedom, gazed at the enemy of all creation.

But the look he received in return was so kindly, and withal so peculiar and so unlike any that he had ever seen before, that his instinct to fly yielded to his curiosity to discover. Romulus did not know that the great house in the grove was an idiot-asylum, nor that the lad with the strange but kindly expression was one of the inmates. He knew only that kindness was there. The look which he saw was not the hard and cruel one of the menagerie-keeper, nor the empty, idle, curious one of the spectators, countenancing by their presence and supporting with their money the infamous and exclusively human practice of capturing wild animals and keeping them all their lives in the torture of captivity. So deeply interested was Romulus in what he saw that he forgot his fear and cocked his head on one side and made a queer grimace; and his motions and attitude were so comical that Moses, the idiot, grinned at him through the pickets.

But the grin was not the only manifestation of pleasure that Moses gave. A peculiar vermicular movement, beginning at his feet and ending at his head, was the precursor of a slow, vacant guffaw that expressed the most intense delight of which he was capable. Moses never before had seen so queer a creature as this little brown man all covered with hair; he never before had seen even a monkey, that common joy of ordinary childhood, and remoter from resemblance to human kind than was Romulus. Moses was nineteen; but, although his voice was childlike no longer and his face was covered with unsightly short hair, and he was large and strong, running mostly to legs and arms, he was simple and innocent. His clothes were much too small, and a thick growth of wild hair topped his poll, otherwise innocent of covering.

Thus gazed these two strange beings at each other, held by sympathy and curiosity. Neither had the power of speech, and hence neither could lie to the other. Was it instinct which made Romulus believe that of all the bipedal devils which infested the face of the earth there was one of so gentle spirit that it could love him? And was it by instinct that Romulus, ignorant as he was of the larger ways of the world, discovered that his own mind was the firmer and cleverer of the two? And, feeling the hitherto unimaginable sweetness of freedom, did there come to him a knowledge that this fellow-being was a prisoner, as he himself had been, and longed for a taste of the open fields? And if Romulus so had reasoned, was it a sense of chivalry or a desire for companionship that led him to the rescue of this one weaker and more unfortunate than he?

He went cautiously to the fence, and put through his hand and touched Moses. The lad, much pleased, took the hand of the ape in his, and at once there was a good understanding between them. Romulus teased the boy to follow him, by going away a few steps and looking back, and then going and pulling his hand through the fence—doing this repeatedly—until his intention worked its way into the idiot's mind. The fence was too high to be scaled; but now that the desire for freedom had invaded his being, Moses crushed the pickets with his huge feet and emerged from his prison.

These two, then, were at large. The heavens were lifted higher and the horizon was extended. At a convenient ditch they slaked their thirst, and in an orchard they found ripe apricots; but what can satisfy the hunger of an ape or an idiot? The world was wide and sweet and beautiful, and the exquisite sense of boundless freedom worked like rich old wine in unaccustomed veins. These all brought infinite delight to Romulus and his charge as over the fields they went.

I will not tell particularly of all they did that wild, mad, happy afternoon, while drunk and reeling with freedom. I might say in passing that at one place they tore open the cage of a canary-bird swinging in a cherry-tree out of sight of the house, and at another they unbuckled the straps which bound a baby in a cart, and might have made off with it but for fear of arrest; but these things have no relation to the climax of their adventures, now hastening to accomplishment.

When the sun had sunk lower in the yellow splendour of the west and the great nickel dome of the observatory on Mount Hamilton had changed from silver to copper, the two revellers, weary and now hungry again, came upon a strange and perplexing place. It was a great oak with its long, cone-shaped shadow pointed towards the east and the cool depths of its foliage that first attracted them. About the tree were mounds with wooden head-boards, which wiser ones would have known the meaning of. But how could an ape or an idiot know of a freedom so sweet and silent and unencompassed and unconditional as death? And how could they know that the winners of so rich a prize should be mourned, should be wetted with tears, should be placed in

11

the ground with the strutting pomp of grief? Knowing nothing at all of things like this, how could they know that this shabby burying-ground upon which they had strayed was so unlike that one which, in clear sight some distance away, was ordered in walks and drive-ways and ornamented with hedges, and foun- tains, and statues, and rare plants, and costly monuments—ah, my friends, how, without money, may we give adequate expres- sion to grief? And surely grief without evidence of its existence is the idlest of indulgences!

But there was no pomp in the shadow of the oak, for the bro- ken fence setting apart this place from the influence of Christian civilization enclosed graves holding only such bones as could not rest easy in soil across which was flung the shadow of the cross. Romulus and Moses knew nothing of these things; knew nothing of laws prohibiting disinterment within two years; knew nothing of a strange, far-away people from Asia, who, scorning the foreign Christian soil upon which they walked, despising the civilization out of which they wrung money, buried their dead in obedience to law which they had not the strength to re- sist, and two years afterwards dug up the bones and sent them to the old home to be interred for everlasting rest in the soil made and nourished by a god of their own.

Should either Romulus or Moses judge between these peo- ples? They were in better business than that.

Their examination of a strange brick furnace in which print- ed prayers were burned, and of a low brick altar covered with the grease of used-up tapers, had hardly been finished when an approaching cloud of dust along the broken fence warned them to the exercise of caution. Romulus was the quicker to escape, for a circus-train makes a trail of dust along the road, and with swift alacrity he sprang into the boughs of the oak, the heavy Moses clambering laboriously after, emitting guffaws in praise of the superior agility of his guardian. It made Moses laugh again to see the little hairy man stretch himself on a branch and sigh with the luxurious comfort of repose, and he nearly had fallen in trying to imitate the nimble Romulus. But they were still and silent when the cloud of dust, parting at a gate, gave forth into the enclosure a small cavalcade of carriages and wagons.

There was a grave newly dug, and towards this came the procession,—a shallow grave, for one must not lie too deep in the Christian soil of the white barbarian,—but it was so small a grave! Even Romulus could have filled it, and, as for Moses, it was hardly too large for his feet.

For little Wang Tai was dead, and in this small grave were her fragile bones to rest for twenty-four months under three feet of Christian law. Interest tempered the fright which Romulus and Moses felt when from the forward carriage came the sound of rasping oboes, belly-less fiddles, brazen tom-toms, and harsh cymbals, playing a dirge for little Wang Tai; playing less for godly protection of her tiny soul than for its exemption from the torture of devils.

With the others there came forth a little woman all bent with grief and weeping, for little Wang Tai had a mother, and every mother has a mother's heart. She was only a little yellow woman from Asia, with queer wide trousers for skirts and rocker-soled shoes that flapped against her heels. Her uncovered black hair was firmly knotted and securely pinned, and her eyes were black of colour and soft of look, and her face, likely blank in content, was wet with tears and drawn with suffering. And there sat upon her, like a radiance from heaven, the sweetest, the saddest, the deepest, the tenderest of all human afflictions,—the one and the only one that time can never heal.

So they interred little Wang Tai, and Romulus and Moses saw it all, and paper prayers were burned in the oven, and tapers were lighted at the altar; and for the refreshment of the angels that should come to bear little Wang Tai's soul to the farther depths of blue heaven some savoury viands were spread upon the grave. The grave filled, the diggers hid their spades behind the oven, Romulus watching them narrowly. The little bent woman gathered her grief to her heart and bore it away; and a cloud of dust, widening away alongside the broken fence, disappeared in the distance. The dome of Mount Hamilton had changed from copper to gold; the purple canyons of the Santa Cruz Mountains looked cold against the blazing orange of the western sky; the crickets set up their cheerful notes in the great old oak, and night fell softly as a dream.

Four hungry eyes saw the viands of the grave, and four greedy nostrils inhaled the aroma. Down dropped Romulus, and with less skill down fell Moses. Little Wang Tai's angels must go supperless to heaven this night—and it is a very long road from Christendom to heaven! The two outlaws snatched, and scrambled, and fought, and when all of this little was eaten they set their minds to other enterprises. Romulus fetched the spades and industriously began to dig into Wang Tai's grave, and Moses, crowing and laughing, fell to as assistant, and as the result of their labour the earth flew to either side. Only three feet of loose Christian law covered little Wang Tai!

★★★★★★

A small yellow woman, moaning with grief, had tossed all night on her hard bed of matting and her harder pillow of hollowed wood. Even the familiar raucous sounds of early morning in the Chinese quarter of San Jose, remindful of that far-distant country which held all of her heart not lying dead under Christian sod, failed to lighten the burden which sat upon her. She saw the morning sun push its way through a sea of amber and the nickel dome of the great observatory on Mount Hamilton standing ebony against the radiant East. She heard the Oriental jargon of the early hucksters who cried their wares in the ill-smelling alleys, and with tears she added to the number of pearls which the dew had strewn upon the porch. She was only a small yellow woman from Asia, all bent with grief; and what of happiness could there be for her in the broad sunshine which poured forth from the windows of heaven, inviting the living babies of all present mankind to find life and health in its luxurious enfolding? She saw the sun climb the skies with imperious magnificence, and whispering voices from remote Cathay tempered the radiance of the day with memories of the past.

Could you, had your hearts been breaking and your eyes

14

blinded with tears, have seen with proper definition the figures of a strange procession which made its way along the alley under the porch? There were white men with three prisoners—three who so recently had tested the sweets of freedom, and they had been dragged back to servitude. Two of these had been haled from the freedom of life and one from the freedom of death, and all three had been found fast asleep in the early morning beside the open grave and empty coffin of little Wang Tai. There were wise men abroad, and they said that little Wang Tai, through imperfect medical skill, had been interred alive, and that Romulus and Moses, by means of their impish pranks, had brought her to life after raising her from the grave. But wherefore the need of all this talk? Is it not enough that these two brigands were whipped and sent back into servitude, and that when the little yellow woman from Asia had gathered her baby to her breast the windows of her soul were opened to receive the warmth of the yellow sunshine that poured in a flood from heaven?

The Hero of the Plague

(A story from *The Ape, the Idiot & Other People*)

1

On a sweltering July day a long and ungainly shadow, stretching thirty feet upon the ground, crept noiselessly up an avenue leading to a fashionable hotel at a great summer resort. The sun was setting, and its slanting rays caused the shadow to assume the appearance of an anamorphosis of ludicrous proportions. It was a timid shadow—perhaps a shadow of strange and unnerving experiences.

The original of it was worthy of study. He was a short, stout, stoop-shouldered man; his hair was ragged and dusty, his beard straggling and scant. His visible clothing consisted of a slouch hat, torn around the rim and covered with dust; a woollen shirt; a pair of very badly soiled cotton trousers; suspenders made of rawhide strips, fastened to his trousers with wooden pins, and the strangest of old boots, which turned high up at the toes like canoes (being much too long for his feet), and which had a rakish aspect.

The man's face was a protest against hilarity. Apparently he had all the appurtenances of natural manhood, yet his whole expression would have at once aroused sympathy, for it was a mixture of childishness, confidence, timidity, humility, and honesty. His look was vague and uncertain, and seemed to be searching hopelessly for a friend—for the guidance of natures that were stronger and minds that were clearer. He could not have been older than thirty-five years, and yet his hair and beard were gray, and his face was lined with wrinkles. Occasionally he would make a movement as if to ward off a sudden and vicious blow.

He carried a knotty stick, and his ample trousers-pockets were filled to such an extent that they made him appear very wide in the hips and very narrow in the shoulders. Their contents were a mystery. The pockets at least produced the good effect of toning down the marvellous ellipticity of his legs, and in doing this they performed a valuable service.

"Hullo! who are you?" gruffly demanded a porter employed in the hotel, as the disreputable-looking man was picking his way with great nicety up the broad interior stairs, afraid that his dusty boots would deface the polished brasses under foot.

"Baker," promptly replied the man, in a small, timid voice, coming to a halt and humbly touching his hat.

"Baker? Well, what's your other name?"

"Mine?"

"Yes, yours."

The stranger was evidently puzzled by the question. He looked vacantly around the ceiling until his gaze rested upon a glass chandelier above him; but, finding no assistance there, his glance wandered to an oriel, in which there was a caged mocking-bird.

"Jess Baker—that's all," he answered at last, in his thin voice and slow, earnest manner.

"What! don't know your other name?"

"No, I reckin not," said Baker, after a thoughtful pause. "I reckin it's jess Baker—that's all."

"Didn't they ever call you anything else?"

"Me?"

"Yes, you."

Again Baker looked helplessly around until he found the chandelier, and then his eyes sought the oriel. Then he started as if he had received a blow, and immediately reached down and felt his ankles.

"Yes, sir," he answered.

"What was it?"

"Hunder'd'n One," he quietly said, looking at his questioner with a shade of fear and suspicion in his face.

The porter believed that a lunatic stood before him. He asked:

"Where are you from?"

"Georgy."

"What part of Georgia?"

Again was Baker at sea, and again did his glance seek the chandelier and the oriel.

"Me?" he asked.

"Yes, you. What part of Georgia are you from?"

"Jess Georgy," he finally said.

"What do you want here?"

"Well, I'll tell you. I want you to hire me," he replied, with a faint look of expectancy.

"What can you do?"

"Me?"

"Yes, you."

"Oh, well, I'll tell you. Most everything."

"What salary do you want?"

"Me?"

"Of course you."

"Want?"

"Yes."

"Oh, well, about five dollars a day, I reckin."

The porter laughed coarsely. "You needn't talk to me about it," he said; "I'm not the proprietor."

"The which?" asked Baker.

"The boss."

"Oh, ain't you?" and then he looked very much puzzled indeed.

The porter had had sufficient amusement, and so he demanded, in a brusque and menacing tone, "Now, say—you get away from here quick! We don't want no crazy tramps around here. You understand?"

Baker did not stir, but stood looking helplessly at the porter, surprised and grieved.

"Get out, I say, or I'll set the dogs on you!"

A look of deep mortification settled on Baker's face, but he was not frightened; he did not move a muscle, except to glance quickly around for the dogs.

"Ain't you going, you crazy old tramp? If you don't I'll lock you up and send for the sheriff;" and the porter rattled some keys in his pocket.

Instantly a great horror overspread the countenance of Baker from Georgia. He looked wildly about and seemed ready to run, and laboured with an imaginary weight that clung to his ankles. He took a single step in his agitation, and suddenly realized that no such encumbrance detained him. He shook off the delusion and sprang to the bottom of the stairs. His whole appearance had changed. Humility had given way to uncontrollable fear, and he had become a fleeing wild beast that was hunted for its life. He sprang through the outer door and reached the ground in another bound, and gathered his strength for immediate flight from terrors without a name.

"Stop, there!" called a stern, full voice.

Baker obeyed instantly; obeyed as might a man long accustomed to the most servile obedience; as might a dog that has been beaten until his spirit is broken. He bared his head, and stood in the warm glow of the fading light, meek and submissive. All signs of fear had disappeared from his face; but he was no longer the Baker from Georgia who, a few minutes ago, had trudged along the gravelled walk after the ungainly shadow. He had sought a thing and had not found it—had bitten a rosy apple and was choked with dust. Even the rakish boots looked submissive, and showed their brass teeth in solemn acquiescence to an inevitability; and somehow they looked not nearly so rakish as formerly.

The voice that had checked Baker had not a kindly tone; it was that of a suspicious man, who believed that he had detected a thief in the act of making off with dishonest booty stored in ample pockets. Yet his face had a generous look, though anger made his eyes harsh. The two men surveyed each other, anger disappearing from the face of one to give place to pity, the other regarding him with mild docility.

"Come along with me," said the gentleman to Baker.

Evidently Baker had heard those words before, for he followed quietly and tamely, with his dusty old hat in his left hand and his head bowed upon his breast. He walked so slowly that the gentleman turned to observe him, and found him moving laboriously, with his feet wide apart and his right hand grasping an invisible something that weighted down his ankles. They were now passing the end of the hotel on their way to the rear, when they came near a hitching-post, to which rings were affixed with staples. Baker had been looking around for something, and, as the gentleman (who was Mr. Clayton, the proprietor of the hotel) stopped near the post, Baker walked straight up to it, without having looked to the left or the right. Upon reaching it he dropped the invisible something that he carried in his right hand, laid his hat on the ground, slipped the rawhide suspenders from his shoulders, unbuttoned his shirt, pulled it over his head, and laid it on the grass alongside his hat. He then humbly embraced the post and crossed his hands over a ring to which a chain was attached. He laid his cheek against his bare right arm and waited patiently, without having uttered a protest or made an appeal. The old boots looked up wistfully into his sorrowing face.

His naked back glistened white. It was a map on which were traced a record of the bloody cruelties of many years; it was a fine piece of mosaic—human flesh inlaid with the venom of the lash. There were scars, and seams, and ridges, and cuts that crossed and recrossed each other in all possible directions. Thus stood Baker for some time, until Mr. Clayton kindly called to him:

"Put on your shirt."

He proceeded to obey silently, but was confused and embarrassed at this unexpected turn of events. He hesitated at first, however, for he evidently did not understand how he could put on his shirt until his hands had been released.

"Your hands are not chained," explained Mr. Clayton.

The revelation was so unexpected that it almost startled the man from Georgia. He pulled out one hand slowly, that a sudden jerk might not lacerate his wrist. Then he pulled out the other, resumed his shirt and hat, picked up the imaginary weight, and shuffled along slowly after his leader.

"What is your name?" asked the gentleman.

"Hunder'd'n One."

They were soon traversing the corridor in the servants' quarter of the hotel, when Baker halted and ventured to say:

"I reckin you'r in the wrong curryder." He was examining the ceiling, the floor, and the numbers on the doors.

"No, this is right," said the gentleman.

Again Baker hobbled along, never releasing his hold on the invisible weight. They halted at No. 13. Said Baker, with a shade of pity in his voice,—

"'Taint right. Wrong curryder. Cell hunder'd'n one's mine."

"Yes, yes; but we'll put you in this one for the present," replied the gentleman, as he opened the door and ushered Baker within. The room was comfortably furnished, and this perplexed Baker more and more.

"Hain't you got it wrong?" he persisted. "Lifer, you know. Hunder'd'n One—lifer—plays off crazy—forty lashes every Monday. Don't you know?"

"Yes, yes, I know; but we'll not talk about that now."

They brought a good supper to his room, and he ate ravenously. They persuaded him to wash in a basin in the room, though he begged hard to be permitted to go to the pump. Later that night the gentleman went to his room and asked him if he wanted anything.

"Well, I'll tell you. You forgot to take it off," Baker replied, pointing to his ankles.

The gentleman was perplexed for a moment, and then he stooped and unlocked and removed an imaginary ball and chain. Baker seemed relieved. Said the gentleman, as Baker was preparing for bed:

"This is not a penitentiary. It is my house, and I do not whip anybody. I will give you all you want to eat, and good clothes, and you may go wherever you please. Do you understand?"

Baker looked at him with vacant eyes and made no reply. He undressed, lay down, sighed wearily, and fell asleep.

2

A stifling Southern September sun beat down upon the mountains and valleys. The thrush and the mocking-bird had been driven to cool places, and their songs were not heard in the trees. The hotel was crowded with refugees from Memphis. A terrible scourge was sweeping through Tennessee, and its black shadow was creeping down to the Gulf of Mexico; and as it crept it mowed down young and old in its path.

"Well, Baker, how are you getting along?" It was the round, cheerful voice of Mr. Clayton.

The man from Georgia was stooping over a pail, scouring it with sand and a cloth. Upon hearing the greeting he hung the cloth over the pail and came slowly to the perpendicular, putting his hands, during the operation, upon the small of his back, as if the hinges in that region were old and rusty and needed care.

"Oh, well, now, I'll tell you. Nothin' pertickler to complain on, excep'——"

"Well?"

"I don't believe it's quite exactly right."

"Tell me about it."

"Well, now, you see—there ain't nobody a-listenin', is there?"

"No."

"I think they ought to give me one more piece, anyway."

"Piece of what?"

"Mebbe two more pieces."

"Of what?"

"Pie. It was pie I was a-talkin' about all the time."

"Don't they give you sufficient?"

"Pie?"

"Yes."

"No, sir; not nigh enough. An'—an'—come here closter. I'm a-gittin' weak—I'm a-starvin'!" he whispered.

"You shall not starve. What do you want?"

"Well, now, I was jess a-thinkin' that one or two more pieces fur dinner every day—every day——"

"Pie?"

"Yes, sir; pie. I was a-talkin' about pie."

"You shall certainly have it; but don't they give you any?"

"What? Pie?"

"Yes."

"Oh, well, they do give me some."

"Every day?"

"Yes, sir; every day."

"How much do they give you?"

"Pie?"

"Yes."

"Well, I'll tell you. About two pieces, I believe."

"Aren't you afraid that much more than that would make you sick?"

"Oh, well, now, I'm a-goin' to tell you about that, too, 'cause you don't know about it. You see, I'm mostly used to gittin' sick, an' I ain't mostly used to eatin' of pie." He spoke then, as he always spoke, with the most impressive earnestness.

Baker had undergone a great change within the two months that had passed over him at the hotel. Kindness had driven away the vacant look in his eyes and his mind was stronger. He had found that for which his meagre soul had yearned—a sympathizing heart and a friend. He was fat, sleek, and strong. His old boots—the same as of yore, for he would not abandon them—looked less foolish and seemed almost cheerful. Were they not always in an atmosphere of gentleness and refinement, and did they not daily tread the very ground pressed by the bravest and richest boots in the land? It is true that they were often covered with slops and chickens' feathers, but this served only to bring

23

out in bolder relief the elevating influences of a healthy morality and a generous prosperity that environed them. There are many boots that would have been spoiled by so sudden an elevation into a higher sphere of life; but the good traits of Baker's boots were strengthened not only by a rooting up of certain weaknesses, but also by the gaining of many good qualities which proved beneficial; and to the full extent of their limited capability did they appreciate the advantages which their surroundings afforded, and looked up with humble gratitude whenever they would meet a friend.

There were six hundred guests at the hotel, and they all knew Baker and had a kind word to give him. But they could never learn anything about him other than that his name was Baker—"jess Baker, that's all"—and that he came from Georgia—"jess Georgy." Occasionally a stranger would ask him with urgent particularity concerning his past history, but he then would merely look helpless and puzzled and would say nothing. As to his name, it was "jess Baker;" but on rare occasions, when pressed with hard cruelty, his lips could be seen to form the words, "Hunder'd'n One," as though wondering how they would sound if he should utter them, and then the old blank, suffering look would come into his face. It had become quite seldom that he dodged an imaginary blow, and the memory of the ball and chain was buried with other bitter recollections of the past. He had free access to every part of the house, and was discreet, diligent, faithful, and honest. Sometimes the porters would impose upon his unfailing willingness and great strength by making him carry the heaviest trunks up three or four flights of stairs.

One day the shadow of death that was stealing southward passed over the house containing so much life, and happiness, and wealth, and beauty. The train passed as usual, and among the passengers who alighted was a man who walked to the counter in a weary, uncertain manner. One or two persons were present who knew him, and upon grasping his hand they found that it was cold. This was strange, for the day was very hot. In his eyes was a look of restlessness and anxiety, but he said that he had only a pain across the forehead, and that after needed rest it would pass away. He was conducted to a room, and there he fell across the bed, quite worn out, he said. He complained of slight cramps in the legs and thought that they had been caused by climbing the stairs. After a half-hour had passed he rang his bell violently and sent for the resident physician. That gentleman went to see him, and after remaining a few minutes went to the office, looking anxious and pale. He was a tall, quiet man, with white hair. He asked for Mr. Clayton, but when he was informed that that gentleman was temporarily absent he asked for Baker.

"Is your patient very ill, doctor?" inquired the cashier, privately and with a certain dread.

"I want Baker," said the doctor, somewhat shortly.

"Nothing serious, I hope."

"Send me Baker instantly."

The physician had a secret of life and death. To treat it wisely he required confidants of courage, sagacity, patience, tact, and prompt action. There were only two to whom he should impart it,—one was the proprietor and the other the man from Georgia.

When Baker had come the physician led him upstairs to the floor which held the patient's room, brought him to the window at the end of the corridor and turned him so that the light fell full upon his face.

"Baker, can you keep a secret?"

"Me?"

"Yes; can you keep a secret?"

"Well, let me tell you about it; I don't know; mebbe I can."

"Have you ever seen people die?"

"Oh, yes, sir!"

"A great many in the same house?"

"Yes, sir; yes, sir."

"Baker," said the physician, placing his hand gently on the broad shoulder before him, and looking the man earnestly in the eyes, and speaking very impressively—"Baker, are you afraid to die?"

"Me?"

"Yes."

"Die?"

"Yes."

There was no expression whatever upon his patient, gentle face. He gazed past the physician through the window and made no reply.

"Are you afraid of death, Baker?"

"Who? Me?"

"Yes."

There was no sign that he would answer the question or even that he comprehended it. He shifted his gaze to his upturned boot-toes and communed with them, but still kept silence.

"There is a man here, Baker, who is very ill, and I think that he will die. I want someone to help me take care of him. If you go into his room, perhaps you, too, will die. Are you afraid to go?"

"Was you a-talkin' 'bout wantin' me to wait on him?"

"Yes."

A brighter look came into Baker's face and he said:

"Oh, now, I'll tell you; I'll go."

They entered the stranger's room and found him suffering terribly. The physician already had put him under vigorous treatment, but he was rapidly growing worse. Baker regarded him attentively a moment, and then felt his pulse and put his hand on the sufferer's forehead. A look of intelligence came into his sad, earnest face, but there was not a trace of pallor or fear. He beckoned the physician to follow him out to the passage, and the two went aside, closing the door.

"He's a-goin' to die," said Baker, simply and quietly.

"Yes; but how do you know?"

"Well, I'll tell you about that; I know."

"Have you seen it before?"

"Hunderds."

"Are you afraid of it?"

"Me?"

"Yes."

"Oh, well, they all ought to know it," he said, with a sweep of his hand towards the corridors.

"Hurry and find Mr. Clayton first and bring him to me."

Baker met Mr. Clayton at the main entrance below and beckoned him to follow. He led the way into a dark room stored with boxes and then into the farther corner of it. There he stood Mr. Clayton with his back against the wall and looked straight into his face. His manner was so mysterious, and there was so strange an expression in his face,—a kind of empty exaltation it seemed,—and his familiarity in touching Mr. Clayton's person was so extraordinary, that that gentleman was alarmed for Baker's sanity. Then Baker leaned forward and whispered one terrible word,—

"*Cholery!*"

Cholera! Great God! No wonder that Mr. Clayton turned deathly pale and leaned heavily against the wall.

At midnight the stranger died, and none in the house had heard of the frightful danger which had come to assail them. The physician and Baker had been with him constantly, but their efforts had availed nothing; and after preparing him for the grave they went out and locked the door. Mr. Clayton was waiting for them. The anxious look in the faces of the two gentlemen was intensified; Baker's evinced nothing but calm consciousness of responsibility. The guests were slumbering.

"We must alarm the house," whispered Mr. Clayton.

The doctor shook his head sadly. "If we do," he said, "there will be a panic; and, besides, the night air of these mountains is very cool, and if they go from their warm beds into it, likely without taking time to dress, the danger will be great."

They both seemed helpless and undecided, and in need of someone to choose between two evils for them. They turned to Baker in silence and for his decision. He seemed to have expected it, for without a word, without submitting it for their concurrence, he went to the end of that passage and rapped upon a door. There was an answer, Baker mentioned his name, the door was opened, and the dreadful news was quietly impart-ed. The guest was terror-stricken, but a word from Baker gave him heart, and he hastily but quietly began preparations to leave the house. Thus went Baker from one door to another, impos-ing silence and care and careful dressing, and advising the peo-ple to take with them such bedding as they could. Mr. Clayton and the physician, observing the remarkable success of Baker's method, adopted it, and soon the three men had the great house swarming. It was done swiftly, quietly, and without panic, and the house became empty.

But selfishness appeared without shame or covering. Every-one in the house wanted Baker's assistance, for all the porters had fled, and there was none other than he to work. So he stag-gered and toiled under the weight of enormous trunks; listened to a hundred orders at once; bore frightened children and faint-ing women in his strong, sure arms; laboured until his face was haggard and his knees trembled from exhaustion. He did the work of fifty men—a hundred men.

The seeds of the plague had been sown. Towards morning the physician retired to his room, stricken down. Baker admin-istered to his needs, and discovered a surprising knowledge of the malady and its treatment. A few of those who had scattered about in the surrounding hills were taken down and brought to the house moaning with fear and pain. Baker treated them all. Mr. Clayton and a few other stout hearts provided him with whatever he ordered, and assisted in watching and in adminis-tering the simple remedies under his direction. These were such as the resources of the hotel permitted,—warm blankets, hot brandy, with water and sugar, or pepper and salt in hot water, heated bricks at the feet, and rubbing the body with spirits of camphor. Many recovered, others grew worse; the physician was saved.

At sunrise, while Baker was working vigorously on a pa-tient, he suddenly straightened himself, looked around some-what anxiously, and reeled backward to the wall. The strong man had collapsed at last. Leaning against the partition, and spreading out his arms against it to keep from falling, he worked his way a few feet to the door, and when he turned to go out his hand slipped on the door-facing and he fell heavily upon his face in the passage. He lay still for a moment, and then crawled slowly to the end of the passage and lay down. He had not said a word nor uttered a groan. It was there, silent, alone, and uncomplaining, that Mr. Clayton found this last victim of the plague waiting patiently for death. Others were hastily summoned. They put him upon a bed, and were going to undress him and treat him, but he firmly stopped them with uplifted hand, and his sunken eyes and anxious face implored more eloquently than his words, when he said:

"No, no! Now, let me tell you: Go an' take care of 'em."

Mr. Clayton sent them away, he alone remaining.

"Here, Baker; take this," he gently urged.

But the man from Georgia knew better. "No, no," he said; "it won't do no good." His speech was faint and laboured. "I'll tell you: I'm struck too hard. It won't do no good. I'm so tired. . . . I'll go quick . . . 'cause I'm . . . so tired."

His extreme exhaustion made him an easy prey. Death sat upon his face, and was reflected from his hollow, suffering, mournful eyes. In an hour they were dimmer; then he became cold and purple. In another hour his pulse was not perceptible. After two more hours his agony had passed.

"Baker, do you want anything?" asked Mr. Clayton, trying to rouse him.

"Me?" very faintly came the response.

"Yes. Do you want anything?"

"Oh, . . . I'll tell you: The governor . . . he found out my brother . . . done it . . . an' . . . an' he's goin' to . . . pardon me. . . . Fifteen years, an' played off . . . played off crazy . . . .Forty lashes every Monday . . . mornin' . . . . Cell hunder'd'n one's mine. . . . Well, I'll tell you: Governor's goin' to . . . pardon me out."

He ceased his struggling to speak. A half-hour passed in silence, and then he roused himself feebly and whispered:

"He'll . . . pardon . . . me."

The old boots stared blankly and coldly at the ceiling; their patient expression no longer bore a trace of life or suffering, and their calm repose was undisturbed by the song of the mocking-bird in the oriel.

His Unconquerable Enemy

(A story from *The Ape, the Idiot & Other People*)

I was summoned from Calcutta to the heart of India to perform a difficult surgical operation on one of the women of
a great *rajah's* household. I found the *rajah* a man of a noble
character, but possessed, as I afterwards discovered, of a sense
of cruelty purely Oriental and in contrast to the indolence of
his disposition. He was so grateful for the success that attended
my mission that he urged me to remain a guest at the palace as
long as it might please me to stay, and I thankfully accepted the
invitation.

One of the male servants early attracted my notice for his
marvellous capacity of malice. His name was Neranya, and I am
certain that there must have been a large proportion of Malay
blood in his veins, for, unlike the Indians (from whom he differed
also in complexion), he was extremely alert, active, nervous, and
sensitive. A redeeming circumstance was his love for his master.
Once his violent temper led him to the commission of an atrocious crime,—the fatal stabbing of a dwarf. In punishment for
this the rajah ordered that Neranya's right arm (the offending
one) be severed from his body. The sentence was executed in a
bungling fashion by a stupid fellow armed with an axe, and I,
being a surgeon, was compelled, in order to save Neranya's life,
to perform an amputation of the stump, leaving not a vestige of
the limb remaining.

After this he developed an augmented fiendishness. His love
for the *rajah* was changed to hate, and in his mad anger he flung

discretion to the winds. Driven once to frenzy by the *rajah's* scornful treatment, he sprang upon the *rajah* with a knife, but, fortunately, was seized and disarmed. To his unspeakable dismay the *rajah* sentenced him for this offence to suffer amputation of the remaining arm. It was done as in the former instance. This had the effect of putting a temporary curb on Neranya's spirit, or, rather, of changing the outward manifestations of his diabolism. Being armless, he was at first largely at the mercy of those who ministered to his needs,—a duty which I undertook to see was properly discharged, for I felt an interest in this strangely distorted nature. His sense of helplessness, combined with a damnable scheme for revenge which he had secretly formed, caused Neranya to change his fierce, impetuous, and unruly conduct into a smooth, quiet, insinuating bearing, which he carried so artfully as to deceive those with whom he was brought in contact, including the *rajah* himself.

Neranya, being exceedingly quick, intelligent, and dexterous, and having an unconquerable will, turned his attention to the cultivating of an enlarged usefulness of his legs, feet, and toes, with so excellent effect that in time he was able to perform wonderful feats with those members. Thus his capability, especially for destructive mischief, was considerably restored.

One morning the *rajah's* only son, a young man of an uncommonly amiable and noble disposition, was found dead in bed. His murder was a most atrocious one, his body being mutilated in a shocking manner, but in my eyes the most significant of all the mutilations was the entire removal and disappearance of the young prince's arms.

The death of the young man nearly brought the *rajah* to the grave. It was not, therefore, until I had nursed him back to health that I began a systematic inquiry into the murder. I said nothing of my own discoveries and conclusions until after the rajah and his officers had failed and my work had been done; then I submitted to him a written report, making a close analysis of all the circumstances and closing by charging the crime to Neranya. The *rajah*, convinced by my proof and argument, at once ordered Neranya to be put to death, this to be accomplished slowly and with frightful tortures. The sentence was so cruel and revolting that it filled me with horror, and I implored that the wretch be shot. Finally, through a sense of gratitude to me, the *rajah* relaxed. When Neranya was charged with the crime he denied it, of course, but, seeing that the *rajah* was convinced, he threw aside all restraint, and, dancing, laughing, and shrieking in the most horrible manner, confessed his guilt, gloated over it, and reviled the *rajah* to his teeth,—this, knowing that some fearful death awaited him.

The *rajah* decided upon the details of the matter that night, and in the morning he informed me of his decision. It was that Neranya's life should be spared, but that both of his legs should be broken with hammers, and that then I should amputate the limbs at the trunk! Appended to this horrible sentence was a provision that the maimed wretch should be kept and tortured at regular intervals by such means as afterwards might be devised.

Sickened to the heart by the awful duty set out for me, I nevertheless performed it with success, and I care to say nothing more about that part of the tragedy. Neranya escaped death very narrowly and was a long time in recovering his wonted vitality. During all these weeks the *rajah* neither saw him nor made inquiries concerning him, but when, as in duty bound, I made official report that the man had recovered his strength, the *rajah's* eyes brightened, and he emerged with deadly activity from the stupor into which he so long had been plunged.

The *rajah's* palace was a noble structure, but it is necessary here to describe only the grand hall. It was an immense chamber, with a floor of polished, inlaid stone and a lofty, arched ceiling. A soft light stole into it through stained glass set in the roof and in high windows on one side. In the middle of the room was a rich fountain, which threw up a tall, slender column of water, with smaller and shorter jets grouped around it. Across one end of the hall, half-way to the ceiling, was a balcony, which communicated with the upper story of a wing, and from which a flight of stone stairs descended to the floor of the hall. During the hot summers this room was delightfully cool; it was the *rajah's* favourite lounging-place, and when the nights were hot he had his cot taken thither, and there he slept.

This hall was chosen for Neranya's permanent prison; here was he to stay so long as he might live, with never a glimpse of the shining world or the glorious heavens. To one of his nervous, discontented nature such confinement was worse than death. At the *rajah's* order there was constructed for him a small pen of open iron-work, circular, and about four feet in diameter, elevated on four slender iron posts, ten feet above the floor, and placed between the balcony and the fountain. Such was Neranya's prison. The pen was about four feet in depth, and the pen-top was left open for the convenience of the servants whose duty it should be to care for him. These precautions for his safe confinement were taken at my suggestion, for, although the man was now deprived of all four of his limbs, I still feared that he might develop some extraordinary, unheard-of power for mischief. It was provided that the attendants should reach his cage by means of a movable ladder.

All these arrangements having been made and Neranya hoisted into his cage, the *rajah* emerged upon the balcony to see him for the first time since the last amputation. Neranya had been lying panting and helpless on the floor of his cage, but when his quick ear caught the sound of the *rajah's* footfall he squirmed about until he had brought the back of his head against the railing, elevating his eyes above his chest, and enabling him to peer through the open-work of the cage. Thus the two deadly enemies faced each other. The *rajah's* stern face paled at sight of the hideous, shapeless thing which met his gaze; but he soon recovered, and the old hard, cruel, sinister look returned. Neranya's black hair and beard had grown long, and they added to the natural ferocity of his aspect. His eyes blazed upon the *rajah* with a terrible light, his lips parted, and he gasped for breath; his face was ashen with rage and despair, and his thin, distended nostrils quivered.

The *rajah* folded his arms and gazed down from the balcony upon the frightful wreck that he had made. Oh, the dreadful pathos of that picture; the inhumanity of it; the deep and dismal tragedy of it! Who might look into the wild, despairing heart of the prisoner and see and understand the frightful turmoil there; the surging, choking passion; unbridled but impotent ferocity; frantic thirst for a vengeance that should be deeper than hell! Neranya gazed, his shapeless body heaving, his eyes aflame; and then, in a strong, clear voice, which rang throughout the great hall, with rapid speech he hurled at the *rajah* the most insulting defiance, the most awful curses. He cursed the womb that had conceived him, the food that should nourish him, the wealth that had brought him power; cursed him in the name of Buddha and all the wise men; cursed by the sun, the moon, and the stars; by the continents, mountains, oceans, and rivers; by all things living; cursed his head, his heart, his entrails; cursed in a whirl-wind of unmentionable words; heaped unimaginable insults and contumely upon him; called him a knave, a beast, a fool, a liar, an infamous and unspeakable coward.

The *rajah* heard it all calmly, without the movement of a muscle, without the slightest change of countenance; and when the poor wretch had exhausted his strength and fallen helpless and silent to the floor, the *rajah*, with a grim, cold smile, turned and strode away.

The days passed. The *rajah*, not deterred by Neranya's curses often heaped upon him, spent even more time than formerly in the great hall, and slept there oftener at night; and finally Neranya wearied of cursing and defying him, and fell into a sullen silence. The man was a study for me, and I observed every change in his fleeting moods. Generally his condition was that of miserable despair, which he attempted bravely to conceal. Even the boon of suicide had been denied him, for when he would wriggle into an erect position the rail of his pen was a foot above his head, so that he could not clamber over and break his skull on the stone floor beneath; and when he had tried to starve himself the attendants forced food down his throat; so that he abandoned such attempts.

At times his eyes would blaze and his breath would come in gasps, for imaginary vengeance was working within him; but steadily he became quieter and more tractable, and was pleasant and responsive when I would converse with him. Whatever might have been the tortures which the *rajah* had decided on, none as yet had been ordered; and although Neranya knew that they were in contemplation, he never referred to them or complained of his lot.

The awful climax of this situation was reached one night, and even after this lapse of years I cannot approach its description without a shudder.

It was a hot night, and the *rajah* had gone to sleep in the great hall, lying on a high cot placed on the main floor just underneath the edge of the balcony. I had been unable to sleep in my own apartment, and so I had stolen into the great hall through the heavily curtained entrance at the end farthest from the balcony. As I entered I heard a peculiar, soft sound above the patter of the fountain. Neranya's cage was partly concealed from my view by the spraying water, but I suspected that the unusual sound came from him. Stealing a little to one side, and crouching against the dark hangings of the wall, I could see him in the faint light which dimly illuminated the hall, and then I discovered that my surmise was correct—Neranya was quietly at work. Curious to learn more, and knowing that only mischief could have been inspiring him, I sank into a thick robe on the floor and watched him.

To my great astonishment Neranya was tearing off with his teeth the bag which served as his outer garment. He did it cautiously, casting sharp glances frequently at the rajah, who, sleeping soundly on his cot below, breathed heavily. After starting a strip with his teeth, Neranya, by the same means, would attach it to the railing of his cage and then wriggle away, much after the manner of a caterpillar's crawling, and this would cause the strip to be torn out the full length of his garment. He repeated this operation with incredible patience and skill until his entire garment had been torn into strips. Two or three of these he tied end to end with his teeth, lips, and tongue, tightening the knots by placing one end of the strip under his body and drawing the other taut with his teeth. In this way he made a line several feet long, one end of which he made fast to the rail with his mouth. It then began to dawn upon me that he was going to make an insane attempt—impossible of achievement without hands, feet, arms, or legs—to escape from his cage! For what purpose? The *rajah* was asleep in the hall—ah! I caught my breath.

Oh, the desperate, insane thirst for revenge which could have unhinged so clear and firm a mind! Even though he should accomplish the impossible feat of climbing over the railing of his cage that he might fall to the floor below (for how could he slide down the rope?), he would be in all probability killed or stunned; and even if he should escape these dangers it would be impossible for him to clamber upon the cot without rousing the *rajah*, and impossible even though the *rajah* were dead! Amazed at the man's daring, and convinced that his sufferings and brooding had destroyed his reason, nevertheless I watched him with breathless interest.

With other strips tied together he made a short swing across one side of his cage. He caught the long line in his teeth at a point not far from the rail; then, wriggling with great effort to an upright position, his back braced against the rail, he put his chin over the swing and worked toward one end. He tightened the grasp of his chin on the swing, and with tremendous exertion, working the lower end of his spine against the railing, he began gradually to ascend the side of his cage. The labour was so great that he was compelled to pause at intervals, and his breathing was hard and painful; and even while thus resting he was in a position of terrible strain, and his pushing against the swing caused it to press hard against his windpipe and nearly strangle him.

After amazing effort he had elevated the lower end of his body until it protruded above the railing, the top of which was now across the lower end of his abdomen. Gradually he worked his body over, going backward, until there was sufficient excess of weight on the outer side of the rail; and then, with a quick lurch, he raised his head and shoulders and swung into a horizontal position on top of the rail. Of course, he would have fallen to the floor below had it not been for the line which he held in his teeth. With so great nicety had he estimated the distance between his mouth and the point where the rope was fastened to the rail, that the line tightened and checked him just as he reached the horizontal position on the rail. If one had told me beforehand that such a feat as I had just seen this man accomplish was possible, I should have thought him a fool.

Neranya was now balanced on his stomach across the top of the rail, and he eased his position by bending his spine and hanging down on either side as much as possible. Having rested thus for some minutes, he began cautiously to slide off backward, slowly paying out the line through his teeth, finding almost a fatal difficulty in passing the knots. Now, it is quite possible that the line would have escaped altogether from his teeth laterally when he would slightly relax his hold to let it slip, had it not been for a very ingenious plan to which he had resorted.

This consisted in his having made a turn of the line around his neck before he attacked the swing, thus securing a threefold control of the line,—one by his teeth, another by friction against his neck, and a third by his ability to compress it between his cheek and shoulder. It was quite evident now that the minutest details of a most elaborate plan had been carefully worked out by him before beginning the task, and that possibly weeks of difficult theoretical study had been consumed in the mental preparation. As I observed him I was reminded of certain hitherto unaccountable things which he had been doing for some weeks past—going through certain hitherto inexplicable motions, undoubtedly for the purpose of training his muscles for the immeasurably arduous labour which he was now performing.

A stupendous and seemingly impossible part of his task had been accomplished. Could he reach the floor in safety? Gradually he worked himself backward over the rail, in imminent danger of falling; but his nerve never wavered, and I could see a wonderful light in his eyes. With something of a lurch, his body fell against the outer side of the railing, to which he was hanging by his chin, the line still held firmly in his teeth. Slowly he slipped his chin from the rail, and then hung suspended by the line in his teeth. By almost imperceptible degrees, with infinite caution, he descended the line, and, finally, his unwieldy body rolled upon the floor, safe and unhurt!

What miracle would this superhuman monster next accomplish? I was quick and strong, and was ready and able to intercept any dangerous act; but not until danger appeared would I interfere with this extraordinary scene.

I must confess to astonishment upon having observed that Neranya, instead of proceeding directly toward the sleeping *rajah*, took quite another direction. Then it was only escape, after all, that the wretch contemplated, and not the murder of the *rajah*. But how could he escape? The only possible way to reach the outer air without great risk was by ascending the stairs to the balcony and leaving by the corridor which opened upon it, and thus fall into the hands of some British soldiers quartered thereabout, who might conceive the idea of hiding him; but surely it was impossible for Neranya to ascend that long flight of stairs! Nevertheless, he made directly for them, his method of progression this: He lay upon his back, with the lower end of his body toward the stairs; then bowed his spine upward, thus drawing his head and shoulders a little forward; straightened, and then pushed the lower end of his body forward a space equal to that through which he had drawn his head; repeating this again and again, each time, while bending his spine, preventing his head from slipping by pressing it against the floor. His progress was laborious and slow, but sensible; and, finally, he arrived at the foot of the stairs.

It was manifest that his insane purpose was to ascend them. The desire for freedom must have been strong within him! Wriggling to an upright position against the newel-post, he looked up at the great height which he had to climb and sighed;

but there was no dimming of the light in his eyes. How could he accomplish the impossible task?

His solution of the problem was very simple, though daring and perilous as all the rest. While leaning against the newel-post he let himself fall diagonally upon the bottom step, where he lay partly hanging over, but safe, on his side. Turning upon his back, he wriggled forward along the step to the rail and raised himself to an upright position against it as he had against the newel-post, fell as before, and landed on the second step. In this manner, with inconceivable labour, he accomplished the ascent of the entire flight of stairs.

It being apparent to me that the *rajah* was not the object of Neranya's movements, the anxiety which I had felt on that account was now entirely dissipated. The things which already he had accomplished were entirely beyond the nimblest imagination. The sympathy which I had always felt for the wretched man was now greatly quickened; and as infinitesimally small as I knew his chances for escape to be, I nevertheless hoped that he would succeed. Any assistance from me, however, was out of the question; and it never should be known that I had witnessed the escape.

Neranya was now upon the balcony, and I could dimly see him wriggling along toward the door which led out upon the balcony. Finally he stopped and wriggled to an upright position against the rail, which had wide openings between the balusters. His back was toward me, but he slowly turned and faced me and the hall. At that great distance I could not distinguish his features, but the slowness with which he had worked, even before he had fully accomplished the ascent of the stairs, was evidence all too eloquent of his extreme exhaustion. Nothing but a most desperate resolution could have sustained him thus far, but he had drawn upon the last remnant of his strength. He looked around the hall with a sweeping glance, and then down upon the *rajah*, who was sleeping immediately beneath him, over twenty feet below. He looked long and earnestly, sinking lower, and lower, and lower upon the rail.

Suddenly, to my inconceivable astonishment and dismay, he toppled through and shot downward from his lofty height! I held my breath, expecting to see him crushed upon the stone floor beneath; but instead of that he fell full upon the *rajah's* breast, driving him through the cot to the floor. I sprang forward with a loud cry for help, and was instantly at the scene of the catastrophe. With indescribable horror I saw that Neranya's teeth were buried in the *rajah's* throat! I tore the wretch away, but the blood was pouring from the *rajah's* arteries, his chest was crushed in, and he was gasping in the agony of death. People came running in, terrified. I turned to Neranya. He lay upon his back, his face hideously smeared with blood. Murder, and not escape, had been his intentions from the beginning; and he had employed the only method by which there was ever a possibility of accomplishing it. I knelt beside him, and saw that he too was dying; his back had been broken by the fall. He smiled sweetly into my face, and a triumphant look of accomplished revenge sat upon his face even in death.

The Permanent Stiletto

(A story from *The Ape, the Idiot & Other People*)

I had sent in all haste for Dr. Rowell, but as yet he had not arrived, and the strain was terrible. There lay my young friend upon his bed in the hotel, and I believed that he was dying. Only the jewelled handle of the knife was visible at his breast; the blade was wholly sheathed in his body.

"Pull it out, old fellow," begged the sufferer through white, drawn lips, his gasping voice being hardly less distressing than the unearthly look in his eyes.

"No, Arnold," said I, as I held his hand and gently stroked his forehead. It may have been instinct, it may have been a certain knowledge of anatomy that made me refuse.

"Why not? It hurts," he gasped. It was pitiful to see him suffer, this strong, healthy, daring, reckless young fellow.

Dr. Rowell walked in—a tall, grave man, with gray hair. He went to the bed and I pointed to the knife-handle, with its great, bold ruby in the end and its diamonds and emeralds alternating in quaint designs in the sides. The physician started. He felt Arnold's pulse and looked puzzled.

"When was this done?" he asked.

"About twenty minutes ago," I answered.

The physician started out, beckoning me to follow.

"Stop!" said Arnold. We obeyed. "Do you wish to speak of me?" he asked.

"Yes," replied the physician, hesitating.

"Speak in my presence then," said my friend; "I fear nothing."

It was said in his old, imperious way, although his suffering must have been great.

"If you insist——"

"I do."

"Then," said the physician, "if you have any matters to adjust they should be attended to at once. I can do nothing for you."

"How long can I live?" asked Arnold.

The physician thoughtfully stroked his gray beard. "It depends," he finally said; "if the knife be withdrawn you may live three minutes; if it be allowed to remain you may possibly live an hour or two—not longer."

Arnold never flinched.

"Thank you," he said, smiling faintly through his pain; "my friend here will pay you. I have some things to do. Let the knife remain." He turned his eyes to mine, and, pressing my hand, said, affectionately, "And I thank you, too, old fellow, for not pulling it out."

The physician, moved by a sense of delicacy, left the room, saying, "Ring if there is a change. I will be in the hotel office." He had not gone far when he turned and came back. "Pardon me," said he, "but there is a young surgeon in the hotel who is said to be a very skilful man. My specialty is not surgery, but medicine. May I call him?"

"Yes," said I, eagerly; but Arnold smiled and shook his head. "I fear there will not be time," he said. But I refused to heed him and directed that the surgeon be called immediately. I was writing at Arnold's dictation when the two men entered the room.

There was something of nerve and assurance in the young surgeon that struck my attention. His manner, though quiet, was bold and straightforward and his movements sure and quick. This young man had already distinguished himself in the performance of some difficult hospital laparotomies, and he was at that sanguine age when ambition looks through the spectacles of experiment. Dr. Raoul Entrefort was the newcomer's name. He was a Creole, small and dark, and he had travelled and studied in Europe.

43

"Speak freely," gasped Arnold, after Dr. Entrefort had made an examination.

"What think you, doctor?" asked Entrefort of the older man.

"I think," was the reply, "that the knife-blade has penetrated the ascending aorta, about two inches above the heart. So long as the blade remains in the wound the escape of blood is comparatively small, though certain; were the blade withdrawn the heart would almost instantly empty itself through the aortal wound."

Meanwhile, Entrefort was deftly cutting away the white shirt and the undershirt, and soon had the breast exposed. He examined the gem-studded hilt with the keenest interest.

"You are proceeding on the assumption, doctor," he said, "that this weapon is a knife."

"Certainly," answered Dr. Rowell, smiling; "what else can it be?"

"It *is* a knife," faintly interposed Arnold.

"Did you see the blade?" Entrefort asked him, quickly.

"I did—for a moment."

Entrefort shot a quick look at Dr. Rowell and whispered, "Then it is *not* suicide." Dr. Rowell looked puzzled and said nothing.

"I must disagree with you, gentlemen," quietly remarked Entrefort; "this is not a knife." He examined the handle very narrowly. Not only was the blade entirely concealed from view within Arnold's body, but the blow had been so strongly delivered that the skin was depressed by the guard. "The fact that it is not a knife presents a very curious series of facts and contingencies," pursued Entrefort, with amazing coolness, "some of which are, so far as I am informed, entirely novel in the history of surgery."

A quizzical expression, faintly amused and manifestly interested, was upon Dr. Rowell's face. "What is the weapon, doctor?" he asked.

"A stiletto."

Arnold started. Dr. Rowell appeared confused. "I must confess," he said, "my ignorance of the differences among these penetrating weapons, whether dirks, daggers, stilettos, poniards, or bowie-knives."

"With the exception of the stiletto," explained Entrefort, "all the weapons you mention have one or two edges, so that in penetrating they cut their way. A stiletto is round, is ordinarily about half an inch or less in diameter at the guard, and tapers to a sharp point. It penetrates solely by pushing the tissues aside in all directions. You will understand the importance of that point."

Dr. Rowell nodded, more deeply interested than ever.

"How do you know it is a stiletto, Dr. Entrefort?" I asked.

"The cutting of these stones is the work of Italian lapidaries," he said, "and they were set in Genoa. Notice, too, the guard. It is much broader and shorter than the guard of an edged weapon; in fact, it is nearly round. This weapon is about four hundred years old, and would be cheap at twenty thousand florins. Observe, also, the darkening colour of your friend's breast in the immediate vicinity of the guard; this indicates that the tissues have been bruised by the crowding of the 'blade,' if I may use the term."

"What has all this to do with me?" asked the dying man.

"Perhaps a great deal, perhaps nothing. It brings a single ray of hope into your desperate condition."

Arnold's eyes sparkled and he caught his breath. A tremor passed all through him, and I felt it in the hand I was holding. Life was sweet to him, then, after all—sweet to this wild daredevil who had just faced death with such calmness! Dr. Rowell, though showing no sign of jealousy, could not conceal a look of incredulity.

"With your permission," said Entrefort, addressing Arnold, "I will do what I can to save your life."

"You may," said the poor boy.

"But I shall have to hurt you."

"Well."

"Perhaps very much."

"Well."

"And even if I succeed (the chance is one in a thousand) you will never be a sound man, and a constant and terrible danger will always be present."

"Well."

Entrefort wrote a note and sent it away in haste by a bell-boy.

"Meanwhile," he resumed, "your life is in imminent danger from shock, and the end may come in a few minutes or hours from that cause. Attend without delay to whatever matters may require settling, and Dr. Rowell," glancing at that gentleman, "will give you something to brace you up. I speak frankly, for I see that you are a man of extraordinary nerve. Am I right?"

"Be perfectly candid," said Arnold.

Dr. Rowell, evidently bewildered by his cyclonic young associate, wrote a prescription, which I sent by a boy to be filled. With unwise zeal I asked Entrefort,—

"Is there not danger of lockjaw?"

"No," he replied; "there is not a sufficiently extensive injury to peripheral nerves to induce traumatic tetanus."

I subsided. Dr. Rowell's medicine came and I administered a dose. The physician and the surgeon then retired. The poor sufferer straightened up his business. When it was done he asked me,—

"What is that crazy Frenchman going to do to me?"

"I have no idea; be patient."

In less than an hour they returned, bringing with them a keen-eyed, tall young man, who had a number of tools wrapped in an apron. Evidently he was unused to such scenes, for he became deathly pale upon seeing the ghastly spectacle on my bed. With staring eyes and open mouth he began to retreat towards the door, stammering,—

"I—I can't do it."

"Nonsense, Hippolyte! Don't be a baby. Why, man, it is a case of life and death!"

"But—look at his eyes! he is dying!"

Arnold smiled. "I am not dead, though," he gasped.

"I—I beg your pardon," said Hippolyte.

Dr. Entrefort gave the nervous man a drink of brandy and then said,—

"No more nonsense, my boy; it must be done. Gentlemen, allow me to introduce Mr. Hippolyte, one of the most original, ingenious, and skilful machinists in the country."

Hippolyte, being modest, blushed as he bowed. In order to conceal his confusion he unrolled his apron on the table with considerable noise of rattling tools.

"I have to make some preparations before you may begin, Hippolyte, and I want you to observe me that you may become used not only to the sight of fresh blood, but also, what is more trying, the odour of it."

Hippolyte shivered. Entrefort opened a case of surgical instruments.

"Now, doctor, the chloroform," he said, to Dr. Rowell.

"I will not take it," promptly interposed the sufferer; "I want to know when I die."

"Very well," said Entrefort; "but you have little nerve now to spare. We may try it without chloroform, however. It will be better if you can do without. Try your best to lie still while I cut."

"What are you going to do?" asked Arnold.

"Save your life, if possible."

"How? Tell me all about it."

"Must you know?"

"Yes."

"Very well, then. The point of the stiletto has passed entirely through the aorta, which is the great vessel rising out of the heart and carrying the aerated blood to the arteries. If I should withdraw the weapon the blood would rush from the two holes in the aorta and you would soon be dead. If the weapon had been a knife, the parted tissue would have yielded, and the blood would have been forced out on either side of the blade and would have caused death. As it is, not a drop of blood has escaped from the aorta into the thoracic cavity. All that is left for us to do, then, is to allow the stiletto to remain permanently in the aorta. Many difficulties at once present themselves, and I do not wonder at Dr. Rowell's look of surprise and incredulity."

That gentleman smiled and shook his head.

"It is a desperate chance," continued Entrefort, "and is a novel case in surgery; but it is the only chance. The fact that the weapon is a stiletto is the important point—a stupid weapon, but a blessing to us now. If the assassin had known more she would have used——"

Upon his employment of the noun "assassin" and the feminine pronoun "she," both Arnold and I started violently, and I cried out to the man to stop.

"Let him proceed," said Arnold, who, by a remarkable effort, had calmed himself.

"Not if the subject is painful," Entrefort said.

"It is not," protested Arnold; "why do you think the blow was struck by a woman?"

"Because, first, no man capable of being an assassin would use so gaudy and valuable a weapon; second, no man would be so stupid as to carry so antiquated and inadequate a thing as a stiletto, when that most murderous and satisfactory of all penetrating and cutting weapons, the bowie-knife, is available. She was a strong woman, too, for it requires a good hand to drive a stiletto to the guard, even though it miss the sternum by a hair's breadth and slip between the ribs, for the muscles here are hard and the intercostal spaces narrow. She was not only a strong woman, but a desperate one also."

"That will do," said Arnold. He beckoned me to bend closer. "You must watch this man; he is too sharp; he is dangerous."

"Then," resumed Entrefort, "I shall tell you what I intend to do. There will undoubtedly be inflammation of the aorta, which, if it persist, will cause a fatal aneurism by a breaking down of the aortal walls; but we hope, with the help of your youth and health, to check it.

"Another serious difficulty is this: With every inhalation, the entire thorax (or bony structure of the chest) considerably expands. The aorta remains stationary. You will see, therefore, that as your aorta and your breast are now held in rigid relation to each other by the stiletto, the chest, with every inhalation, pulls the aorta forward out of place about half an inch. I am certain that it is doing this, because there is no indication of an escape of arterial blood into the thoracic cavity; in other words, the mouths of the two aortal wounds have seized upon the blade with a firm hold and thus prevent it from slipping in and out. This is a very fortunate occurrence, but one which will cause pain for some time. The aorta, you may understand, being made by the stiletto to move with the breathing, pulls the heart backward and forward with every breath you take; but that organ, though now undoubtedly much surprised, will accustom itself to its new condition.

"What I fear most, however, is the formation of a clot around the blade. You see, the presence of the blade in the aorta has already reduced the blood-carrying capacity of that vessel; a clot, therefore, need not be very large to stop up the aorta, and, of course, if that should occur death would ensue. But the clot, if one form, may be dislodged and driven forward, in which event it may lodge in any one of the numerous branches from the aorta and produce results more or less serious, possibly fatal. If, for instance, it should choke either the right or the left carotid, there would ensue atrophy of one side of the brain, and consequently paralysis of half the entire body; but it is possible that in time there would come about a secondary circulation from the other side of the brain, and thus restore a healthy condition. Or the clot (which, in passing always from larger arteries to smaller, must unavoidably find one not sufficiently large to carry it, and must lodge somewhere) may either necessitate amputation of one of the four limbs or lodge itself so deep within the body that it cannot be reached with the knife. You are beginning to realize some of the dangers which await you."

Arnold smiled faintly.

"But we shall do our best to prevent the formation of a clot," continued Entrefort; "there are drugs which may be used with effect."

"Are there more dangers?"

"Many more; some of the more serious have not been mentioned. One of these is the probability of the aortal tissues pressing upon the weapon relaxing their hold and allowing the blade to slip. That would let out the blood and cause death. I am uncertain whether the hold is now maintained by the pressure of the tissues or the adhesive quality of the serum which was set free by the puncture. I am convinced, though, that in either event the hold is easily broken and that it may give way at any moment, for it is under several kinds of strains. Every time the heart contracts and crowds the blood into the aorta, the latter expands a little, and then contracts when the pressure is removed. Any unusual exercise or excitement produces stronger and quicker heart-beats, and increases the strain on the adhesion of the aorta to the weapon. A fright, fall, a jump, a blow on the chest—any of these might so jar the heart and aorta as to break the hold."

Entrefort stopped.

"Is that all?" asked Arnold.

"No; but is not that enough?"

"More than enough," said Arnold, with a sudden and dangerous sparkle in his eyes. Before any of us could think, the desperate fellow had seized the handle of the stiletto with both hands in a determined effort to withdraw it and die. I had had no time to order my faculties to the movement of a muscle, when Entrefort, with incredible alertness and swiftness, had Arnold's wrists. Slowly Arnold relaxed his hold.

"There, now!" said Entrefort, soothingly; "that was a careless act and might have broken the adhesion! You'll have to be careful."

Arnold looked at him with a curious combination of expressions.

"Dr. Entrefort," he quietly remarked, "you are the devil."

Bowing profoundly, Entrefort replied: "You do me too great honour;" then he whispered to his patient: "If you do *that*"—with a motion towards the hilt—"I will have *her* hanged for

50

murder."

Arnold started and choked, and a look of horror overspread his face. He withdrew his hands, took one of mine in both of his, threw his arms upon the pillow above his head, and, holding my hand, firmly said to Entrefort,—

"Proceed with your work."

"Come closer, Hippolyte," said Entrefort, "and observe narrowly. Will you kindly assist me, Dr. Rowell?" That gentleman had sat in wondering silence.

Entrefort's hand was quick and sure, and he used the knife with marvellous dexterity. First he made four equidistant incisions outward from the guard and just through the skin. Arnold held his breath and ground his teeth at the first cut, but soon regained command of himself. Each incision was about two inches long. Hippolyte shuddered and turned his head aside. Entrefort, whom nothing escaped, exclaimed,—

"Steady, Hippolyte! Observe!"

Quickly was the skin peeled back to the limit of the incisions. This must have been excruciatingly painful. Arnold groaned, and his hands were moist and cold. Down sank the knife into the flesh from which the skin had been raised, and blood flowed freely; Dr. Rowell handled the sponge. The keen knife worked rapidly. Arnold's marvellous nerve was breaking down. He clutched my hand fiercely; his eyes danced; his mind was weakening. Almost in a moment the flesh had been cut away to the bones, which were now exposed,—two ribs and the sternum. A few quick cuts cleared the weapon between the guard and the ribs.

"To work, Hippolyte—be quick!"

The machinist had evidently been coached before he came. With slender, long-fingered hands, which trembled at first, he selected certain tools with nice precision, made some rapid measurements of the weapon and of the cleared space around it, and began to adjust the parts of a queer little machine. Arnold watched him curiously.

"What——" he began to say; but he ceased; a deeper pallor set on his face, his hands relaxed, and his eyelids fell.

"Thank God!" exclaimed Entrefort; "he has fainted—he can't stop us now. Quick, Hippolyte!"

The machinist attached the queer little machine to the handle of the weapon, seized the stiletto in his left hand, and with his right began a series of sharp, rapid movements backward and forward.

"Hurry, Hippolyte!" urged Entrefort.

"The metal is very hard."

"Is it cutting?"

"I can't see for the blood."

In another moment something snapped. Hippolyte started; he was very nervous. He removed the little machine.

"The metal is very hard," he said; "it breaks the saws."

He adjusted another tiny saw and resumed work. After a little while he picked up the handle of the stiletto and laid it on the table. He had cut it off, leaving the blade inside Arnold's body.

"Good, Hippolyte!" exclaimed Entrefort. In a minute he had closed the bright end of the blade from view by drawing together the skin-flaps and sewing them firmly.

Arnold returned to consciousness and glanced down at his breast. He seemed puzzled. "Where is the weapon?" he asked.

"Here is part of it," answered Entrefort, holding up the handle.

"And the blade——"

"That is an irremovable part of your internal machinery." Arnold was silent. "It had to be cut off," pursued Entrefort, "not only because it would be troublesome and an undesirable ornament, but also because it was advisable to remove every possibility of its withdrawal." Arnold said nothing. "Here is a prescription," said Entrefort; "take the medicine as directed for the next five years without fail."

"What for? I see that it contains muriatic acid."

"If necessary I will explain five years from now."

"If I live."

"If you live."

Arnold drew me down to him and whispered, "Tell her to fly

at once; this man may make trouble for her."

Was there ever a more generous fellow?

★★★★★★

I thought that I recognized a thin, pale, bright face among the passengers who were leaving an Australian steamer which had just arrived at San Francisco.

"Dr. Entrefort!" I cried.

"Ah!" he said, peering up into my face and grasping my hand; "I know you now, but you have changed. You remember that I was called away immediately after I had performed that crazy operation on your friend. I have spent the intervening four years in India, China, Tibet, Siberia, the South Seas, and God knows where not. But wasn't that a most absurd, hare-brained experiment that I tried on your friend! Still, it was all that could have been done. I have dropped all that nonsense long ago. It is better, for more reasons than one, to let them die at once. Poor fellow! he bore it so bravely! Did he suffer much afterwards? How long did he live? A week—perhaps a month?"

"He is alive yet."

"What!" exclaimed Entrefort, startled.

"He is, indeed, and is in this city."

"Incredible!"

"It is true; you shall see him."

"But tell me about him now!" cried the surgeon, his eager eyes glittering with the peculiar light which I had seen in them on the night of the operation. "Has he regularly taken the medicine which I prescribed?"

"He has. Well, the change in him, from what he was before the operation, is shocking. Imagine a young dare-devil of twenty-two, who had no greater fear of danger or death than of a cold, now a cringing, cowering fellow; apparently an old man, nursing his life with pitiful tenderness, fearful that at any moment something may happen to break the hold of his aorta-walls on the stiletto-blade; a confirmed hypochondriac, peevish, melancholic, unhappy in the extreme. He keeps himself confined as closely as possible, avoiding all excitement and exercise, and even reads nothing exciting. The constant danger has worn out the last shred of his manhood and left him a pitiful wreck. Can nothing be done for him?"

"Possibly. But has he consulted no physician?"

"None whatever; he has been afraid that he might learn the worst."

"Let us find him at once. Ah, here comes my wife to meet me! She arrived by the other steamer."

I recognized her immediately and was overcome with astonishment.

"Charming woman," said Entrefort; "you'll like her. We were married three years ago at Bombay. She belongs to a noble Italian family and has travelled a great deal."

He introduced us. To my unspeakable relief she remembered neither my name nor my face. I must have appeared odd to her, but it was impossible for me to be perfectly unconcerned. We went to Arnold's rooms, I with much dread. I left her in the reception-room and took Entrefort within. Arnold was too greatly absorbed in his own troubles to be dangerously excited by meeting Entrefort, whom he greeted with indifferent hospitality.

"But I heard a woman's voice," he said. "It sounds——" He checked himself, and before I could intercept him he had gone to the reception-room; and there he stood face to face with the beautiful adventuress,—none other than Entrefort's wife now,— who, wickedly desperate, had driven a stiletto into Arnold's vitals in a hotel four years before because he had refused to marry her. They recognized each other instantly and both grew pale; but she, quicker witted, recovered her composure at once and advanced towards him with a smile and an extended hand. He stepped back, his face ghastly with fear.

"Oh!" he gasped, "the excitement, the shock,—it has made the blade slip out! The blood is pouring from the opening,—it burns,—I am dying!" and he fell into my arms and instantly expired.

The autopsy revealed the surprising fact that there was no

blade in his thorax at all; it had been gradually consumed by the muriatic acid which Entrefort had prescribed for that very purpose, and the perforations in the aorta had closed up gradually with the wasting of the blade and had been perfectly healed for a long time. All his vital organs were sound. My poor friend, once so reckless and brave, had died simply of a childish and groundless fear, and the woman unwittingly had accomplished her revenge.

Over an Absinthe Bottle

(A story from *The Ape, the Idiot & Other People*)

Arthur Kimberlin, a young man of very high spirit, found himself a total stranger in San Francisco one rainy evening, at a time when his heart was breaking; for his hunger was of that most poignant kind in which physical suffering is forced to the highest point without impairment of the mental functions. There remained in his possession not a thing that he might have pawned for a morsel to eat; and even as it was, he had stripped his body of all articles of clothing except those which a remaining sense of decency compelled him to retain. Hence it was that cold assailed him and conspired with hunger to complete his misery. Having been brought into the world and reared a gentleman, he lacked the courage to beg and the skill to steal. Had not an extraordinary thing occurred to him, he either would have drowned himself in the bay within twenty-four hours or died of pneumonia in the street.

He had been seventy hours without food, and his mental desperation had driven him far in its race with his physical needs to consume the strength within him; so that now, pale, weak, and tottering, he took what comfort he could find in the savoury odours which came steaming up from the basement kitchens of the restaurants in Market Street, caring more to gain them than to avoid the rain. His teeth chattered; he shambled, stooped, and gasped. He was too desperate to curse his fate—he could only long for food. He could not reason; he could not understand that ten thousand hands might gladly have fed him; he could think only of the hunger which consumed him, and of food that could give him warmth and happiness.

When he had arrived at Mason Street, he saw a restaurant a little way up that thoroughfare, and for that he headed, crossing the street diagonally. He stopped before the window and ogled the steaks, thick and lined with fat; big oysters lying on ice; slices of ham as large as his hat; whole roasted chickens, brown and juicy. He ground his teeth, groaned, and staggered on.

A few steps beyond was a drinking-saloon, which had a private door at one side, with the words "Family Entrance" painted thereon. In the recess of the door (which was closed) stood a man. In spite of his agony, Kimberlin saw something in this man's face that appalled and fascinated him. Night was on, and the light in the vicinity was dim; but it was apparent that the stranger had an appearance of whose character he himself must have been ignorant. Perhaps it was the unspeakable anguish of it that struck through Kimberlin's sympathies. The young man came to an uncertain halt and stared at the stranger. At first he was unseen, for the stranger looked straight out into the street with singular fixity, and the death-like pallor of his face added a weirdness to the immobility of his gaze. Then he took notice of the young man.

"Ah," he said, slowly and with peculiar distinctness, "the rain has caught you, too, without overcoat or umbrella! Stand in this doorway—there is room for two."

The voice was not unkind, though it had an alarming hardness. It was the first word that had been addressed to the sufferer since hunger had seized him, and to be spoken to at all, and have his comfort regarded in the slightest way, gave him cheer. He entered the embrasure and stood beside the stranger, who at once relapsed into his fixed gaze at nothing across the street. But presently the stranger stirred himself again.

"It may rain a long time," said he; "I am cold, and I observe that you tremble. Let us step inside and get a drink."

He opened the door and Kimberlin followed, hope beginning to lay a warm hand upon his heart. The pale stranger led the way into one of the little private booths with which the place was furnished. Before sitting down he put his hand into his pocket and drew forth a roll of bank-bills.

"You are younger than I," he said; "won't you go to the bar and buy a bottle of absinthe, and bring a pitcher of water and some glasses? I don't like for the waiters to come around. Here is a twenty-dollar bill."

Kimberlin took the bill and started down through the corridor towards the bar. He clutched the money tightly in his palm; it felt warm and comfortable, and sent a delicious tingling through his arm. How many glorious hot meals did that bill represent? He clutched it tighter and hesitated. He thought he smelled a broiled steak, with fat little mushrooms and melted butter in the steaming dish. He stopped and looked back towards the door of the booth. He saw that the stranger had closed it. He could pass it, slip out the door, and buy something to eat. He turned and started, but the coward in him (there are other names for this) tripped his resolution; so he went straight to the bar and made the purchase. This was so unusual that the man who served him looked sharply at him.

"Ain't goin' to drink all o' that, are you?" he asked.

"I have friends in the box," replied Kimberlin, "and we want to drink quietly and without interruption. We are in Number 7."

"Oh, beg pardon. That's all right," said the man.

Kimberlin's step was very much stronger and steadier as he returned with the liquor. He opened the door of the booth. The stranger sat at the side of the little table, staring at the opposite wall just as he had stared across the street. He wore a wide-brimmed, slouch hat, drawn well down. It was only after Kimberlin had set the bottle, pitcher, and glasses on the table, and seated himself opposite the stranger and within his range of vision, that the pale man noticed him.

"Oh! you have brought it? How kind of you! Now please lock the door."

Kimberlin had slipped the change into his pocket, and was in

58

the act of bringing it out when the stranger said,—

"Keep the change. You will need it, for I am going to get it back in a way that may interest you. Let us first drink, and then I will explain."

The pale man mixed two drinks of absinthe and water, and the two drank. Kimberlin, unsophisticated, had never tasted the liquor before, and he found it harsh and offensive; but no sooner had it reached his stomach than it began to warm him, and sent the most delicious thrill through his frame.

"It will do us good," said the stranger; "presently we shall have more. Meanwhile, do you know how to throw dice?"

Kimberlin weakly confessed that he did not.

"I thought not. Well, please go to the bar and bring a dice-box. I would ring for it, but I don't want the waiters to be coming in."

Kimberlin fetched the box, again locked the door, and the game began. It was not one of the simple old games, but had complications, in which judgment, as well as chance, played a part. After a game or two without stakes, the stranger said,—

"You now seem to understand it. Very well—I will show you that you do not. We will now throw for a dollar a game, and in that way I shall win the money that you received in change. Otherwise I should be robbing you, and I imagine you cannot afford to lose. I mean no offence. I am a plain-spoken man, but I believe in honesty before politeness. I merely want a little di-version, and you are so kind-natured that I am sure you will not object."

"On the contrary," replied Kimberlin, "I shall enjoy it."

"Very well; but let us have another drink before we start. I believe I am growing colder."

They drank again, and this time the starving man took his liquor with relish—at least, it was something in his stomach, and it warmed and delighted him.

The stake was a dollar a side. Kimberlin won. The pale stranger smiled grimly, and opened another game. Again Kimberlin won. Then the stranger pushed back his hat and fixed that still gaze upon his opponent, smiling yet. With this full view of the pale stranger's face, Kimberlin was more appalled than ever. He had begun to acquire a certain self-possession and ease, and his marvelling at the singular character of the adventure had begun to weaken, when this new incident threw him back into confusion. It was the extraordinary expression of the stranger's face that alarmed him. Never upon the face of a living being had he seen a pallor so death-like and chilling. The face was more than pale; it was white.

Kimberlin's observing faculty had been sharpened by the absinthe, and, after having detected the stranger in an absent-minded effort two or three times to stroke a beard which had no existence, he reflected that some of the whiteness of the face might be due to the recent removal of a full beard. Besides the pallor, there were deep and sharp lines upon the face, which the electric light brought out very distinctly. With the exception of the steady glance of the eyes and an occasional hard smile, that seemed out of place upon such a face, the expression was that of stone inartistically cut. The eyes were black, but of heavy expression; the lower lip was purple; the hands were fine, white, and thin, and dark veins bulged out upon them. The stranger pulled down his hat.

"You are lucky," he said. "Suppose we try another drink. There is nothing like absinthe to sharpen one's wits, and I see that you and I are going to have a delightful game."

After the drink the game proceeded. Kimberlin won from the very first, rarely losing a game. He became greatly excited. His eyes shone; colour came to his cheeks. The stranger, having exhausted the roll of bills which he first produced, drew forth another, much larger and of higher denominations. There were several thousand dollars in the roll. At Kimberlin's right hand were his winnings,—something like two hundred dollars. The stakes were raised, and the game went rapidly on. Another drink was taken. Then fortune turned the stranger's way, and he won easily. It went back to Kimberlin, for he was now playing with all the judgment and skill he could command. Once only did it occur to him to wonder what he should do with the money if he should quit winner; but a sense of honour decided him that it would belong to the stranger.

By this time the absinthe had so sharpened Kimberlin's faculties that, the temporary satisfaction which it had brought to his hunger having passed, his physical suffering returned with increased aggressiveness. Could he not order a supper with his earnings? No; that was out of the question, and the stranger said nothing about eating. Kimberlin continued to play, while the manifestations of hunger took the form of sharp pains, which darted through him viciously, causing him to writhe and grind his teeth. The stranger paid no attention, for he was now wholly absorbed in the game. He seemed puzzled and disconcerted. He played with great care, studying each throw minutely. No conversation passed between them now. They drank occasionally, the dice continued to rattle, the money kept piling up at Kimberlin's hand.

The pale man began to behave strangely. At times he would start and throw back his head, as though he were listening. For a moment his eyes would sharpen and flash, and then sink into heaviness again. More than once Kimberlin, who had now begun to suspect that his antagonist was some kind of monster, saw a frightfully ghastly expression sweep over his face, and his features would become fixed for a very short time in a peculiar grimace. It was noticeable, however, that he was steadily sinking deeper and deeper into a condition of apathy. Occasionally he would raise his eyes to Kimberlin's face after the young man had made an astonishingly lucky throw, and keep them fixed there with a steadiness that made the young man quail.

The stranger produced another roll of bills when the second was gone, and this had a value many times as great as the others together. The stakes were raised to a thousand dollars a game, and still Kimberlin won. At last the time came when the stranger braced himself for a final effort. With speech somewhat thick, but very deliberate and quiet, he said,—

"You have won seventy-four thousand dollars, which is exactly the amount I have remaining. We have been playing for several hours. I am tired, and I suppose you are. Let us finish the game. Each will now stake his all and throw a final game for it."

Without hesitation, Kimberlin agreed. The bills made a considerable pile on the table. Kimberlin threw, and the box held but one combination that could possibly beat him; this combination might be thrown once in ten thousand times. The starving man's heart beat violently as the stranger picked up the box with exasperating deliberation. It was a long time before he threw. He made his combinations and ended by defeating his opponent. He sat looking at the dice a long time, and then he slowly leaned back in his chair, settled himself comfortably, raised his eyes to Kimberlin's, and fixed that unearthly stare upon him. He said not a word; his face contained not a trace of emotion or intelligence. He simply looked. One cannot keep one's eyes open very long without winking, but the stranger did. He sat so motionless that Kimberlin began to be tortured.

"I will go now," he said to the stranger—said that when he had not a cent and was starving.

The stranger made no reply, but did not relax his gaze; and under that gaze the young man shrank back in his own chair, terrified. He became aware that two men were cautiously talking in an adjoining booth. As there was now a deathly silence in his own, he listened, and this is what he heard:

"Yes; he was seen to turn into this street about three hours ago."

"And he had shaved?"

"He must have done so; and to remove a full beard would naturally make a great change in a man."

"But it may not have been he."

"True enough; but his extreme pallor attracted attention. You know that he has been troubled with heart-disease lately, and it has affected him seriously."

"Yes, but his old skill remains. Why, this is the most daring bank-robbery we ever had here. A hundred and forty-eight thousand dollars—think of it! How long has it been since he was let out of Joliet?"

"Eight years. In that time he has grown a beard, and lived by dice-throwing with men who thought they could detect him if he should swindle them; but that is impossible. No human being can come winner out of a game with him. He is evidently not here; let us look farther."

Then the two men clinked glasses and passed out.

The dice-players—the pale one and the starving one—sat gazing at each other, with a hundred and forty-eight thousand dollars piled up between them. The winner made no move to take in the money; he merely sat and stared at Kimberlin, wholly unmoved by the conversation in the adjoining room. His imperturbability was amazing, his absolute stillness terrifying.

Kimberlin began to shake with an ague. The cold, steady gaze of the stranger sent ice into his marrow. Unable to bear longer this unwavering look, Kimberlin moved to one side, and then he was amazed to discover that the eyes of the pale man, instead of following him, remained fixed upon the spot where he had sat, or, rather, upon the wall behind it. A great dread beset the young man. He feared to make the slightest sound. Voices of men in the bar-room were audible, and the sufferer imagined that he heard others whispering and tip-toeing in the passage outside his booth. He poured out some absinthe, watching his strange companion all the while, and drank alone and unnoticed.

He took a heavy drink, and it had a peculiar effect upon him: he felt his heart bounding with alarming force and rapidity, and breathing was difficult. Still his hunger remained, and that and the absinthe gave him an idea that the gastric acids were destroying him by digesting his stomach. He leaned forward and whispered to the stranger, but was given no attention. One of the man's hands lay upon the table; Kimberlin placed his upon it, and then drew back in terror—the hand was as cold as a stone.

The money must not lie there exposed. Kimberlin arranged it into neat parcels, looking furtively every moment at his immovable companion, and *in mortal fear that he would stir*! Then he sat back and waited. A deadly fascination impelled him to move back into his former position, so as to bring his face directly before the gaze of the stranger. And so the two sat and stared at each other.

Kimberlin felt his breath coming heavier and his heart-beats growing weaker, but these conditions gave him comfort by reducing his anxiety and softening the pangs of hunger. He was growing more and more comfortable and yawned. If he had dared he might have gone to sleep.

Suddenly a fierce light flooded his vision and sent him with a bound to his feet. Had he been struck upon the head or stabbed to the heart? No; he was sound and alive. The pale stranger still sat there staring at nothing and immovable; but Kimberlin was no longer afraid of him. On the contrary, an extraordinary buoyancy of spirit and elasticity of body made him feel reckless and daring. His former timidity and scruples vanished, and he felt equal to any adventure. Without hesitation he gathered up the money and bestowed it in his several pockets.

"I am a fool to starve," he said to himself, "with all this money ready to my hand."

As cautiously as a thief he unlocked the door, stepped out, reclosed it, and boldly and with head erect stalked out upon the street. Much to his astonishment, he found the city in the bustle of the early evening, yet the sky was clear. It was evident to him that he had not been in the saloon as long as he had supposed. He walked along the street with the utmost unconcern of the dangers that beset him, and laughed softly but gleefully. Would he not eat now—ah, would he not? Why, he could buy a dozen restaurants! Not only that, but he would hunt the city up and down for hungry men and feed them with the fattest steaks, the juiciest roasts, and the biggest oysters that the town could supply. As for himself, he must eat first; after that he would set up a great establishment for feeding other hungry mortals without charge. Yes, he would eat first; if he pleased, he would eat till he should burst. In what single place could he find sufficient to satisfy his hunger? Could he live sufficiently long to have an ox killed and roasted whole for his supper?

Besides an ox he would order two dozen broiled chickens, fifty dozen oysters, a dozen crabs, ten dozen eggs, ten hams, eight young pigs, twenty wild ducks, fifteen fish of four different kinds, eight salads, four dozen bottles each of claret, burgundy, and champagne; for pastry, eight plum-puddings, and for dessert, bushels of nuts, ices, and confections. It would require time to prepare such a meal, and if he could only live until it could be made ready it would be infinitely better than to spoil his appetite with a dozen or two meals of ordinary size. He thought he could live that long, for he felt amazingly strong and bright. Never in his life before had he walked with so great ease and lightness; his feet hardly touched the ground—he ran and leaped. It did him good to tantalize his hunger, for that would make his relish of the feast all the keener. Oh, but how they would stare when he would give his order, and how comically they would hang back, and how amazed they would be when he would throw a few thousands of dollars on the counter and tell them to take their money out of it and keep the change! Really, it was worthwhile to be so hungry as that, for then eating became an unspeakable luxury.

And one must not be in too great a hurry to eat when one is so hungry—that is beastly. How much of the joy of living do rich people miss from eating before they are hungry—before they have gone three days and nights without food! And how manly it is, and how great self-control it shows, to dally with starvation when one has a dazzling fortune in one's pocket and every restaurant has an open door! To be hungry without money—that is despair; to be starving with a bursting pocket—that is sublime! Surely the only true heaven is that in which one famishes in the presence of abundant food, which he might have for the taking, and then a gorged stomach and a long sleep.

The starving wretch, speculating thus, still kept from food. He felt himself growing in stature, and the people whom he met became pygmies. The streets widened, the stars became suns and dimmed the electric lights, and the most intoxicating odours and the sweetest music filled the air. Shouting, laughing, and singing, Kimberlin joined in a great chorus that swept over the city, and then———

★★★★★★

The two detectives who had traced the famous bank-robber to the saloon in Mason Street, where Kimberlin had encountered the stranger of the pallid face, left the saloon; but, unable to pursue the trail farther, had finally returned. They found the door of booth No. 7 locked. After rapping and calling and receiving no answer, they burst open the door, and there they saw two men—one of middle age and the other very young—sitting perfectly still, and in the strangest manner imaginable staring at each other across the table. Between them was a great pile of money, arranged neatly in parcels. Near at hand were an empty absinthe bottle, a water-pitcher, glasses, and a dice-box, with the dice lying before the elder man as he had thrown them last. One of the detectives covered the elder man with a revolver and commanded,—

"Throw up your hands!"

But the dice-thrower paid no attention. The detectives exchanged startled glances. They looked closer into the faces of the two men, and then they discovered that both were dead.

The Inmate of the Dungeon

(A story from *The Ape, the Idiot & Other People*)

After the Board of State Prison Directors, sitting in session at the prison, had heard and disposed of the complaints and petitions of a number of convicts, the warden announced that all who wished to appear had been heard. Thereupon a certain uneasy and apprehensive expression, which all along had sat upon the faces of the directors, became visibly deeper. The chairman—a nervous, energetic, abrupt, incisive man—glanced at a slip of paper in his hand, and said to the warden,—

"Send a guard for convict No. 14,208."

The warden started and became slightly pale. Somewhat confused, he haltingly replied, "Why, he has expressed no desire to appear before you."

"Nevertheless, you will send for him at once," responded the chairman.

The warden bowed stiffly and directed a guard to produce the convict. Then, turning to the chairman, he said,—

"I am ignorant of your purpose in summoning this man, but of course I have no objection. I desire, however, to make a statement concerning him before he appears."

"When we shall have called for a statement from you," coldly responded the chairman, "you may make one."

The warden sank back into his seat. He was a tall, fine-looking man, well-bred and intelligent, and had a kindly face. Though ordinarily cool, courageous, and self-possessed, he was unable to conceal a strong emotion, which looked much like fear. A heavy silence fell upon the room, disturbed only by the official stenographer, who was sharpening his pencils. A stray beam of light from the westering sun slipped into the room between the edge of the window-shade and the sash, and fell across the chair reserved for the convict. The uneasy eyes of the warden finally fell upon this beam and there his glance rested. The chairman, without addressing any one particularly, remarked,—

"There are ways of learning what occurs in a prison without the assistance of either the warden or the convicts."

Just then the guard appeared with the convict, who shambled in painfully and laboriously, as with a string he held up from the floor the heavy iron ball which was chained to his ankles. He was about forty-five years old. Undoubtedly he once had been a man of uncommon physical strength, for a powerful skeleton showed underneath the sallow skin which covered his emaciated frame. His sallowness was peculiar and ghastly. It was partly that of disease, and partly of something worse; and it was this something that accounted also for his shrunken muscles and manifest feebleness.

There had been no time to prepare him for presentation to the board. As a consequence, his unstockinged toes showed through his gaping shoes; the dingy suit of prison stripes which covered his gaunt frame was frayed and tattered; his hair had not been recently cut to the prison fashion, and, being rebellious, stood out upon his head like bristles; and his beard, which, like his hair, was heavily dashed with gray, had not been shaved for weeks. These incidents of his appearance combined with a very peculiar expression of his face to make an extraordinary picture. It is difficult to describe this almost unearthly expression. With a certain suppressed ferocity it combined an inflexibility of purpose that sat like an iron mask upon him.

His eyes were hungry and eager; they were the living part of him, and they shone luminous from beneath shaggy brows. His forehead was massive, his head of fine proportions, his jaw square and strong, and his thin, high nose showed traces of an ancestry that must have made a mark in some corner of the world at some time in history. He was prematurely old; this was seen in his gray hair and in the uncommonly deep wrinkles which lined his forehead and the corners of his eyes and of his mouth.

Upon stumbling weakly into the room, faint with the labour of walking and of carrying the iron ball, he looked around eagerly, like a bear driven to his haunches by the hounds. His glance passed so rapidly and unintelligently from one face to another that he could not have had time to form a conception of the persons present, until his swift eyes encountered the face of the warden. Instantly they flashed; he craned his neck forward; his lips opened and became blue; the wrinkles deepened about his mouth and eyes; his form grew rigid, and his breathing stopped. This sinister and terrible attitude—all the more so because he was wholly unconscious of it—was disturbed only when the chairman sharply commanded, "Take that seat."

The convict started as though he had been struck, and turned his eyes upon the chairman. He drew a deep inspiration, which wheezed and rattled as it passed into his chest. An expression of excruciating pain swept over his face. He dropped the ball, which struck the floor with a loud sound, and his long, bony fingers tore at the striped shirt over his breast. A groan escaped him, and he would have sunk to the floor had not the guard caught him and held him upright. In a moment it was over, and then, collapsing with exhaustion, he sank into the chair. There he sat, conscious and intelligent, but slouching, disorganized, and indifferent.

The chairman turned sharply to the guard. "Why did you manacle this man," he demanded, "when he is evidently so weak, and when none of the others were manacled?"

"Why, sir," stammered the guard, "surely you know who this man is: he is the most dangerous and desperate——"

"We know all about that. Remove his manacles."

The guard obeyed. The chairman turned to the convict, and in a kindly manner said, "Do you know who we are?"

The convict got himself together a little and looked steadily at the chairman. "No," he replied, after a pause. His manner was direct, and his voice was deep, though hoarse.

"We are the State Prison Directors. We have heard of your case, and we want you to tell us the whole truth about it."

The convict's mind worked slowly, and it was some time before he could comprehend the explanation and request. When he had accomplished that task he said, very slowly, "I suppose you want me to make a complaint, sir."

"Yes,—if you have any to make."

The convict was getting himself in hand. He straightened up, and gazed at the chairman with a peculiar intensity. Then firmly and clearly he answered, "I've no complaint to make."

The two men sat looking at each other in silence, and as they looked a bridge of human sympathy was slowly reared between them. The chairman rose, passed around an intervening table, went up to the convict, and laid a hand on his gaunt shoulder. There was a tenderness in his voice that few men had ever heard there.

"I know," said he, "that you are a patient and uncomplaining man, or we should have heard from you long ago. In asking you to make a statement I am merely asking for your help to right a wrong, if a wrong has been done. Leave your own wishes entirely out of consideration, if you prefer. Assume, if you will, that it is not our intention or desire either to give you relief or to make your case harder for you. There are fifteen hundred human beings in this prison, and they are under the absolute control of one man. If a serious wrong is practised upon one, it may be upon others. I ask you in the name of common humanity, and as one man of another, to put us in the way of working justice in this prison. If you have the instincts of a man within you, you will comply with my request. Speak out, therefore, like a man, and have no fear of anything."

The convict was touched and stung. He looked up steadily into the chairman's face, and firmly said, "There is nothing in this world that I fear." Then he hung his head, and presently he raised it and added, "I will tell you all about it."

At that moment he shifted his position so as to bring the

beam of light perpendicularly across his face and chest, and it seemed to split him in twain. He saw it, and feasted his gaze upon it as it lay upon his breast. After a time he thus proceeded, speaking very slowly, and in a strangely monotonous voice:

"I was sent up for twenty years for killing a man. I hadn't been a criminal: I killed him without thinking, for he had robbed me and wronged me. I came here thirteen years ago. I had trouble at first—it galled me to be a convict; but I got over that, because the warden that was here then understood me and was kind to me, and he made me one of the best men in the prison. I don't say this to make you think I'm complaining about the present warden, or that he didn't treat me kindly: I can take care of myself with him. I am not making any complaint. I ask no man's favour, and I fear no man's power."

"That is all right. Proceed."

"After the warden had made a good man out of me I worked faithfully, sir; I did everything they told me to do; I worked willingly and like a slave. It did me good to work, and I worked hard. I never violated any of the rules after I was broken in. And then the law was passed giving credits to the men for good conduct. My term was twenty years, but I did so well that my credits piled up, and after I had been here ten years I could begin to see my way out. There were only about three years left. And, sir, I worked faithfully to make those years good. I knew that if I did anything against the rules I should lose my credits and have to stay nearly ten years longer. I knew all about that, sir: I never forgot it. I wanted to be a free man again, and I planned to go away somewhere and make the fight all over,—to be a man in the world once more."

"We know all about your record in the prison. Proceed."

"Well, it was this way. You know they were doing some heavy work in the quarries and on the grades, and they wanted the strongest men in the prison. There weren't very many: there never are very many strong men in a prison. And I was one of 'em that they put on the heavy work, and I did it faithfully. They used to pay the men for extra work,—not pay 'em money, but

71

the value of the money in candles, tobacco, extra clothes, and things like that. I loved to work, and I loved to work extra, and so did some of the other men. On Saturdays the men who had done extra work would fall in and go up to the captain of the guard, and he would give to each man what was coming to him. He had it all down in a book, and when a man would come up and call for what was due him the captain would give it to him, whatever he wanted that the rules allowed.

"One Saturday I fell in with the others. A good many were ahead of me in the line, and when they got what they wanted they fell into a new line, waiting to be marched to the cells. When my turn in the line came I went up to the captain and said I would take mine in tobacco. He looked at me pretty sharply, and said, 'How did you get back in that line?' I told him I belonged there,—that I had come to get my extra. He looked at his book, and he said, 'You've had your extra: you got tobacco.' And he told me to fall into the new line. I told him I hadn't received any tobacco; I said I hadn't got my extra, and hadn't been up before. He said, 'Don't spoil your record by trying to steal a little tobacco. Fall in.' . . . It hurt me, sir. I hadn't been up; I hadn't got my extra; and I wasn't a thief, and I never had been a thief, and no living man had a right to call me a thief. I said to him, straight, 'I won't fall in till I get my extra, and I'm not a thief, and no man can call me one, and no man can rob me of my just dues.' He turned pale, and said, 'Fall in, there.' I said, 'I won't fall in till I get my dues.'

"With that he raised his hand as a signal, and the two guards behind him covered me with their rifles, and a guard on the west wall, and one on the north wall, and one on the portico in front of the arsenal, all covered me with rifles. The captain turned to a trusty and told him to call the warden. The warden came out, and the captain told him I was trying to run double on my extra, and said I was impudent and insubordinate and refused to fall in. The warden said, 'Drop that and fall in.' I told him I wouldn't fall in. I said I hadn't run double, that I hadn't got my extra, and that I would stay there till I died before I would be robbed of it. He asked the captain if there wasn't some mistake, and the captain looked at his book and said there was no mistake; he said he remembered me when I came up and got the tobacco and he saw me fall into the new line, but he didn't see me get back in the old line. The warden didn't ask the other men if they saw me get my tobacco and slip back into the old line. He just ordered me to fall in. I told him I would die before I would do that. I said I wanted my just dues and no more, and I asked him to call on the other men in line to prove that I hadn't been up.

"He said, 'That's enough of this.' He sent all the other men to the cells, and left me standing there. Then he told two guards to take me to the cells. They came and took hold of me, and I threw them off as if they were babies. Then more guards came up, and one of them hit me over the head with a club, and I fell. And then, sir,"—here the convict's voice fell to a whisper,—"and then he told them to take me to the dungeon."

The sharp, steady glitter of the convict's eyes failed, and he hung his head and looked despairingly at the floor.

"Go on," said the chairman.

"They took me to the dungeon, sir. Did you ever see the dungeon?"

"Perhaps; but you may tell us about it."

The cold, steady gleam returned to the convict's eyes, as he fixed them again upon the chairman.

"There are several little rooms in the dungeon. The one they put me in was about five by eight. It has steel walls and ceiling, and a granite floor. The only light that comes in passes through a slit in the door. The slit is an inch wide and five inches long. It doesn't give much light, because the door is thick. It's about four inches thick, and is made of oak and sheet-steel, bolted through. The slit runs this way,"—making a horizontal motion in the air,—"and it is four inches above my eyes when I stand on tiptoe. And I can't look out at the factory-wall forty feet away unless I hook my fingers in the slit and pull myself up."

He stopped and regarded his hands, the peculiar appearance of which we all had observed. The ends of the fingers were uncommonly thick; they were red and swollen, and the knuckles were curiously marked with deep white scars.

"Well, sir, there wasn't anything at all in the dungeon, but they gave me a blanket, and they put me on bread and water. That's all they ever give you in the dungeon. They bring the bread and water once a day, and that is at night, because if they come in the daytime it lets in the light.

"The next night after they put me in—it was Sunday night— the warden came with the guard and asked me if I was all right. I said I was. He said, 'Will you behave yourself and go to work tomorrow?' I said, 'No, sir; I won't go to work till I get what is due me.' He shrugged his shoulders, and said, 'Very well: maybe you'll change your mind after you have been in here a week.'

"They kept me there a week. The next Sunday night the warden came and said, 'Are you ready to go to work to-morrow?' and I said, 'No; I will not go to work till I get what is due me.' He called me hard names. I said it was a man's duty to demand his rights, and that a man who would stand to be treated like a dog was no man at all."

The chairman interrupted. "Did you not reflect," he asked, "that these officers would not have stooped to rob you?—that it was through some mistake they withheld your tobacco, and that in any event you had a choice of two things to lose,—one a plug of tobacco, and the other seven years of freedom?"

"But they angered me and hurt me, sir, by calling me a thief, and they threw me in the dungeon like a beast . . . . I was standing for my rights, and my rights were my manhood; and that is something a man can carry sound to the grave, whether he's bond or free, weak or powerful, rich or poor."

"Well, after you refused to go to work what did the warden do?"

The convict, although tremendous excitement must have surged and boiled within him, slowly, deliberately, and weakly came to his feet. He placed his right foot on the chair, and rested his right elbow on the raised knee. The index finger of his right hand, pointing to the chairman and moving slightly to lend emphasis to his narrative, was the only thing that modified the rigid immobility of his figure. Without a single change in the pitch or modulation of his voice, never hurrying, but speaking with the slow and dreary monotony with which he had begun, he nevertheless—partly by reason of these evidences of his incredible self-control—made a formidable picture as he proceeded:

"When I told him that, sir, he said he'd take me to the ladder and see if he couldn't make me change my mind . . . . Yes, sir; he said he'd take me to the ladder." (Here there was a long pause.) "And I a human being, with flesh on my bones and the heart of a man in my body. The other warden hadn't tried to break my spirit on the ladder. He did break it, though; he broke it clear to the bottom of the man inside of me; but he did it with a human word, and not with the dungeon and the ladder. I didn't believe the warden when he said he would take me to the ladder. I couldn't imagine myself alive and put through at the ladder, and I couldn't imagine any human being who could find the heart to put me through. If I had believed him I would have strangled him then and there, and got my body full of lead while doing it. No, sir; I could not believe it.

"And then he told me to come on. I went with him and the guards. He brought me to the ladder. I had never seen it before. It was a heavy wooden ladder, leaned against the wall, and the bottom was bolted to the floor and the top to the wall. A whip was on the floor." (Again there was a pause.) "The warden told me to strip, sir, and I stripped . . . . And still I didn't believe he would whip me. I thought he just wanted to scare me.

"Then he told me to face up to the ladder. I did so, and reached my arms up to the straps. They strapped my arms to the ladder, and stretched so hard that they pulled me up clear of the floor. Then they strapped my legs to the ladder. The warden then picked up the whip. He said to me, 'I'll give you one more chance: will you go to work tomorrow?' I said, 'No; I won't go to work till I get my dues.' 'Very well,' said he, 'you'll get your dues now.' And then he stepped back and raised the whip. I turned my head and looked at him, and I could see it in his eyes that he meant to strike . . . . And when I saw that, sir, I felt that something inside of me was about to burst."

The convict paused to gather up his strength for the crisis of his story, yet not in the least particular did he change his position, the slight movement of his pointing finger, the steady gleam of his eye, or the slow monotony of his speech. I had never witnessed any scene so dramatic as this, and yet all was absolutely simple and unintentional. I had been thrilled by the greatest actors, as with matchless skill they gave rein to their genius in tragic situations; but how inconceivably tawdry and cheap such pictures seemed in comparison with this! The clap-trap of the music, the lights, the posing, the wry faces, the gasps, lunges, staggerings, rolling eyes,—how flimsy and colourless, how mocking and grotesque, they all appeared beside this simple, uncouth, but genuine expression of immeasurable agony!

The stenographer held his pencil poised above the paper, and wrote no more.

"And then the whip came down across my back. The something inside of me twisted hard and then broke wide open, and went pouring all through me like melted iron. It was a hard fight to keep my head clear, but I did it. And then I said to the warden this: 'You've struck me with a whip, in cold blood. You've tied me up hand and foot, to whip me like a dog. Well, whip me, then, till you fill your belly with it. You are a coward. You are lower, and meaner, and cowardlier than the lowest and meanest dog that ever yelped when his master kicked him. You were born a coward. Cowards will lie and steal, and you are the same as a thief and liar. No hound would own you for a friend. Whip me hard and long, you coward. Whip me, I say. See how good a coward feels when he ties up a man and whips him like a dog. Whip me till the last breath quits my body; if you leave me alive I will kill you for this.'

"His face got white. He asked me if I meant that, and I said, 'Yes; before God I do.' Then he took the whip in both hands and came down with all his might."

"That was nearly two years ago," said the chairman. "You

would not kill him now, would you?"

"Yes. I will kill him if I get a chance; and I feel it in me that the chance will come."

"Well, proceed."

"He kept on whipping me. He whipped me with all the strength of both hands. I could feel the broken skin curl up on my back, and when my head got too heavy to hold it straight it hung down, and I saw the blood on my legs and dripping off my toes into a pool of it on the floor. Something was straining and twisting inside of me again. My back didn't hurt much; it was the thing twisting inside of me that hurt. I counted the lashes, and when I counted to twenty-eight the twisting got so hard that it choked me and blinded me; . . . and when I woke up I was in the dungeon again, and the doctor had my back all plastered up, and he was kneeling beside me, feeling my pulse."

The prisoner had finished. He looked around vaguely, as though he wanted to go.

"And you have been in the dungeon ever since?"

"Yes, sir; but I don't mind that."

"How long?"

"Twenty-three months."

"On bread and water?"

"Yes; but that was all I wanted."

"Have you reflected that so long as you harbor a determination to kill the warden you may be kept in the dungeon? You can't live much longer there, and if you die there you will never find the chance you want. If you say you will not kill the warden he may return you to the cells."

"But that would be a lie, sir; I will get a chance to kill him if I go to the cells. I would rather die in the dungeon than be a liar and sneak. If you send me to the cells I will kill him. But I will kill him without that. I will kill him, sir . . . .And he knows it."

Without concealment, but open, deliberate, and implacable, thus in the wrecked frame of a man, so close that we could have touched it, stood Murder,—not boastful, but relentless as death.

"Apart from weakness, is your health good?" asked the chairman.

"Oh, it's good enough," wearily answered the convict. "Sometimes the twisting comes on, but when I wake up after it I'm all right."

The prison surgeon, under the chairman's direction, put his ear to the convict's chest, and then went over and whispered to the chairman.

"I thought so," said that gentleman. "Now, take this man to the hospital. Put him to bed where the sun will shine on him, and give him the most nourishing food."

The convict, giving no heed to this, shambled out with a guard and the surgeon.

★★★★★★

The warden sat alone in the prison office with No. 14,208. That he at last should have been brought face to face, and alone, with the man whom he had determined to kill, perplexed the convict. He was not manacled; the door was locked, and the key lay on the table between the two men. Three weeks in the hospital had proved beneficial, but a deathly pallor was still in his face.

"The action of the directors three weeks ago," said the warden, "made my resignation necessary. I have awaited the appointment of my successor, who is now in charge. I leave the prison today. In the meantime, I have something to tell you that will interest you. A few days ago a man who was discharged from the prison last year read what the papers have published recently about your case, and he has written to me confessing that it was he who got your tobacco from the captain of the guard. His name is Salter, and he looks very much like you. He had got his own extra, and when he came up again and called for yours the captain, thinking it was you, gave it to him. There was no intention on the captain's part to rob you."

The convict gasped and leaned forward eagerly.

"Until the receipt of this letter," resumed the warden, "I had opposed the movement which had been started for your pardon; but when this letter came I recommended your pardon, and it has been granted. Besides, you have a serious heart trouble. So you are now discharged from the prison."

The convict stared and leaned back speechless. His eyes shone with a strange, glassy expression, and his white teeth glistened ominously between his parted lips. Yet a certain painful softness tempered the iron in his face.

"The stage will leave for the station in four hours," continued the warden. "You have made certain threats against my life." The warden paused; then, in a voice that slightly wavered from emotion, he continued: "I shall not permit your intentions in that regard—for I care nothing about them—to prevent me from discharging a duty which, as from one man to another, I owe you. I have treated you with a cruelty the enormity of which I now comprehend. I thought I was right. My fatal mistake was in not understanding your nature. I misconstrued your conduct from the beginning, and in doing so I have laid upon my conscience a burden which will embitter the remaining years of my life. I would do anything in my power, if it were not too late, to atone for the wrong I have done you. If, before I sent you to the dungeon, I could have understood the wrong and foreseen its consequences, I would cheerfully have taken my own life rather than raised a hand against you. The lives of us both have been wrecked; but your suffering is in the past,—mine is present, and will cease only with my life. For my life is a curse, and I prefer not to keep it."

With that the warden, very pale, but with a clear purpose in his face, took a loaded revolver from a drawer and laid it before the convict.

"Now is your chance," he said, quietly: "no one can hinder you."

The convict gasped and shrank away from the weapon as from a viper.

"Not yet—not yet," he whispered, in agony.

The two men sat and regarded each other without the movement of a muscle.

"Are you afraid to do it?" asked the warden.

A momentary light flashed in the convict's eyes.

"No!" he gasped; "you know I am not. But I can't—not yet,—not yet."

The convict, whose ghastly pallor, glassy eyes, and gleaming teeth sat like a mask of death upon his face, staggered to his feet.

"You have done it at last! you have broken my spirit. A human word has done what the dungeon and the whip could not do . . . .It twists inside of me now . . . .I could be your slave for that human word." Tears streamed from his eyes. "I can't help crying. I'm only a baby, after all—and I thought I was a man."

He reeled, and the warden caught him and seated him in the chair. He took the convict's hand in his and felt a firm, true pressure there. The convict's eyes rolled vacantly. A spasm of pain caused him to raise his free hand to his chest; his thin, gnarled fingers—made shapeless by long use in the slit of the dungeon-door—clutched automatically at his shirt. A faint, hard smile wrinkled his wan face, displaying the gleaming teeth more freely.

"That human word," he whispered,—"if you had spoken it long ago,—if—but it's all—it's all right—now. I'll go—I'll go to work—tomorrow."

There was a slightly firmer pressure of the hand that held the warden's; then it relaxed. The fingers which clutched the shirt slipped away, and the hand dropped to his side. The weary head sank back and rested on the chair; the strange, hard smile still sat upon the marble face, and a dead man's glassy eyes and gleaming teeth were upturned towards the ceiling.

A Game of Honour

(A story from *The Ape, the Idiot & Other People*)

Four of the five men who sat around the card-table in the cabin of the *Merry Witch* regarded the fifth man with a steady, implacable look of scorn. The solitary one could not face that terrible glance. His head drooped, and his gaze rested upon some cards which he idly fumbled as he waited, numbed and listless, to hear his sentence.

The more masterful one of the four made a disdainful gesture towards the craven one, and thus addressed the others:

"Gentlemen, none of us can have forgotten the terms of our compact. It was agreed at the beginning of this expedition that only men of unflinching integrity should be permitted to participate in its known dangers and possible rewards. To find and secure the magnificent treasure which we are seeking with a sure prospect of discovering it, we must run the risk of encounters with savage Mexican soldiers and marines, and take all the other dangerous chances of which you are aware. As the charterer of this vessel and the leader of the expedition I have exercised extraordinary care in selecting my associates. We have been and still are equals, and my leadership as the outfitter of the expedition gives me no advantage in the sharing of the treasure. As such leader, however, I am in authority, and have employed, unsuspected by you, many devices to test the manhood of each of you. Were it not for the fact that I have exhausted all reasonable resources to this end, and have found all of you trustworthy except one, I would not now be disclosing the plan which I have been pursuing."

The three others, who had been gazing at the crestfallen one, now stared at their leader with a startled interest.

"The final test of a man's character," calmly pursued the leader, "is the card-table. Whatever there may be in him of weakness, whether it be a mean avarice, cowardice, or a deceitful disposition, will there inevitably appear. If I were the president of a bank, the general of an army, or the leader of any other great enterprise I would make it a point to test the character of my subordinates in a series of games at cards, preferably played for money. It is the only sure test of character that the wisdom of the ages has been able to devise."

He paused, and then turned his scornful glance upon the cringing man, who meanwhile had mustered courage to look up, and was employing his eyes as well as his ears to comprehend the strange philosophy of his judge. Terror and dismay were elements of the expression which curiously wrinkled his white face, as though he found himself standing before a court of inscrutable wisdom and relentless justice. But his glance fell instantly when it encountered that of his judge, and his weak lower lip hung trembling.

"We have all agreed," impressively continued the leader, "that the one found guilty of deceiving or betraying the others to the very smallest extent should pay the penalty which we are all sworn to exact. A part of this agreement, as we all remember, is that the one found derelict shall be the first to insist on the visitation of the penalty, and that should he fail to do so—but I trust that it is unnecessary to mention the alternative."

There was another pause, and the culprit sat still, hardly breathing, and permitting the cards to slip from his fingers to the floor.

"Mr. Rossiter," said the leader, addressing the hapless man in a tone so hard and cold that it congealed the marrow which it pierced, "have you any suggestion to make?"

The doomed man made such a pitiful struggle for self-mastery as the gallows often reveals. If there was a momentary flash of hope based on a transient determination to plead, it faded instantly before the stern and implacable eyes that greeted him from all sides of the table. Certainly there was a fierce struggle under which his soul writhed, and which showed in a passing flush that crimsoned his face. That went by, and an acceptance of doom sat upon him. He raised his head and looked firmly at the leader, and as he did so his chest expanded and his shoulders squared bravely.

"Captain," said he, with a very good voice, "whatever else I may be, I am not a coward. I have cheated. In doing so I have betrayed the confidence of all. I remember the terms of the compact. Will you kindly summon the skipper?"

Without any change of countenance, the leader complied.

"Mr. Rossiter," he said to the skipper, "has a request to make of you, and whatever it may be I authorize you to comply with it."

"I wish," asked Mr. Rossiter of the skipper, "that you would lower a boat and put me aboard, and that you would furnish the boat with one oar and nothing else whatever."

"Why," exclaimed the skipper, aghast, looking in dismay from one to another of the men, "the man is insane! There is no land within five hundred miles. We are in the tropics, and a man couldn't live four days without food or water, and the sea is alive with sharks. Why, this is suicide!"

The leader's face darkened, but before he could speak Mr. Rossiter calmly remarked,—

"That is my own affair, sir;" and there was a fine ring in his voice.

★★★★★★

The man in the boat, bareheaded and stripped nearly naked in the broiling sun, was thus addressing something which he saw close at hand in the water:

"Let me see. Yes, I think it is about four days now that we have travelled together, but I am not very positive about that. You see, if it hadn't been for you I should have died of loneliness . . . .Say! aren't you hungry, too? I was a few days ago, but

I'm only thirsty now. You've got the advantage of me, because you don't get thirsty. As for your being hungry—ha, ha, ha! Who ever heard of a shark that wasn't always hungry? Oh, I know well enough what's in your mind, companion mine, but there's time enough for that. I hate to disturb the pleasant relation which exists between us at present. That is to say—now, here is a witticism—I prefer the outside relation to the inside intimacy. Ha, ha, ha! I knew you'd laugh at that, you sly old rogue!

"What a very sly, patient old shark you are! Don't you know that if you didn't have those clumsy fins, and that dreadfully homely mouth away down somewhere on the underside of your body, and eyes so grotesquely wide apart, and should go on land and match your wit against the various and amusing species of sharks which abound there, your patience in pursuing a manifest advantage would make you a millionaire in a year? Can you get that philosophy through your thick skull, my friend?

"There, there, there! Don't turn over like that and make a fool of yourself by opening your pretty mouth and dazzling the midday sun with the gleam of your white belly. I'm not ready yet. God! how thirsty I am! Say, did you ever feel like that? Did you ever see blinding flashes that tear through your brain and turn the sun black?

"You haven't answered my question yet. It's a hypothetical question—yes, hypothetical. I'm sure that's what I want to say. Hypo—hypothetical question. Question; yes, that's right. Now, suppose you'd been a pretty wild young shark, and had kept your mother anxious and miserable, and had drifted into gambling and had gone pretty well to the dogs. Do sharks ever go to the dogs? Now, that's a poser. Sharks; dogs. Oh, what a very ridiculously, sublimely amusing old shark! Dreadfully discreet you are. Never disclose your hand except on a showdown. What a glum old villain you are!

"Pretty well to the dogs, and then braced up and left home to make a man of yourself. Think of a shark making a man of himself! And then—easy there! Don't get excited. I only staggered that time and didn't quite go overboard. And don't let my gesticulations excite you. Keep your mouth shut, my friend; you're not pretty when you smile like that. As I was saying—oh!...

"How long was I that way, old fellow? Good thing for me that you don't know how to climb into a boat when a fellow is that way. Were you ever that way, partner? Come on like this: Biff! Big blaze of red fire in your head. Then—then—well, after awhile you come out of it, with the queerest and crookedest of augers boring through your head, and a million tadpoles of white fire darting in every direction through the air. Don't ever get that way, my friend, if you can possibly keep out of it. But then, you never get thirsty. Let me see. The sun was over there when the red fire struck, and it's over here now. Shifted about thirty degrees. Then, I was that way about two hours.

"Where are those dogs? Do they come to you or do you go to them? That depends. Now, say you had some friends that wanted to do you a good turn; wanted to straighten you up and make a man of you. They had ascertained the exact situation of a wonderful treasure buried in an island of the Pacific. All right. They knew you had some of the qualities useful for such an expedition—reckless dare-devil, afraid of nothing—things like that. Understand, my friend? Well, all swore oaths as long as your leg—as long as your—oh, my! Think of a shark having a leg! Ha, ha, ha! Long as your leg! Oh, my! Pardon my levity, old man, but I must laugh. Ha, ha, ha! Oh, my!

"All of you swore—you and the other sharks. No lying; no deceit; no swindling. First shark that makes a slip is to call the skipper and be sent adrift with one oar and nothing else. And all, my friend, after you had pledged your honour to your mother, your God, yourself, and your friends, to be a true and honourable shark. It isn't the hot sun broiling you and covering you with bursting blisters, and changing the marrow of your bones to melted iron and your blood to hissing lava—it isn't the sun that hurts; and the hunger that gnaws your intestines to rags, and the thirst that changes your throat into a funnel of hot brass, and blinding bursts of red fire in your head, and lying dead in the waist of the boat while the sun steals thirty degrees of time out the sky, and a million fiery tadpoles darting through the air—none of them hurts so much as something infinitely deeper and more cruel,—your broken pledge of honour to your mother, your God, yourself, and your friends. That is what hurts, my friend.

"It is late, old man, to begin life all over again while you are in the article of death, and resolve to be good when it is no longer possible to be bad. But that is our affair, yours and mine; and just at this time we are not choosing to discuss the utility of goodness. But I don't like that sneer in your glance. I have only one oar, and I will cheerfully break it over your wretched head if you come a yard nearer. . . .

"Aha! Thought I was going over, eh? See; I can stand steady when I try. But I don't like that sneer in your eyes. You don't believe in the reformation of the dying, eh? You are a contemptible dog; a low, mean, outcast dog. You sneer at the declaration of a man that he can and will be honest at last and face his Maker humbly, but still as a man. Come, then, my friend, and let us see which of us two is the decent and honourable one. Stake your manhood against mine, and stake your life with your manhood. We'll see which is the more honorable of the two; for I tell you now, Mr. Shark, that we are going to gamble for our lives and our honour.

"Come up closer and watch the throw. No? Afraid of the oar? You sneaking coward! You would be a decent shark at last did the oar but split your skull. See this visiting card, you villain? Look at it as I hold it up. There is printing on one side; that is my name; it is I. The other side is blank; that is you. Now, I am going to throw this into the water. If it falls name up, I win; if blank side up, you win. If I win, I eat you; if you win, you eat me. Is that a go?

"Hold on. You see, I can throw a card so as to bring uppermost either side I please. That wouldn't be fair. For this, the last game of my life, is to be square. So I fold one end down on this side, and the other down on that side. When you throw a card folded like that no living shark, whether he have legs or only a tail, can know which side will fall uppermost. That is a square game, old man, and it will settle the little difference that has existed between you and me for four days past—a difference of ten or fifteen feet.

"Mind you, if I win, you are to come alongside the boat and I am to kill you and eat you. That may sustain my life until I am picked up. If you win, over I go and you eat me. Are you in the game? Well, here goes, then, for life or death . . . .Ah! you have won! And this is a game of honour!"

★★★★★★

A black-smoking steamer was steadily approaching the drifting boat, for the lookout had reported the discovery, and the steamer was bearing down to lend succour. The captain, standing on the bridge, saw through his glass a wild and nearly naked man making the most extraordinary signs and gestures, staggering and lurching in imminent danger of falling overboard. When the ship had approached quite near the captain saw the man toss a card into the water, and then stand with an ominous rigidity, the meaning of which was unmistakable. He sounded a blast from the whistle, and the drifting man started violently and turned to see the steamer approaching, and observed hasty preparations for the lowering of a boat. The outcast stood immovable, watching the strange apparition, which seemed to have sprung out of the ocean.

The boat touched the water and shot lustily forward.

"Pull with all your might, lads, for the man is insane, and is preparing to leap overboard. A big shark is lying in wait for him, and the moment he touches the water he is gone."

The men did pull with all their might and hallooed to the drifting one and warned him of the shark.

"Wait a minute," they cried, "and we'll take you on the ship!"

The purpose of the men seemed at last to have dawned upon the understanding of the outcast. He straightened himself as well as he could into a wretched semblance of dignity, and hoarsely replied,—

87

"No; I have played a game and lost; an honest man will pay a debt of honour."

And with such a light in his eyes as comes only into those whose vision has penetrated the most wonderful of all mysteries, he leaped forth into the sea.

Treacherous Velasco

(A story from *The Ape, the Idiot & Other People*)

Sitting at the open window of her room in the upper storey of the farmhouse, on the Rancho San Gregorio, Señora Violante Ovando de McPherson watched, with the deepest interest, a cloud of dust which rose in the still May air far down the valley; for it was evident that the colour in her cheeks and the sparkle in her violet-black eyes spoke a language of devotion and happiness. Her husband was coming home, and with him his *vaqueros*, after a tedious drive of cattle to San Francisco. He had been gone but a month; but what an interminable absence that is to a wife of a year! She had watched the fading of the wild golden poppies; she had seen the busy workers of the bee-hives laying up their stores of honey culled from the myriads of flowers which carpeted the valley; and she had ridden over the Gabilan Hills to see the thousands of her husband's cattle which dotted them.

She had been respectful of her housekeeping duties, and had directed Alice, the sewing-girl, in the making of garments for the approaching hot season. Yet, busy as she thought she was, and important as she imagined herself to be in the management of the great ranch, time had dragged itself by in manacles. But now was coming the cloud of dust to lift the cloud of loneliness; and if ever a young wife's heart quickened with gladness, it was hers.

Presently the fine young Scotchman leaped from his horse, clasped his wife in his arms, asked a few hurried questions concerning her welfare during his absence, untied a small buckskin bag which depended from the pommel of his saddle, and, re-marking, "I thought you might need some spending-money, Vi-olante," held up the bag containing gold, containing a hundred times more gold than her simple tastes and restricted opportuni-ties would permit her to employ. But was not her Robert the most generous of men? Other eyes than hers saw it—those of Basilio Velasco, one of the *vaqueros*; a small, swarthy man, with the blackest and sharpest of eyes, in which just then was a strange glitter.

What a handsome couple were the young husband and wife, as, arm-in-arm, they entered the house—he so large, and red, and masculine; she so dark, and reliant, and feminine! Beautiful Spanish girls were plentiful in those youthful days of California; but Violante had been known as the most beautiful of all the maidens between the Santa Barbara Channel and the Bay of Monterey. Hard-headed and fiery-tempered Scotch Presbyte-rian; gentle, patient, and faithful Catholic; they were the happiest and most devoted of couples.

"Well, little Violante," he said, "take the bag up to your room, and give us dinner; for before we rest we must ride over to the range and look after the cattle, and after that you and I shall have a good, long visit."

These pleasant duties were quickly dispatched, and the dusty men, led by her husband, galloped away. From the open window of her room she saw the receding cloud of dust, wondering at that urgent sense of duty which could make so fond a husband leave her, even though for a short time, after so long a separa-tion. Thus she sat, dreamily thinking of her great happiness in having him once again at home, and drinking in the rich per-fume of the racemes of wisteria-blossoms which covered the massive vine against the house. This old vine, springing from the ground beneath the window at which she sat, spread its long arms almost completely over that part of the wall, divided on either side for the window, and hung gracefully from beneath the eaves, embowering their lovely owner in a tangled mass of purple blossoms.

It was an exquisite picture—the pretty wife sitting there, in the whitest of lawns, looking out over the hills from this frame of gorgeous flowers—all the more charming from her unconsciousness of its beauty. Behind her, at the opposite side of the room, sat her maid, Alice, sewing in silence.

As the *señora* looked dreamily over the hills, she became aware of the peculiar actions of a man on horseback, who was approaching the house from the direction in which her husband and the *vaqueros* had disappeared. That which summoned her attention was the fact that the man was approaching by an irregular route, which no ordinary circumstance would have required. He had such a way of keeping behind the trees that she could not determine his identity. It looked strange and mysterious, and something impelled her to drop the lace curtain over the window, for behind it she could watch without danger of being seen.

The horseman disappeared, and this made her uneasiness all the greater, but she said nothing to Alice. Soon she noticed the man on foot approaching the house, in a watchful, skulking fashion, slipping from one tree or one bit of shrubbery to another. Then, with a swift run, he came near, and, stealthily and noiselessly as a cat, began to ascend to her window by clambering up the wisteria-vine. Her spirit quailed and her cheeks blanched when she saw the naked blade of a dagger held between his teeth. She understood his mission—it was her life and the gold; and the glittering eyes of the robber she recognized as those of Basilio Velasco. After a moment of nerveless terror the ancient resisting blood of the Ovandos sprang into alert activity, and this gentlest and sweetest of young women armed her soul to meet Death on his own ground and his own terms, and try the issue with him.

She gave no alarm, for there was none in the house except herself and Alice. To have given way to fear would have destroyed her only hope of life. Quietly, in a low tone, she said,—

"Alice, listen, but do not say a word." There was an impressiveness in her manner that startled the nervous, timid girl; but there were also in it a strength and a self-reliance that reassured her. She dropped her work and regarded her mistress with wonder. "Look in the second drawer of the bureau. You will find a pistol there. Bring it to me quickly, without a word, for a man is clambering up the vine under my window to rob me, and if we make any outcry or lose our heads we are dead. Place full confidence in me, and it will be all right."

Alice, numb and nervous with fear, found the pistol and brought it to her mistress.

"Go and sit down and keep quiet," she was told; and this she did.

Violante, seeing that the weapon was loaded, cocked it, and glanced out the window. Basilio was climbing very slowly and carefully, fearing that the least disturbance of the vine would alarm the *señora*. When he had come sufficiently near to make her aim sure, Violante suddenly thrust aside the curtain, leaned out the window, and brought the barrel of the weapon in line with Velasco's head.

"What do you want, Basilio?" she asked.

Hearing the musical voice, the Spaniard quickly looked up. Had the bullet then imprisoned in the weapon been sent crashing through his vitals, he would have received hardly a greater shock than that which quivered through his nerves when he saw the black barrel of the pistol, the small but steady hand which held it aimed at his brain, and the pale and beautiful face above it. Thus holding the robber at her mercy, she said firmly to the girl,—

"Alice, there is nothing to fear now. Run as fast as you can to the west end of the house, about a hundred yards away, and you will find this man's horse tied there somewhere in the shrubbery. Mount it, and ride as fast as God will let you. Find my husband, and tell him I have a robber as prisoner."

The girl, almost fainting, passed out of the room, found the horse, and galloped away, leaving these two mortal enemies facing each other.

Velasco had heard all this, and he heard the horse clattering up the road to the range beyond the hills of Gabilan. The picture of a fierce and angry young Scotchman dashing up to the house and slaying him without a parley needed no elaboration in his dazed imagination. He gazed steadily at the *señora* and she at him; and, while he saw a strange pity and a sorrow in her glance, he saw also an unyielding determination. He could not speak, for the knife between his teeth held his tongue a prisoner. If only he could plead with her and beg for his life!

"Basilio," she quietly said, seeing that he was preparing to release one hand by finding a firmer hold for the other, "if you take either of your hands away from the vine I will shoot you. Keep perfectly still. If you make the least movement, I will shoot. You have seen me throw apples in the air and send a bullet through every one with this pistol."

There was no boastfulness in this, and Velasco knew it to be true.

"I would have given you money, Basilio, if you had asked me for it; but to come thus with a knife! You would have killed me, Basilio, and I have never been unkind to you."

If he could only remove the dagger from his mouth! Surely one so kind and gentle as she would let him go in peace if he could only plead with her! But to let the dagger fall from his teeth would be to disarm himself, and he was hardly ready for that; and there was much thinking and planning to be done within a very few minutes.

Velasco, still with his gaze on the black hole in the pistol-barrel, soon made a discouraging discovery; the position in which he had been arrested was insecure and uncomfortable, and the unusual strain that it brought upon his muscles became painful and exhausting. To shift his position even in the smallest way would be to invite the bullet. As the moments flew the strain upon particular sets of muscles increased his pain with alarming rapidity, and unconsciously he began to speculate upon the length of time that remained before his suffering would lead him into recklessness and death. While he was thus approaching a very agony of pain, with the end of all human endurance not far away, another was suffering in a different manner, but hardly less severely.

The beautiful *señora* held the choice of two lives in the barrel of her pistol; but that she should thus hold any life at all was a matter that astounded, perplexed, and agonized her; that she had the courage to be in so extraordinary a position amazed her beyond estimation. Now, when one reflects that one is courageous, one's courage is questionable. And then, she was really so tender-hearted that she wondered if she could make good her threat to shoot if the murderer should move. That he believed she would was sufficient.

But after the arrival of her husband—what then? With his passionate nature could he resist the temptation to cut the fellow's throat before her very eyes? That was too horrible to think of. But—God!—the robber himself had a knife! By thus summoning her husband was she not inviting him to a mortal struggle with a desperate man better armed than he? It would have been easy to liberate Basilio and let him go his way; but she knew that her husband would follow and find him. Now that the mischief of notifying him had been done, it was best to keep the prisoner with her, that she might plead for his life. Therein lay her hope that she could avert the shedding of blood by either of the men.

Her suspense; her self-questionings; her dread of a terrible termination to an incident which already had assumed the shape of a tragedy; her fearful responsibility; the menacing possibility that she herself, in simple defence of her life, might have to kill Basilio; her trepidation on the score of her aim and the reliability of the pistol—all these things and others were wearing her out; and at last she, too, began to wonder how long she could bear the strain, and whether or not her husband would arrive in time to save her.

Meanwhile, Velasco, racked to the marrow by the pains which tortured him, and driven by a desire to drop the dagger and plead for his life and by fear of parting with his weapon, was urged to despair, and finally to desperation. All the supplication that his face and eyes could show pleaded eloquently for him, and with this silent pleading came evidence of his physical agony. The muscles of his arms and legs twitched and trembled, and his laboured breathing hissed as it split upon the edge of the knife. He was unable longer to control the muscles of his lips; the keen edge of his weapon found a way into the flesh at either side of his mouth, and two small streams of blood trickled down his chin and fell upon his breast.

Not for a moment did he take his gaze from her eyes; and thus these two regarded each other in a silence and a stillness that were terrible. A crisis had to come. Here was a test of nerve that inevitably would make a victim of one or the other. The spectacle of the man's agony, the pitiful sight of his imploring look, were more than the feminine flesh of which Violante was composed could bear.

The crash came—Basilio was the first to break down. Whether voluntarily or not, he released his hold upon the knife, which went clattering through the vine-branches to the ground. In another instant his tongue, now free, began pouring forth a supplication in the Spanish language with an eloquence which Violante had never heard equalled.

"Oh, *señora!*" he said, "who but an angel could show a mercy tenderer than human? And yet, as I hope for the mercy of the Holy Virgin, there are a sweetness and a kindness in your face that belong to an angel of mercy. Oh, Mother of God! surely thy unworthy son has been brought into this strait for the trying of his soul, and for its chastisement and purification at the hands of thy sweetest and gentlest of daughters; for thou hast put it into her heart—which is as pure as her face is beautiful—to spare me from a most horrible end. Thou hast whispered into her mother-soul that one of thy sons, however base and undeserving, should not be sent unshriven to the judgment-seat of the most Holy Christ, thy son.

"Through the holy church thou hast enlightened her soul to the duties of a Christian, for in her beautiful face shines the radiance of heaven.—Ah, *señora!* see me plead for mercy! Behold the agonies which beset me, and let my sufferings unlock the door of your heart. Let me go in peace, señora; and you shall find in me a slave all the days of my life—the humblest and most devoted of slaves, happy if you beat me, glorying in my slavery if you starve me, and giving praise to Almighty God if you trample me under your feet. *Señora, señora*, release me, for time is pressing—I can barely escape if you let me go this instant. Would you have my blood on your hands? Can you face the Virgin with that? Oh, *señora—señora*——"

Her head swam, and all her senses were afloat in a sea of agonies. Still she looked down into his eyes as he continued his pleadings, but the outlines of his body were wavering and uncertain, and inexpressible suffering numbed her faculties. Still she listened vaguely to his outpouring of speech; and it was not until her husband, with two of his *vaqueros*, dashed up on horseback that either of these two strangely situated sufferers was aware of his approach. Seeing him, Violante threw her arms abroad, and the pistol went flying to the ground; and then she sank down to the floor, and the brilliant sunshine became night and the shining glories of the day all nothingness.

✶✶✶✶✶✶

She awoke and found herself lying on her bed, with her husband sitting beside her, caressing her hands and watching her anxiously. It was a little time before she could summon her faculties to exercise and to an understanding of her husband's endearing words; but, seeing him safe with her, her next thought was of Velasco.

"Where is Basilio?" she asked, starting up and looking fearfully about.

"He is safe, my dear one. Think no more of Basilio, who would have harmed my Violante. Be calm, for my sake, sweet wife."

"Oh, I can't, I can't! You must tell me about Basilio." And, in a frightened whisper, she asked, "Did you kill him?"

"No, loved one; Basilio is alive."

96

She sank back upon her pillow. "God be praised!" she whispered.

Suddenly she started again and looked keenly into her husband's eyes. "You have never deceived me," she hurriedly said; "but, Robert, I must know the truth. Have no fear—I can bear it. For God's sake, my husband, tell me the truth!"

Alarmed, he took her in his arms, and said, "Be calm, my Violante; for as the Almighty is my witness, Basilio is alive."

"Alive! alive!" she cried; "what does that mean? You are keeping something back, my husband. I know your passionate nature too well—you could not let him off so easily. Tell me the whole truth, Robert, or I shall go mad!"

There was a frantic earnestness in this that would have made evasion unwise.

"I will, Violante; I will. Listen—for upon my soul, this is the whole truth: When I saw you drop the pistol and sink back upon the floor, I knew that you had fainted. I ordered the *vaqueros* to secure the weapon and make Basilio descend to the ground. Then I ran upstairs, placed you on the bed, loosened your clothing, and did what I could to restore you. But you remained unconscious——"

"Basilio! Basilio! tell me about him."

"I went to the window and sent one of the men to the *hacienda* for a doctor for you, and told the other to bring Basilio to this room. He came in very weak and trembling, for he had fallen from the vine and was slightly stunned, but not much hurt. He expected me to kill him here in this room, but I could not do that—I was afraid on your account, Violante. He was very quiet and ill——"

"Hurry, Robert, hurry!"

"He said nothing. I spoke to him. He hung his head and asked me if I would let him pray. I told him I would not kill him. A great light broke over his face. He fell at my feet and clasped my knees and kissed my boots and wept like a child. It was pitiful, Violante."

"Poor Basilio!"

"He begged me to punish him. He removed his shirt and implored me to beat him. I told him I would not touch him. He said he would be your slave and mine all his life; but he insisted that he must make some physical atonement—he must be punished. 'Very well,' I said. Then I turned to Nicolas and told him to give Basilio some light punishment, as that would relieve his mind. Nicolas took him down and lashed him to the back of a horse, and turned the animal into the horse-corral. Then Nicolas came back and told me what he had done. I replied that it was all right, and that as soon as I could leave you I would go and release Basilio. And then I told Nicolas to go to the range and look up Alice and bring her home, for she was too weak to come back with me."

"And Basilio is in the corral now?"

"Yes."

"How was he lashed to the horse?"

"I don't know—Nicolas didn't tell me; but you may be sure that he is all right."

She threw her arms around her husband's neck and kissed him again and again, saying, "My noble, generous husband! I love you a thousand times more than ever. Now go, Robert, at once, and release Basilio."

"I can't leave you, dear."

"You must—you shall! I am fully recovered. If you don't go, I will."

"Very well."

No sooner had he left the room than she sprang out of the bed, caught up a penknife, and noiselessly followed him; he did not suspect her presence close behind him as he went towards the corral. When they had gone thus a short distance from the house her alert ear caught a peculiar sound that sent icicles through her body. They were feeble cries of human agony, and they came from a direction other than that of the corral. Heedlessly, and therefore unwisely, she ran towards their source, without having summoned her husband, and soon she came upon a fearful spectacle.

McPherson pursued his way to the corral; but when he arrived there he was surprised not to find Basilio in the enclosure. The gate was closed—the horse to which he was lashed could not have escaped through it. Looking about, he read the signs of a commotion that must have occurred among the horses, caused, undoubtedly, by the strange sight of a man lashed in some peculiar way to the back of one of their number. The ground was torn by flying hoofs in all directions; there had been a wild stampede among the animals. Even when he entered, possibly more than a half-hour after Basilio was introduced among them, they were huddled in a corner, and snorted in alarm when he approached them.

The horse to which Nicolas had lashed Basilio was not to be seen. Annoyed at the stupidity of Nicolas, McPherson looked about until he found the place in the fence through which Basilio's horse had broken; only two of the rails had been thrown down. Alarmed and distressed, McPherson leaped over the fence, took up the trail of the horse, and followed it, running. Presently he discovered that the horse, in his mad flight, had broken through the fence enclosing the apiary, and had played havoc among the twenty or more bee-hives therein. Then McPherson saw a spectacle that for a little while took all the strength out of his body.

The *señora*, guided by a quicker sense than that of her husband, had gone straight to the apiary. There she saw the horse, with Basilio, naked to the waist, strapped upon his back, the animal plunging madly among the bee-hives, kicking them to fragments as the vicious insects plied him with their stings. Basilio was tied with his face to the sun, which poured its fierce rays into his eyes; for Nicolas was devoted to the *señora*, and he had been determined to make matters as uncomfortable for the ingrate as possible. Upon Basilio's unprotected body the bees swarmed by hundreds, giving him a score of stings to one for the horse, and he was utterly helpless to protect himself. Already the poison of a thousand stings had been poured into his face and body; his features were hideously swollen and distorted, and his chest was puffed out of resemblance to a human shape, and was livid and ghastly.

Without a moment's hesitation, the *señora* flew through the gate and went to the deliverance of Basilio, praying to God with every breath. His cries were feeble, for his strength was nearly gone, and his incredible agony, aided by the poison of the bees, had sent his wits astray. For Violante to approach the maddened horse and the swarming bees was to offer herself to death; but what cared she for that, when another's life was at stake? Into this desperate situation she threw herself. With the coolness of a trained horsewoman, she finally twisted the fingers of one hand into the frantic horse's nostrils, bringing him instantly under control. In another moment, unmindful of the stings which the bees inflicted upon her face and hands, she had cut Basilio's lashings and caught his shapeless body in her arms as it slipped to the ground. Then, taking him under the arms, she dragged him, with uncommon strength, from the enclosure and away from the murderous assaults of the bees.

He moaned; his head rolled from one side to the other. His eyes were closed by the swelling of the lids, and he could not see her; but even had this not been so, he was past knowing her. She laid him down in the shade of a great oak, and she saw from his faint and interrupted gasps that in another moment all would be over with him. Unconscious of the presence of her husband, who now stood reverently, with uncovered head, behind her, she raised to heaven her blanched face and beautiful eyes, and softly prayed, "Holy mother of Jesus, hear the prayer of thy wretched daughter, and intercede for this unshriven spirit." She glanced down at Basilio, and saw that he was dead. Feebly she staggered to her feet, and, seeing her husband, cried out his name, stretched out her arms towards him, and sank unconscious into his strong grasp; and thus he bore her to the house, kissing her face, while tears streamed down his cheeks.

An Uncommon View of It

(A story from *The Ape, the Idiot & Other People*)

Mr. Clarke Randolph was stupefied by a discovery which he had just made—his wife had proved unfaithful, and the betrayer was his nearest friend, Henry Stockton. If there had been the least chance for a doubt, the unhappy husband would have seized upon it, but there was none whatever.

Let us try to understand what this meant to such a man as Randolph. He was a high-bred, high-spirited man of thirty, descended from a long line of proud and chivalrous men; educated, refined, sensitive, generous, and brave. His fine talents, his dash, his polished manner, his industry, his integrity, his loftiness of character, had lifted him upon the shoulders of popularity and prosperity; so that, in the city of his home, there was not another man of his age, a member of his profession, the law, who was so well known, so well liked, or wielded such a power.

He had been married four years. His wife was beautiful, winning, and intelligent; and she had always had from him the best devotion that a husband could give his wife. He and Stockton had been friends for many years. Next to his wife, Randolph had loved and trusted him above all others.

Such was the situation. At one stroke he had lost his wife, his home, his best friend, his confidence in human nature, his spirit, his ambition. These—and essentially they were all that made up his life, except the operation of purely animal functions—had gone all at once without a moment's warning.

Well, there was something to be done. A keen sense of the

betrayal, a smarting under the gross humiliation, urged him to the natural course of revenge. This, as he sat crouched down in a chair in his locked office, he began systematically to prepare. The first idea—always first in such cases—was to kill. That, in the case of a man of his spirit and temperament, was a matter of course. Fear of the legal consequences found no place within him. Besides, suicide after the killing would settle that exceedingly small part of the difficulty.

So it was first decided that as the result of this discovery three persons had to die,—his wife, his friend, and himself. Very well; that took a load from his mind. An orderly and intelligent arrangement of details now had to be worked out. A plan which would bring the largest results in the satisfaction of a desire for revenge must be chosen. The simple death of those two, the bare stoppage of breath, would be wholly inadequate. First, the manner of taking their lives must have the quality of strength and a force which in itself would have a large element of satisfaction; hence it must be striking, deliberate, brutal if you wish, revolting if you are particular. Second, it must be preceded by exposure, denunciation, publication, scorn, contempt, and terror.

That much was good—what next? There were various available means for taking life. A revolver suggested itself. It makes a dark, red spot; the very sight of the weapon, held steadily and longer than necessary, levelled at the place where the spot is to appear, is terrifying; there is a look of fright; then uplifted arms, an appeal for mercy, a protest of innocence, a cry to God; after that the crash, a white face, a toppling to the floor, eyes rolled upward, bluish lips apart, a dark pool on the carpet—all that was very good. The wretched man felt better now that he was beginning to think so clearly.

But there was poison also—poison in variety: arsenic, which burns and corrodes, causing great pain, often for hours; strychnine, which acts through the nerves, producing convulsions and sometimes a fixed distortion of the features, which even the relaxation of death cannot remove; corrosive sublimate, prussic acid, cyanide of potassium—too quick and deadly. It must be a poison, if poison at all, which will bring about a sensible progression through perceptible stages of suffering, so that during this time the efficiency of physical pain may be raised by the addition of mental suffering.

Were these all the methods? Yes—enough for this purpose. Then, which should it be—revolver or poison? It was a difficult problem. Let it first be settled that the three should be together, locked in a room, and that the two guilty ones should suffer first, one at a time.

The revolver won.

Randolph was in the act of leaving his office to go and buy the weapon, when he was startled by what he saw in his office-mirror. It required a moment for him to recognize his own reflection. His face was unnaturally white; a discoloration was under his eyes, which had a glassy appearance; his lips were pressed tightly together, the corners of his mouth drawn down, large dark veins standing out on his temples. Fearing that if, while in this condition, he should apply to a gunsmith for a revolver he would be refused, he stood for some time before the mirror trying to restore the natural expression of his face. He kneaded his lips to remove their stiffness, pinched his cheeks to bring back their color, rubbed down the ridged veins, and scraped a little of the white plaster from the wall and with it concealed the dark colour under his eyes. Then he went forth with a firm step, bought the revolver without difficulty, tried it, satisfied himself that it was reliable, loaded it, put it into his pocket, and returned to his office.

For there were certain matters of property to be attended to. He had a considerable fortune, all his separate possession; his wife had brought him nothing. He now felt sufficiently clear-minded to dispose of his estate intelligently. He drew his will—a holographic instrument—devising his wealth to various persons and benevolent societies.

He glanced at his office-clock. There would be four long hours yet before the time for going home to dinner. Fortunately for his plans, Stockton was to dine with them that evening, and neither of the guilty ones knew that they had been discovered. How should Randolph employ these weary hours? There was nothing to do, nothing even to think of. He tried to read a newspaper, then a book, and failed; looked out upon the crowds which thronged the street; counted the passing cars awhile; tried other things, failed at everything, and then sat down.

Something was beginning to work in the wretched man. Let us see: his wife, while pretending the warmest affection for him, was receiving the guilty attentions of a traitor in the house; she had betrayed her husband, had wrecked his life, had driven him to his death. Really, therefore, she had swept aside all the obligations which the marriage relation imposed. In essence she was no longer his wife, but a criminal enemy who, with deliberate and abounding malice, had destroyed him. He could go to the grave with a willing heart, but he could not permit her to live and enjoy his downfall and gloat over his destruction.

But would she really do that? And, then,—God!—she was a woman! In spite of all that she had done, she was a woman! A strong man, his strength reinforced by a revolver, employs deception to bring a woman into a room, locks the door, insults, humiliates, and terrifies her, brandishes a revolver, and then kills her like a rat in its hole. Can a brave man, of mature judgment and in possession of his faculties, do such a thing? Why, it would be not only murder, but cowardice as well! No; it could not be done. She was still a woman, with all the weakness, all the frailty which her sex imposed. It could not be done.

After all, it would be far sweeter revenge to let her live, bearing through life a brand of infamy. That would be much better. She would lose her high position and the respect of her friends; the newspapers would publish her shame to the world, pointing her out by name as the depraved woman who had betrayed her husband and driven him to murder and suicide; they would have her portrait in their columns; her name and crime would be hawked upon the street by loud-crying news-boys; sermons denouncing her would be preached in all the churches; her shame would be discussed everywhere—in homes, shops, hotels, and bar-rooms in many cities.

Not only that, but she would be stripped of all the property which she had enjoyed so much. She would be turned adrift upon the streets, for no one would help her, none have a kind word for her, none give her even the respect which money might command. Being thus turned out upon the world all friendless and alone, and being naturally depraved, she would seek the protection of fast and shady men. Thus started, and soon taking to drink, as such women always do, down she would plunge into a reckless and shameless career, sinking lower and lower, losing her beauty; becoming coarse, loud, and vulgar; then, arriving at that stage when her beauty no longer could be a source of revenue, drifting into vile dens, consorting with the lowest and most brutal blackguards, finding herself dragged often before police-magistrates, first for drunkenness and then for theft, serving short terms in prison with others as low; finally, one night brought shrieking with delirium tremens to the police-station, bundled out to the hospital, strapped firmly to an iron bed, and then dying with foul oaths on her lips—such a life would be infinitely worse than death; such revenge immeasurably vaster than that of the pistol. Then it was finally decided that she must live and suffer.

As to the friend—as to Stockton, the betrayer, the sneak, the coward—*he* should die like a dog. *That* decision could not be reconsidered. He should not be granted the privilege of a duel, for not only was he wholly undeserving of such consideration, but by such means his life might be spared. Undoubtedly *she* loved him; perhaps he loved her. He living and the husband killed in a duel, their satisfaction would be doubled—having wrecked and humiliated him and driven him to despair, they then killed him. After that they could enjoy each other's society openly, unmolested, and without fear of detection or punishment. Besides, they might marry and both be happy. This was unthinkable. He must be killed, he must die like a dog, and he must go to his death with a foul stain on his name.

These things being settled, the wretched man reread the will.

As the woman was to live, she must be mentioned in the document. He tore up the will and wrote another, in which he bequeathed her one dollar, setting forth her shame as the reason for so small a bequest. Then he wrote out a separate statement of the whole affair, sealed it, addressed it to the coroner, and placed it in his pocket. It would be found there after awhile.

Well, why this trembling in every member, this unaccountable nausea, this unconquerable feeling of horror and repugnance as the draft of the picture was contemplated? Did instinct arise and dumbly plead for mercy? What mercy had been shown that mercy could be expected? None whatever. There was not only revenge to be satisfied, but justice also. Still, it was horrible! Admit that she deserved it all, deserved even more, she was a woman! No act of hers could deprive her of her natural claims upon the stronger sex. As a woman she had inalienable rights which even she could not forfeit, which men may not withhold. And then, where could be the benefit of adding physical suffering to mental? One surely would weaken the force of the other. The lower she should fall and the deeper her degradation, the smaller would become the efficiency of her mental agony; and yet mental suffering was the kind which it was desired should fall upon her.

It would be well, therefore, to leave her some money—a considerable amount of money—in order that, holding herself above the want which, in her case, would lead to degradation and a blunting of the sensibilities, she might suffer all the more keenly; in order that the memory of her shame might be forever poignant, forever a cause for the sharpest regrets. This would be better in other ways: her shame published, she could never associate with those fine characters who had been her friends; her lover dead and his memory disgraced, he could not be present to console her; for society she would have only those whom her fortune would attract, and they were not of a kind to satisfy such a woman as she; she would always be within sight of the old life and its pleasures, but just beyond the pale—sufficiently near to see and long for, but too far to reach, and forever kept back by the cold glance of contempt and disdain from the high circle in which she had been reared.

Therefore, it were better to leave her the bulk of his fortune. So he tore up the second will and wrote a third, in which, while naming her as his principal legatee, he incorporated the story of her shame. He felt better now than at any other time since his discovery. He walked about the room, looked out the window, then fell into his chair again.

How strangely alike in many respects are all animals, including man! he thought. There are qualities and passions common to them all,—hate, fear, anger, revenge, love, fondness for offspring. In what is man superior to the others? Manifestly in self-control, a sense of justice, the attribute of mercy, the quality of charity, the power to forgive, the force of benevolence, the operation of gratitude; an appreciation of abstractions; an ability to compare, contrast, and adjust; consciousness of an inherent tendency to higher and better achievements. To the extent that he lacks these does he approach more closely to the lower orders. To the degree that the passions common to all have mastery over him does he lack the finer qualities which distinguish his species. The desire to kill when hurt, angered, or threatened is the stronger the lower we descend in the scale of the orders— the lower we descend even among the members of the same order. The least developed men are the most brutal. Revenge is the malice of anger.

It is strange that his thoughts should have taken such a turn!

And then, the fundamental instinct which guards the perpetuation of the species is common to all, and its manifestations are controlled by a universal law, whose simple variations do not impair its integrity. Love and mating—these are the broad lines upon which the perpetuation of the species starts. What possible abstractions are there in them? Is not their character concrete and visible? Whatever fine sentiments are evolved, we know their source and comprehend their function. There is no mystery here.

What is this jealousy, which all animals may have? It is an instinctive resentment, by one of a mated pair, of something which interferes with a pleasant established system, the basis of which is perpetuation of the species. Higher mankind has the ability to dissect it, analyze it, understand it, and guard against its harmful operation; herein lie distinguishing qualities of superiority. If, when his jealousy is roused, he is unable to act any differently from the lion, the horse, or the dog, then, in that regard, he is not superior to them. Man, being an eater of meat, is a savage animal, like the dog, the tiger, the panther, the lion. His passions are strong, as are theirs; but he has qualities which enable him to hold them in check.

If an animal have a strong attachment for his mate, he will fight if she be taken from him; this is the operation of jealousy. If he be a savage animal, he will kill if he can or dare. Few males among the animals will kill their deserting mates; that is left for man, the noblest of the animals. The others are content to kill the seducer. What thankfulness there is for escape from an act, so recently contemplated, which would have placed its perpetrator below the level of the most savage of the brutes! In what, of all that was now proposed to be done, was there any quality to distinguish the acts from those of the most savage brute, except a more elaborate detail, the work of superior malice and ferocity? Is it a wonder that Randolph shuddered when he thought of it?

The broadest characteristic of all animals, including man, is selfishness. In man it reaches its highest form and becomes vanity, pride, and a ridiculous sense of self-importance. But man alone is conscious of its existence, character, and purpose; he alone encourages its rational development and suppresses the most evil of its abuses. The animal which would fight or kill from jealousy is moved by a selfish motive only. It proceeds to satisfy its anger or gratify its revenge without any regard to the ethics, without any thought of its obligations to nature, without the slightest wish to inquire whether there may not be in the cause of its jealousy a natural purpose which is proceeding upon the very lines that led to its mating. A man, however, can think of these things, weigh them carefully, understand them approximately, and then advance in the light of wisdom. If not, he is no better, in this regard, than the animal which cannot so reason and understand.

This manner of thinking was bringing the unhappy man closer to himself.

Then, having faced the proposition that he had been considering his own case all along, he found the situation to be somewhat like this: He had a certain understanding which should operate to remove him from influences which with men of inferior conceptions would be more powerful; not being a brute, he should rise above impulses which a brute is constrained by its nature to obey. So much was clear. Then what should he do? He pondered this long and seriously.

Was it possible to wipe out the past with exposure, humiliation, shame, and blood? He had been proud of her; he had loved her; he had been very, very happy with her. She had been his inspiration; a part of his hopes, ambition, life. True, she had undone all this, but the memory of it remained. Until this recent act of shame, she had been kind, unselfish, gentle, and faithful. Who knows why she fell? Who could sound the depths of this strange mystery; who measure the capacity of her resistance; who judge her frailty with a righteous mind; who say that at that very moment she was not suffering unspeakable things?

And then, was there anyone so noble of character, with integrity so unfailing and so far beyond temptation, that he might say he was better than she? Her weakness—should we presume to call it depravity when we cannot know, and might we with intelligent knowledge of our own conduct lay the whole responsibility upon her, and none upon that which made her? If we are human, let us seek wherein we may convince ourselves that we are not brutes. Compassion is an attribute of a noble character. The test of manhood is the exercise of manly qualities.

What good would come from this revenge of humiliation and exposure? It would not mend the wrong; it would not save life; it would be only proof of the vanity, the sense of self-importance, of the injured one. Would it be possible to spare her? Yes. That finally was settled. She should live; she should have the property; she should be left to enjoy life as best she could without the shadow of a stain upon her name. That were the nobler part, the test of manhood. And then, the past could not be forgotten!

Randolph felt so much better after arriving at this decision that he marvelled at himself. He walked about the room feeling strong and elastic. He tore up the will because it charged her crime upon her; tore up the letter to the coroner; collected all the scraps of paper and carefully burned them. Then he drew a new will, free from stain, leaving all his property to his wife. He did not only that, but he wrote her a letter—formal, of course— merely saying that he had found his life a mistake; this he sealed, addressed, and placed in his pocket.

Stockton—the false friend, the betrayer and destroyer—he should die, he should die like a dog. But not with a stain on his name—that were impossible, because it would reflect upon *her*.

Here was a new situation. The two men would be found dead, likely in the same room—the friend and the husband. What would people think? A duel? For what reason? Murder and suicide? Who had handled the weapon, and for what possible cause? The road which suspicion would travel was too short and wide. The fair name of the wife was to be guarded—that had been decided upon, and now it was the first consideration.

There were other matters to be thought of. Suppose that Stockton had been the husband and Randolph the friend. God! let us think. Have brutes, frenzied with rage and jealousy, the power to hold nature's mirror before the heart, to feel compassion, to exercise charity, to weigh with a steady hand the weaknesses and frailties of their kind, to feel humility, to bow the head before the inscrutable ways of nature? Have they not? No? Well, then, have men? If they have not, they are no better in that regard than brutes. Besides, would it punish Stockton to kill him? There can be no punishment in death; it can be only in dying; but even dying is not unpleasant, and death is the absence of suffering. There was no way under heaven to give him adequate punishment.

Nor was that all. *She* loved him—that must be so. What would be the benefit of removing him from her life? It would be merely revenge—revenge upon both of them; and where lies the nobility of such revenge? If they both should live, both go unexposed, they might be happy together.

After all, whom would that disturb, with whose pleasure interfere? Surely no sound of their happiness could penetrate the grave; violence would be done to none of nature's laws. Why should they not be happy? If they could, why should they not? Was there any reason under the sun that wisdom, charity, compassion, and a high manhood could give why they should not be happy?

But suppose that she should suspect the cause of her husband's suicide; this would likely poison her life, for the consciousness of guilt would give substance to suspicion. The result would be an abhorrence of self, a detestation of the participant in her sin, a belief that the blood of her husband was upon her head, and a long train of evils which would seriously impair, if not wholly destroy, the desired serenity of her life. Was there any way to prevent the birth of such a suspicion?

Yes; there was a way. As soon as Randolph had worked it out he felt as if an enormous load had been removed from him. His eyes shone brightly, his cheeks were flushed, and a look of pride and triumph lighted up his face.

He returned to his chair, removed the revolver from his pocket, and laid it on the table; wrote his wife an affectionate letter, in which he told her that he had just become aware of an incurable ailment which he had not the courage to face through months or years of suffering, and begged her to look to Stockton for friendship and advice; wrote to Stockton, charging him with her protection; burned the last will that he had made and drew a new one, in which he left them the property jointly, on condition that they marry within two years.

Then, with a perfectly clear head, he laid down his pen and

sighed, but his face was bright and tranquil. He picked up the revolver, cocked it, placed the muzzle against his temple, and without the tremor of a nerve he pressed the trigger.

A Story Told by the Sea

(A story from *The Ape, the Idiot & Other People*)

One night, when the storm had come up from the south, apparently for the sole purpose of renewing war with its old enemy, the Peninsula of Monterey, I left the ancient town, crossed the neck of the peninsula, and descended on the other side of the Santa Lucia slope to see the mighty battle on Carmel Bay. The tearing wind, which, charged with needles of rain, assailed me sharply, did nobler work with the ocean and the cypresses, sending the one upon a riotous course and rending the other with groans. I arrived upon a cliff just beyond a pebbly beach, and with bared head and my waistcoat open, stood facing the ocean and the storm. It was not a cold night, though a winter storm was at large; but it was a night of blind agonies and struggles, in which a mad wind lashed the sea and a maddened sea assailed the shore, while a flying rain and a drenching spray dimmed the sombre colours of the scene. It was a night for the sea to talk in its travail and yield up some of its mysteries.

I left the cliff and went a little distance to the neighbourhood of a Chinese fishing-station, where there was a sand-beach; and here, after throwing off my coat and waistcoat, I went down to have a closer touch with my treacherous friend. The surf sprang at me, and the waves, retreating gently, beckoned me to further ventures, which I made with a knowledge of my ground, but with a love of this sweet danger also. A strong breaker lifted me from my footing, but I outwitted it and pursued it in retreat; there came another afterwards, and it was armed, for, towering above me, it came down upon me with a bludgeon, which fell heavily upon me. I seized it, but there my command upon my powers ceased; and the wave, returning, bore me out. A blindness, a vague sense of suffocation, an uncertain effort of instinct to regain my hold upon the ground, a flight through the air, a soft fall upon the sand—it was thus that I was saved; and I still held in my hand the weapon with which my old friend had dealt me the blow.

It was a bottle. Afterwards, in my room at Monterey, I broke it and found within it a writing of uncommon interest. After weeks of study and deciphering (for age and imperfect execution made the task serious and the result uncertain), I put together such fragments of it as had the semblance of coherence; and I found that the sea in its travail had yielded up one of its strangest mysteries. No hope of a profitable answer to this earnest cry for help prompts its publication; it is brought forth rather to show a novel and fearful form of human suffering, and also to give knowledge possibly to some who, if they be yet alive, would rather know the worst than nothing. The following is what my labour has accomplished:

I am Amasa D. Keating, an unhappy wretch, who, with many others, am suffering an extraordinary kind of torture; and so great is the mental disturbance which I suffer, that I fear I shall not be able to make an intelligent report. I am but just from a scene of inconceivable terrors, and, although I am a man of some education and usually equal to the task of intelligent expression, I am now in a condition of violent mental disturbance, and of great physical suffering as well, which I fear will prove a hindrance to the understanding of him who may find this report. At the outset, I most earnestly beg such one to use the swiftest diligence in publishing the matter of this writing, to the end that haply an expedition for our relief may be outfitted without delay; for, if the present state of affairs continue much longer with those whom I have left behind, any measure taken for their relief will be useless. As for myself and my companion, we expect nothing but death.

I will hasten to the material part of my narrative, with the relation only of so much of the beginning as may serve for our identification.

On the 14th of October, 1852, we sailed from Boston in the brig *Hopewell*, Captain Campbell, bound for the islands of the South Pacific Ocean. We carried a cargo of general merchandise, with the purpose of trading with the natives; but we desired also to find some suitable island which we might take possession of in the name of the United States and settle upon for our permanent home. With this end in view, we had formed a company and bought the brig, so that it might remain our property and be used as a means of communication between us and the civilized world. These facts and many others are so familiar to our friends in Boston, that I deem it wholly unnecessary to set them forth in fuller detail. The names of all our passengers and crew stand upon record in Boston, and are not needed to be written here for ampler identification.

No ill-fortune assailed us until we arrived in the neighbourhood of the Falkland Islands. Cape Horn wore its ugliest aspect (for the brig was a slow sailer, and the Antarctic summer was well gone before we had encountered bad weather),—an unusual thing, Captain Campbell assured us; from that time forward we had a series of misfortunes, which ended finally, after two or three months, in a fearful gale, which not only cost some of the crew their lives, but dismasted our vessel. The storm continued, and, the brig being wholly at the mercy of the wind and the sea, we saw that she must founder. We therefore took to the boats with what provisions and other necessary things we could stow away.

With no land in sight, and in the midst of a boiling sea, which appeared every moment to be on the eve of swamping us, we bent to our oars and headed for the northwest. It is hardly necessary to say that we had lost our reckoning; but, after a manner, we made out that we were nearly in longitude 136.30 west, and about upon the Tropic of Capricorn. This would have made our situation about a hundred and seventy miles from a number of small islands lying to the eastward of the one hundred and fortieth meridian. The prospect was discouraging, as there was hardly a sound person in the boats to pull an oar, so badly had the weather used us; and besides that, the ship's instruments had been lost and our provisions were badly damaged.

Nevertheless, we made some headway. The poor abandoned brig, seemingly conscious of our desertion, behaved in a very singular fashion; urged doubtless by the wind, she pursued us with pathetic struggles—now beam on, again stern foremost, and still again plunging forward with her nose under the water. Her pitching and lurching were straining her heavily, and, with her hold full of water, she evidently could live but a few minutes longer. Meanwhile, it was no small matter for us to keep clear of her, for whether we would pull to this side or that she followed us, and sometimes we were in danger. There came an end, however, for the brig, now heavily water-logged, rose majestically on a great wave and came down side on into the trough; she made a brave struggle to right herself, but in another moment she went over upon her beam, settled, steadied herself a moment, and then sank straight down like a mass of lead. This brought upon us a peculiar sense of desolation; for, so far as we knew (and Captain Campbell had sailed these seas before), there was hardly a chance of our gaining land alive.

Much to our surprise, we had not rowed more than twenty knots when (it being about midnight) a fire was sighted off our port bow,—that is to say, due west. This gave us so great courage that we rowed heartily towards it, and at three in the morning, to our unspeakable happiness, we dragged our boats upon a beautiful sand-beach. So exhausted were we that with small loss of time we made ourselves comfortable and soon were sound asleep upon firm ground.

The next sun had done more than half its work before any of us were awake. Excepting some birds of lively plumage, there was not a living thing in sight; but no sooner had we begun to stir about than a number of fine brown men approached us simultaneously from different directions. A belt was around their waists, and from it hung a short garment, made of bark woven into a coarse fabric; and also hanging from the belt was a heavy sword of metal. Undoubtedly the men were savages; but there was a dignity in their manner which set them wholly apart from the known inhabitants of these South Sea Islands. Our captain, who understood many of the languages and dialects of the sub-tropical islanders, found himself at fault in attempting verbal intercourse with these visitors, but it was not long before we found them exceedingly apt in understanding signs. They showed much commiseration for us, and with manifestations of friendship invited us to follow them and test their hospitality. This we were not slow in doing.

The island—we were made to know on the way—was a journey of ten hours long and seven wide, and our eyes gave us proof of its wonderful fecundity of soil, for there were great banana plantations and others of curious kinds of grain. The narrowness of the roads convinced us that there were no wagons or beasts of burden, but there were many evidences of a civilization which, for these parts, was of extraordinary development; such, for instance, as finely cultivated fields and good houses of stone, with such evidences of an æsthetic taste as found expression in the domestic cultivation of many of the beautiful flowers which grew upon the island. These matters I mention with some particularity, in order that the island may be recognized by the rescuers for whom we are eagerly praying.

The town to which we were led is a place of singular beauty. While there is no orderly arrangement of streets (the houses being scattered about confusedly), there is a large sense of comfort and room and a fine character of neatness. The buildings are all of rough stone and are not divided into apartments; the windows and doors are hung with matting, giving testimony of an absence of thieves. A little to one side, upon a knoll, is the house of the king, or chief. It is much like the others, except that it is larger, a chamber in front serving as an executive-room, where the king disposes of the business of his rulership.

Into this audience-room we were led, and presently the king

himself appeared. He was dressed with more barbaric profusion than his subjects; about his neck and in his ears were many fine pieces of jewellery of gold and silver, evidently the work of European artisans, but worn with a complete disregard of their original purpose. The king, a large, strong, and handsome man, received us with a kindly smile; if ever a human face showed kindness of heart, it was his. He had us to understand at once that we were most welcome, that he sympathized with us in our distress, and that all our wants should be attended to until means should be found for restoring us to our country, or sending us whithersoever else we might desire to go.

It was not at all likely, he said (for he spoke German a little), that any vessel from the outside world would ever visit the island, as it appeared to be unknown to navigators, and it was a law upon the island that the inhabitants of no other islands should approach. At certain times of the moon, however, he sent a boat to an island, many leagues away, to bear some rare products of his people in exchange for other commodities, and, should we so desire, we might be taken, one at a time, in the boat, and thus eventually be put in the way of passing vessels.

With what appeared to be an embarrassed hesitation, he informed us that he was compelled to impose a certain mild restraint upon us—one which, he hurried to add, would in no way interfere with our comfort or pleasure. This was that we be kept apart from his people, as they were simple and happy, and he feared that association with us would bring discontent among them. Their present condition had come about solely through the policy of complete isolation which had been followed in the past.

We received this communication with a delight which we took no pains to conceal; and the king seemed touched by our expressions of gratitude. So in a little while we were established as a colony about three miles from the town, the quick hands of the natives having made for us, out of poles, matting, and thatch, a sufficient number of houses for our comfort; and the king placed at our disposal a large acreage for our use, if we should desire to help ourselves with farming; for which purpose an intelligent native was sent to instruct us. It was on the 10th day of May, 1853, that we went upon the island, and the 14th when we went into colony.

I cannot pause to give any further description of this beautiful island and our delightful surroundings, but must hasten away to a relation of the terrible things which presently befell us. We had been upon the island about a month, when the king (who had been to visit us twice) sent a messenger to say that a boat would leave on the morrow, and that if any one of us wished to go he could be taken. The messenger said that the king's best judgment was that the sickly ones ought to go first, as, in the event of serious illness, it would be better that they should die at home. We overlooked this singular and savage way of stating the case, for our sense of gratitude to the king was so great that the expression of a slight wish from him was as binding upon us as law. Hence from our number we selected John Foley, a carpenter, of Boston, as the hardships of the voyage had developed in him a quick consumption, and he had no family or relatives in the colony, as many others of us had. The poor fellow was overcome with gratitude, and he left us the happiest man I ever saw.

I must now mention a very singular thing, which upon the departure of Foley was given a conspicuous place in our attention. We were in a roomy valley, which was nearly surrounded by perpendicular walls of great height, and from no accessible point was the sea visible. On several occasions some of the younger men had sought to leave the valley for the shore, but at each attempt the native guards set over us had suddenly appeared at the few passes which nature had left in the wall, and kindly but firmly had turned our young men back, saying that it was the king's wish we should not leave the valley. The older heads among us discouraged these attempts to escape, holding them to be breaches of faith and hospitality; but the knowledge of being absolute prisoners weighed upon us nevertheless, and became more and more irksome.

When, therefore, our companion was taken away, an organized movement was made among the young men to gain an elevated position commanding a view of the sea, in order to observe the direction taken by Foley's boat. The plan was to divide into bodies and move simultaneously in force upon all the points of egress, and overcome, without any resort to dangerous violence, the two or three guards who had been seen at those points. When our men arrived at these places they encountered the small number it was customary to see, and were pushing their way through, when suddenly there appeared a strong body of natives, who drew their heavy swords and assumed so threatening an attitude that our men lost no time in retreating.

A report of this occurrence was made to the colony, each of the parties of young men having had an exactly similar experience. While there appeared to be no good ground for the feeling of uneasiness which spread throughout the colony, a sense of oppression came over the stronger ones and of fear over the weaker; and, a council having been held, it was decided to ask an explanation of the king.

Other things of some interest had happened; among them, a surreptitious acquiring of considerable knowledge of the island language by me. For this reason I was chosen as ambassador to the king. My mission was a failure, as the king, though gracious, informed me that this plan was necessary in securing complete isolation from his people; and he instructed me to tell my people that any member of our colony found beyond the lines would be punished with death. In addition to this, the king, seemingly hurt that we should have questioned the propriety of his actions, said that thenceforward he himself would make the selections of our people for deportation. The man's evident superiority of character impressed me with no little effect, and the sincerity with which he regarded us as belonging to a race inferior to his in mental and moral strength confounded me and placed me at a disadvantage.

When I took the news to the colony, a mood bordering upon hopelessness came upon our people. The ones of hastier temper suggested a revolt and a seizure of the island; but this was so insane an idea that it was put away at once.

Not long afterwards the king sent for Absalom Maywood, one of our young men, unmarried, but with a mother among us. Maywood, at first very low with scurvy on the brig, had drifted into other ailments, and was now an invalid and much wasted. I will not dwell upon the pathetic parting between him and his aged mother, nor upon the deeper gloom that fell upon the colony. What was becoming of these men? None might know whither they were taken and none could guess their after-fate. Behind our efforts to be cheerful and industrious there were heavy hearts, and possibly thoughts and fears that dared not seek expression.

The third man was taken—again a sickly one—this time a consumptive farmer, named Jackson; and some time afterward a fourth, an elderly woman, with a cancer; she was Mrs. Lyons, formerly a milliner in South Boston. Then the patience and hope which had sustained us gave way, and we were in a condition close upon despair. The cooler ones among the men assembled quietly apart and debated what to do. Our captain, a man quiet and brave, still the leader in our councils, and always advising patience and obedience, presided at this meeting. There was one dreadful thought upon every mind, but no man had the courage to bring it forth; but after there had been some discussion without any profit, Captain Campbell made this speech:

My friends, it does not become us longer to seek to conceal the thought which all of us have, and which, sooner or later, must be spoken. It is a matter of common knowledge that upon many of the islands of these seas there exists the horrible practice of cannibalism.

Not a word was spoken for a long time, and all were glad that it had come out at last. Not one man looked at his neighbour or dared raise his glance from the ground, and there was a weight upon the hearts of all. The captain resumed:

Nevertheless it is extremely difficult to believe that this evil is upon us, for you must have noticed that only the lean and sickly ones have been taken, and surely this cannot mean cannibalism.

Some had not thought of this, and they looked up quickly, with brighter faces; whereupon Captain Campbell proceeded:

You must have observed, however, that all of the sick and weakly have gone, and this brings a new situation upon us. I have an idea, which I will not give expression to now, and my desire in calling you together was to determine its correctness or falsity. For this purpose, some man of daring and agility must risk his life.

Nearly every man present made offer of his services, but the captain shook his head and begged them all to remain quiet.

"It is necessary," he added, "that this man understand the language, and I fear there is not one among you."

Each man, taken aback, looked at his neighbour and then all at me, as I stepped forward. The captain regarded me gratefully and said:

"Let there now be a binding secrecy among us, for the others of the colony must not know now, and perhaps never. If our fear find a ground in truth, there is all the greater reason for keeping these matters secret among ourselves. Is that well understood? Then, Mr. Keating, the plan is this: When the next one of us is taken, you are by strategy, but in no event by violence, to escape from this imprisonment and discover the fate of that one and make report to us."

A week afterwards (these things occurring now with greater frequency) Lemuel Arthur, a young man of twenty-two, was taken away about one o'clock in the afternoon. My whole plan having been studied out, I arrayed myself in the style of the natives, stained my skin with ochre, blackened my eyebrows and hair with a mixture of soot and tallow, and without difficulty slipped by the guards and found myself at large and free upon the island. I gained a high point and saw no sign of a boat making ready to put off with Arthur. When darkness had come I descended to the village. I kept upon the outskirts and remained as much as possible in shadow. I dared not talk with any one, but

I could listen; and presently I learned something that made my heart stand still.

"It has been so long since we had one," said a native to his fellow.

"Yes; and this one will be delicious. They say he is young and fat. Why, we have not touched any since the four men and their woman with the jewellery came upon the island from a wreck."

"True; but this one will not go around among so many of us—many must go without."

"What of that? Those not supplied now will have all the keener relish when their turn comes. All that are left now are good and fat, as the king has taken away all the lean and sickly ones. He would not allow the people to touch them, although some of them begged very hard. So, to make sure, they were placed in the kiln."

So heavy a sickness fell upon me when I heard this that I was near upon a betrayal of my presence; and certainly I lost some of the talk which these men were having. Presently I realized that nothing indicating a horrible fate for my friends had been said; my own fears were sufficient to give a frightful colour to their language. When I looked about me again they were gone, and so with much caution I moved to another part of the town, keeping always in shadow. At a certain place I heard another conversation, as follows:

"Does he know what they will do with him?"

"No; but he fears something. He does not understand the language. He tried to get away this afternoon to go to the seashore, where he thought the boat was waiting, and when they made an effort to keep him quiet he became very angry."

"What did they do then?"

"They took him to the king, who was so kind that the young man became quiet. Our king is so gentle, and they always believe what he tells them,"—whereupon the fellow broke into a hearty laugh.

"And do the others suspect nothing?"

"There is doubt about that. Kololu, the farmer, has reported that they appear uneasy and disturbed, and hold secret meetings."

"What do you think they would do if they should discover everything?"

"Revolt, I think, for they appear to be fighters."

"But they have no arms, and we are more than a hundred to one."

"That is true, and so no lives would be lost on either side. After the revolt they would merely be kept in closer confinement, and no harm would come in the end. They could be taken one at a time, as is the present intention."

"They might refuse to eat sufficient, and hence become lean."

"That would come about surely, but it would last only for a time; for you have noticed that even our own people, when condemned, though they lose flesh at first, invariably become reconciled to their end, and at last become fatter than ever."

The words of this man, who was evidently a functionary of the king, inspired me with so great a horror that I could bear to hear no more; so I moved away, considering whether I should return to the colony and report what I had heard already or remain to see this ghastly tragedy to the end. As there was nothing to be gained by returning at once, I decided to stay, for through the horror of it all might come some suggestion of a means of deliverance.

I soon became aware, by the making of all the people towards a certain quarter, that something of unusual importance was afoot; so as best I could I worked my way around to the point of convergence, which was in the neighbourhood of the king's house, and there I saw an extraordinary preparation under way. A large bonfire was burning in an open place; standing around it, in a circle having a generous radius, were hundreds of the strange half-savages of the island, kept at their proper distance by an armed patrol; in a clear space at one side, on higher ground, was an elevated seat, which I surmised was reserved for the king.

Manifestly a matter of some moment was to be attended to, having likely a ceremonious character.

The most curious feature of all this affair was the activity of a number of workers engaged in dragging large, hot stones from the fire and arranging them in the form of an oblong mound. This mound had one peculiar feature: a hollow space, about six feet long and two feet wide, was left within it, and the men, under the instructions of a leader, were fashioning it to a depth approaching two feet, all the stones being very hot and difficult to handle, even with the aid of barrows.

While they were still at work, the great repressed excitement under which the people labored found an excuse for expression in the arrival of the king, who, tricked out in unusual finery, walked solemnly ahead of his attendants to his elevated seat. Then he gave an order which, from my distance, I could not hear. I pushed a little closer under the safety which the occasion lent, and overheard this conversation:

"How many will get some of it?"

"Only forty, I hear. You know the women are not allowed to have it."

"Yes."

"The leading men will be supplied. It makes them strong and wise. The next one will be given to sixty of the men who carry swords."

"And the next after that?"

"To more of the swordsmen; and so on until they all have had some, and then the common people will be taken in like rotation, but given a smaller allowance."

At this juncture, a strange procession moved from the king's house. It was led by two priests chanting dolefully; behind them walked four men, armed with curious implements—flails, no doubt. Then came four warriors, and behind them, firmly bound and completely naked, walked my young friend, Arthur; after him came six warriors. Arthur's white skin showed in strong contrast to that of the brown men around him. His face was very pale, and his eyes, staring wide, swept a quick glance around for a stray hope.

The group stopped in front of the king; the natives faced and made an obeisance and awaited further orders. Before all this had been done, a man in front of me said to another:

"Those hot stones will cool, I fear."

"There is no danger; they will keep their heat a long time. If they were too hot, they would burn it."

"True."

"They are much too hot now, but it will be some time before they will be needed."

"Will they use the sword first, as they did with those who had the jewellery?"

"No; the best part then was spilled. This is a new idea of the king's. The flails will do just as well and will make it very tender besides. Our king is a wise man."

By this time young Arthur (the king having given his order) was surrounded by the armed men, and between him and them were the four who carried flails. His hands had been bound to a strong post sunk in the ground. The king raised his hand as a signal, and the four men brought down their flails with moderate force upon Arthur's naked body. These implements were heavy, and evidently care was taken not to break the skin. When the poor fellow felt the blows, he shrank and quivered, but uttered no sound. They fell again.

What was I doing all this time? What was I thinking? I do not know; but when the second blows had been delivered and Arthur had cried out in his agony, I sprang through the encircling line of savages, dashed into the midst of the group surrounding the prisoner, snatched a sword from a warrior, leaped upon the king and split his head in twain, turned, cut Arthur's bonds, caught him by the hand, and fled at full speed with him into the darkness. Never had been a surprise more complete— the people had seen one of their own number, as they supposed, free the prisoner and murder their king.

Soon there came a howl, and some started in pursuit; but— there was the body of the king, and the stones were hot and waiting! There was no longer authority! Our pursuers fell off, one by one, and the others, thus discouraged, gave up the chase. We ran to the shore, found a boat, and put out to sea.

We are free—we two; but to what purpose? We have no idea of the direction of the land; we are without food; we dare not return to our friends, for only in the desperate hope of our finding land can there be the least encouragement for their rescue. We have rowed all night; it is now well into the following afternoon; we have had nothing to eat or drink, and we are beginning to suffer; we both are naked and the sun seemingly will burn us up. I therefore make this record with material which I had been prudent to provide for such an emergency, and I shall now give it to the sea, with such earnest prayers for its discovery as can come only from a most unhappy human being in a desperate extremity.

The Monster-Maker

(A story from *The Ape, the Idiot & Other People*)

A young man of refined appearance, but evidently suffering great mental distress, presented himself one morning at the residence of a singular old man, who was known as a surgeon of remarkable skill. The house was a queer and primitive brick affair, entirely out of date, and tolerable only in the decayed part of the city in which it stood. It was large, gloomy, and dark, and had long corridors and dismal rooms; and it was absurdly large for the small family—man and wife—that occupied it. The house described, the man is portrayed—but not the woman. He could be agreeable on occasion, but, for all that, he was but animated mystery. His wife was weak, wan, reticent, evidently miserable, and possibly living a life of dread or horror—perhaps witness of repulsive things, subject of anxieties, and victim of fear and tyranny; but there is a great deal of guessing in these assumptions. He was about sixty-five years of age and she about forty. He was lean, tall, and bald, with thin, smooth-shaven face, and very keen eyes; kept always at home, and was slovenly. The man was strong, the woman weak; he dominated, she suffered.

Although he was a surgeon of rare skill, his practice was almost nothing, for it was a rare occurrence that the few who knew of his great ability were brave enough to penetrate the gloom of his house, and when they did so it was with deaf ear turned to sundry ghoulish stories that were whispered concerning him. These were, in great part, but exaggerations of his experiments in vivisection; he was devoted to the science of surgery.

The young man who presented himself on the morning just mentioned was a handsome fellow, yet of evident weak character and unhealthy temperament—sensitive, and easily exalted or depressed. A single glance convinced the surgeon that his visitor was seriously affected in mind, for there was never bolder skull-grin of melancholia, fixed and irremediable.

A stranger would not have suspected any occupancy of the house. The street door—old, warped, and blistered by the sun—was locked, and the small, faded-green window-blinds were closed. The young man rapped at the door. No answer. He rapped again. Still no sign. He examined a slip of paper, glanced at the number on the house, and then, with the impatience of a child, he furiously kicked the door. There were signs of numerous other such kicks. A response came in the shape of a shuffling footstep in the hall, a turning of the rusty key, and a sharp face that peered through a cautious opening in the door.

"Are you the doctor?" asked the young man.

"Yes, yes! Come in," briskly replied the master of the house.

The young man entered. The old surgeon closed the door and carefully locked it. "This way," he said, advancing to a rickety flight of stairs. The young man followed. The surgeon led the way up the stairs, turned into a narrow, musty-smelling corridor at the left, traversed it, rattling the loose boards under his feet, at the farther end opened a door at the right, and beckoned his visitor to enter. The young man found himself in a pleasant room, furnished in antique fashion and with hard simplicity.

"Sit down," said the old man, placing a chair so that its occupant should face a window that looked out upon a dead wall about six feet from the house. He threw open the blind, and a pale light entered. He then seated himself near his visitor and directly facing him, and with a searching look, that had all the power of a microscope, he proceeded to diagnosticate the case.

"Well?" he presently asked.

The young man shifted uneasily in his seat.

"I—I have come to see you," he finally stammered, "because I'm in trouble."

"Ah!"

"Yes; you see, I—that is—I have given it up."

"Ah!" There was pity added to sympathy in the ejaculation.

"That's it. Given it up," added the visitor. He took from his pocket a roll of banknotes, and with the utmost deliberation he counted them out upon his knee. "Five thousand dollars," he calmly remarked. "That is for you. It's all I have; but I presume—I imagine—no; that is not the word—*assume*—yes; that's the word—assume that five thousand—is it really that much? Let me count." He counted again. "That five thousand dollars is a sufficient fee for what I want you to do."

The surgeon's lips curled pityingly—perhaps disdainfully also. "What do you want me to do?" he carelessly inquired.

The young man rose, looked around with a mysterious air, approached the surgeon, and laid the money across his knee. Then he stooped and whispered two words in the surgeon's ear.

These words produced an electric effect. The old man started violently; then, springing to his feet, he caught his visitor angrily, and transfixed him with a look that was as sharp as a knife. His eyes flashed, and he opened his mouth to give utterance to some harsh imprecation, when he suddenly checked himself. The anger left his face, and only pity remained. He relinquished his grasp, picked up the scattered notes, and, offering them to the visitor, slowly said:

"I do not want your money. You are simply foolish. You think you are in trouble. Well, you do not know what trouble is. Your only trouble is that you have not a trace of manhood in your nature. You are merely insane—I shall not say pusillanimous. You should surrender yourself to the authorities, and be sent to a lunatic asylum for proper treatment."

The young man keenly felt the intended insult, and his eyes flashed dangerously.

"You old dog—you insult me thus!" he cried. "Grand airs, these, you give yourself! Virtuously indignant, old murderer, you! Don't want my money, eh? When a man comes to you himself and wants it done, you fly into a passion and spurn his money; but let an enemy of his come and pay you, and you are only too willing. How many such jobs have you done in this miserable old hole? It is a good thing for you that the police have not run you down, and brought spade and shovel with them. Do you know what is said of you? Do you think you have kept your windows so closely shut that no sound has ever penetrated beyond them? Where do you keep your infernal implements?"

He had worked himself into a high passion. His voice was hoarse, loud, and rasping. His eyes, bloodshot, started from their sockets. His whole frame twitched, and his fingers writhed. But he was in the presence of a man infinitely his superior. Two eyes, like those of a snake, burned two holes through him. An overmastering, inflexible presence confronted one weak and passionate. The result came.

"Sit down," commanded the stern voice of the surgeon.

It was the voice of father to child, of master to slave. The fury left the visitor, who, weak and overcome, fell upon a chair.

Meanwhile, a peculiar light had appeared in the old surgeon's face, the dawn of a strange idea; a gloomy ray, strayed from the fires of the bottomless pit; the baleful light that illumines the way of the enthusiast. The old man remained a moment in profound abstraction, gleams of eager intelligence bursting momentarily through the cloud of sombre meditation that covered his face. Then broke the broad light of a deep, impenetrable determination. There was something sinister in it, suggesting the sacrifice of something held sacred. After a struggle, mind had vanquished conscience.

Taking a piece of paper and a pencil, the surgeon carefully wrote answers to questions which he peremptorily addressed to his visitor, such as his name, age, place of residence, occupation, and the like, and the same inquiries concerning his parents, together with other particular matters.

"Does anyone know you came to this house?" he asked.

"No."

"You swear it?"

"Yes."

"But your prolonged absence will cause alarm and lead to search."

"I have provided against that."

"How?"

"By depositing a note in the post, as I came along, announcing my intention to drown myself."

"The river will be dragged."

"What then?" asked the young man, shrugging his shoulders with careless indifference. "Rapid undercurrent, you know. A good many are never found."

There was a pause.

"Are you ready?" finally asked the surgeon.

"Perfectly." The answer was cool and determined.

The manner of the surgeon, however, showed much perturbation. The pallor that had come into his face at the moment his decision was formed became intense. A nervous tremulousness came over his frame. Above it all shone the light of enthusiasm.

"Have you a choice in the method?" he asked.

"Yes; extreme anæsthesia."

"With what agent?"

"The surest and quickest."

"Do you desire any—any subsequent disposition?"

"No; only nullification; simply a blowing out, as of a candle in the wind; a puff—then darkness, without a trace. A sense of your own safety may suggest the method. I leave it to you."

"No delivery to your friends?"

"None whatever."

Another pause.

"Did you say you are quite ready?" asked the surgeon.

"Quite ready."

"And perfectly willing?"

"Anxious."

"Then wait a moment."

With this request the old surgeon rose to his feet and stretched himself. Then with the stealthiness of a cat he opened the door and peered into the hall, listening intently. There was no sound. He softly closed the door and locked it. Then he closed the window-blinds and locked them. This done, he opened a door leading into an adjoining room, which, though it had no window, was lighted by means of a small skylight. The young man watched closely. A strange change had come over him. While his determination had not one whit lessened, a look of great relief came into his face, displacing the haggard, despairing look of a half-hour before. Melancholic then, he was ecstatic now.

The opening of the second door disclosed a curious sight. In the centre of the room, directly under the skylight, was an operating-table, such as is used by demonstrators of anatomy. A glass case against the wall held surgical instruments of every kind. Hanging in another case were human skeletons of various sizes. In sealed jars, arranged on shelves, were monstrosities of divers kinds preserved in alcohol. There were also, among innumerable other articles scattered about the room, a manikin, a stuffed cat, a desiccated human heart, plaster casts of various parts of the body, numerous charts, and a large assortment of drugs and chemicals. There was also a lounge, which could be opened to form a couch. The surgeon opened it and moved the operating-table aside, giving its place to the lounge.

"Come in," he called to his visitor.

The young man obeyed without the least hesitation.

"Take off your coat."

He complied.

"Lie down on that lounge."

In a moment the young man was stretched at full length, eyeing the surgeon. The latter undoubtedly was suffering under great excitement, but he did not waver; his movements were sure and quick. Selecting a bottle containing a liquid, he carefully measured out a certain quantity. While doing this he asked:

"Have you ever had any irregularity of the heart?"

"No."

The answer was prompt, but it was immediately followed by a quizzical look in the speaker's face.

"I presume," he added, "you mean by your question that it might be dangerous to give me a certain drug. Under the circumstances, however, I fail to see any relevancy in your question."

This took the surgeon aback; but he hastened to explain that he did not wish to inflict unnecessary pain, and hence his question.

He placed the glass on a stand, approached his visitor, and carefully examined his pulse.

"Wonderful!" he exclaimed.

"Why?"

"It is perfectly normal."

"Because I am wholly resigned. Indeed, it has been long since I knew such happiness. It is not active, but infinitely sweet."

"You have no lingering desire to retract?"

"None whatever."

The surgeon went to the stand and returned with the draught.

"Take this," he said, kindly.

The young man partially raised himself and took the glass in his hand. He did not show the vibration of a single nerve. He drank the liquid, draining the last drop. Then he returned the glass with a smile.

"Thank you," he said; "you are the noblest man that lives. May you always prosper and be happy! You are my benefactor, my liberator. Bless you, bless you! You reach down from your seat with the gods and lift me up into glorious peace and rest. I love you—I love you with all my heart!"

These words, spoken earnestly, in a musical, low voice, and accompanied with a smile of ineffable tenderness, pierced the old man's heart. A suppressed convulsion swept over him; intense anguish wrung his vitals; perspiration trickled down his face. The young man continued to smile.

"Ah, it does me good!" said he.

The surgeon, with a strong effort to control himself, sat down upon the edge of the lounge and took his visitor's wrist, counting the pulse.

"How long will it take?" the young man asked.

"Ten minutes. Two have passed." The voice was hoarse.

"Ah, only eight minutes more!... Delicious, delicious! I feel it coming .... What was that?... Ah, I understand. Music .... Beautiful!... Coming, coming .... Is that—that—water?... Trickling? Dripping? Doctor!"

"Well?"

"Thank you, ... thank you .... Noble man, .. my saviour, ... my bene ... bene ... factor .... Trickling, ... trickling .... Dripping, dripping .... Doctor!"

"Well?"

"Doctor!"

"Past hearing," muttered the surgeon.

"Doctor!"

"And blind."

Response was made by a firm grasp of the hand.

"Doctor!"

"And numb."

"Doctor!"

The old man watched and waited.

"Dripping, ... dripping."

The last drop had run. There was a sigh, and nothing more.

The surgeon laid down the hand.

"The first step," he groaned, rising to his feet; then his whole frame dilated. "The first step—the most difficult, yet the simplest. A providential delivery into my hands of that for which I have hungered for forty years. No withdrawal now! It is possible, because scientific; rational, but perilous. If I succeed—*if?* I *shall* succeed. I *will* succeed .... And after success—what?... Yes; what? Publish the plan and the result? The gallows .... So long as *it* shall exist, ... and *I* exist, the gallows. That much .... But how account for its presence? Ah, that pinches hard! I must trust to the future."

He tore himself from the reverie and started.

"I wonder if *she* heard or saw anything."

With that reflection he cast a glance upon the form on the lounge, and then left the room, locked the door, locked also the door of the outer room, walked down two or three corridors, penetrated to a remote part of the house, and rapped at a door. It was opened by his wife. He, by this time, had regained complete mastery over himself.

"I thought I heard someone in the house just now," he said, "but I can find no one."

"I heard nothing."

He was greatly relieved.

"I did hear someone knock at the door less than an hour ago," she resumed, "and heard you speak, I think. Did he come in?"

"No."

The woman glanced at his feet and seemed perplexed.

"I am almost certain," she said, "that I heard foot-falls in the house, and yet I see that you are wearing slippers."

"Oh, I had on my shoes then!"

"That explains it," said the woman, satisfied; "I think the sound you heard must have been caused by rats."

"Ah, that was it!" exclaimed the surgeon. Leaving, he closed the door, reopened it, and said, "I do not wish to be disturbed today." He said to himself, as he went down the hall, "All is clear there."

He returned to the room in which his visitor lay, and made a careful examination.

"Splendid specimen!" he softly exclaimed; "every organ sound, every function perfect; fine, large frame; well-shaped muscles, strong and sinewy; capable of wonderful development—if given opportunity . . . .I have no doubt it can be done. Already I have succeeded with a dog,—a task less difficult than this, for in a man the cerebrum overlaps the cerebellum, which is not the case with a dog. This gives a wide range for accident, with but one opportunity in a lifetime! In the cerebrum, the intellect and the affections; in the cerebellum, the senses and the motor forces; in the medulla oblongata, control of the diaphragm.

In these two latter lie all the essentials of simple existence. The cerebrum is merely an adornment; that is to say, reason and the affections are almost purely ornamental. I have already proved it. My dog, with its cerebrum removed, was idiotic, but it retained its physical senses to a certain degree."

While thus ruminating he made careful preparations. He moved the couch, replaced the operating-table under the sky-light, selected a number of surgical instruments, prepared certain drug-mixtures, and arranged water, towels, and all the accessories of a tedious surgical operation. Suddenly he burst into laughter.

"Poor fool!" he exclaimed. "Paid me five thousand dollars to kill him! Didn't have the courage to snuff his own candle! Singular, singular, the queer freaks these madmen have! You thought you were dying, poor idiot! Allow me to inform you, sir, that you are as much alive at this moment as ever you were in your life. But it will be all the same to you. You shall never be more conscious than you are now; and for all practical purposes, so far as they concern you, you are dead henceforth, though you shall live. By the way, how should you feel *without a head*? Ha, ha, ha!. . . But that's a sorry joke."

He lifted the unconscious form from the lounge and laid it upon the operating-table.

★★★★★★

About three years afterwards the following conversation was held between a captain of police and a detective:

"She may be insane," suggested the captain.

"I think she is."

"And yet you credit her story!"

"I do."

"Singular!"

"Not at all. I myself have learned something."

"What!"

"Much, in one sense; little, in another. You have heard those queer stories of her husband. Well, they are all nonsensical—probably with one exception. He is generally a harmless old fellow, but peculiar. He has performed some wonderful surgical operations. The people in his neighbourhood are ignorant, and they fear him and wish to be rid of him; hence they tell a great many lies about him, and they come to believe their own stories. The one important thing that I have learned is that he is almost insanely enthusiastic on the subject of surgery—especially experimental surgery; and with an enthusiast there is hardly such a thing as a scruple. It is this that gives me confidence in the woman's story."

"You say she appeared to be frightened?"

"Doubly so—first, she feared that her husband would learn of her betrayal of him; second, the discovery itself had terrified her."

"But her report of this discovery is very vague," argued the captain. "He conceals everything from her. She is merely guessing."

"In part—yes; in other part—no. She heard the sounds distinctly, though she did not see clearly. Horror closed her eyes. What she thinks she saw is, I admit, preposterous; but she undoubtedly saw something extremely frightful. There are many peculiar little circumstances. He has eaten with her but few times during the last three years, and nearly always carries his food to his private rooms. She says that he either consumes an enormous quantity, throws much away, or is feeding something that eats prodigiously. He explains this to her by saying that he has animals with which he experiments. This is not true. Again, he always keeps the door to these rooms carefully locked; and not only that, but he has had the doors doubled and otherwise strengthened, and has heavily barred a window that looks from one of the rooms upon a dead wall a few feet distant."

"What does it mean?" asked the captain.

"A prison."

"For animals, perhaps."

"Certainly not."

"Why!"

"Because, in the first place, cages would have been better; in the second place, the security that he has provided is infinitely greater than that required for the confinement of ordinary animals."

"All this is easily explained: he has a violent lunatic under treatment."

"I had thought of that, but such is not the fact."

"How do you know?"

"By reasoning thus: He has always refused to treat cases of lunacy; he confines himself to surgery; the walls are not padded, for the woman has heard sharp blows upon them; no human strength, however morbid, could possibly require such resisting strength as has been provided; he would not be likely to conceal a lunatic's confinement from the woman; no lunatic could consume all the food that he provides; so extremely violent mania as these precautions indicate could not continue three years; if there is a lunatic in the case it is very probable that there should have been communication with someone outside concerning the patient, and there has been none; the woman has listened at the keyhole and has heard no human voice within; and last, we have heard the woman's vague description of what she saw."

"You have destroyed every possible theory," said the captain, deeply interested, "and have suggested nothing new."

"Unfortunately, I cannot; but the truth may be very simple, after all. The old surgeon is so peculiar that I am prepared to discover something remarkable."

"Have you suspicions?"

"I have."

"Of what?"

"A crime. The woman suspects it."

"And betrays it?"

"Certainly, because it is so horrible that her humanity revolts; so terrible that her whole nature demands of her that she hand over the criminal to the law; so frightful that she is in mortal terror; so awful that it has shaken her mind."

"What do you propose to do?" asked the captain.

"Secure evidence. I may need help."

"You shall have all the men you require. Go ahead, but be careful. You are on dangerous ground. You would be a mere plaything in the hands of that man."

Two days afterwards the detective again sought the captain.

"I have a queer document," he said, exhibiting torn fragments of paper, on which there was writing. "The woman stole it and brought it to me. She snatched a handful out of a book, getting only a part of each of a few leaves."

These fragments, which the men arranged as best they could, were (the detective explained) torn by the surgeon's wife from the first volume of a number of manuscript books which her husband had written on one subject,—the very one that was the cause of her excitement. "About the time that he began a certain experiment three years ago," continued the detective, "he removed everything from the suite of two rooms containing his study and his operating-room. In one of the bookcases that he removed to a room across the passage was a drawer, which he kept locked, but which he opened from time to time.

As is quite common with such pieces of furniture, the lock of the drawer is a very poor one; and so the woman, while making a thorough search yesterday, found a key on her bunch that fitted this lock. She opened the drawer, drew out the bottom book of a pile (so that its mutilation would more likely escape discovery), saw that it might contain a clew, and tore out a handful of the leaves. She had barely replaced the book, locked the drawer, and made her escape when her husband appeared. He hardly ever allows her to be out of his sight when she is in that part of the house."

The fragments read as follows:

> . . . the motory nerves. I had hardly dared to hope for such a result, although inductive reasoning had convinced me of its possibility, my only doubt having been on the score of my lack of skill. Their operation has been only slightly impaired, and even this would not have been the case had the operation been performed in infancy, before the intellect had sought and obtained recognition as an essential part of

the whole. Therefore I state, as a proved fact, that the cells of the motory nerves have inherent forces sufficient to the purposes of those nerves. But hardly so with the sensory nerves. These latter are, in fact, an offshoot of the former, evolved from them by natural (though not essential) heterogeneity, and to a certain extent are dependent on the evolution and expansion of a contemporaneous tendency, that developed into mentality, or mental function.

Both of these latter tendencies, these evolvements, are merely refinements of the motory system, and not independent entities; that is to say, they are the blossoms of a plant that propagates from its roots. The motory system is the first . . . nor am I surprised that such prodigious muscular energy is developing. It promises yet to surpass the wildest dreams of human strength. I account for it thus: The powers of assimilation had reached their full development. They had formed the habit of doing a certain amount of work. They sent their products to all parts of the system.

As a result of my operation the consumption of these products was reduced fully one-half; that is to say, about one-half of the demand for them was withdrawn. But force of habit required the production to proceed. This production was strength, vitality, energy. Thus double the usual quantity of this strength, this energy, was stored in the remaining . . . developed a tendency that did surprise me. Nature, no longer suffering the distraction of extraneous interferences, and at the same time being cut in two (as it were), with reference to this case, did not fully adjust herself to the new situation, as does a magnet, which, when divided at the point of equilibrium, renews itself in its two fragments by investing each with opposite poles; but, on the contrary, being severed from laws that theretofore had controlled her, and possessing still that mysterious tendency to develop into something more potential and complex, she blindly (having lost her lantern) pushed her demands for material that would secure this development, and as blindly used it when it was given her.

Hence this marvellous voracity, this insatiable hunger, this wonderful ravenousness; and hence also (there being nothing but the physical part to receive this vast storing of energy) this strength that is becoming almost hourly herculean, almost daily appalling. It is becoming a serious . . . narrow escape today. By some means, while I was absent, it unscrewed the stopper of the silver feeding-pipe (which I have already herein termed 'the artificial mouth'), and, in one of its curious antics, allowed all the chyle to escape from its stomach through the tube.

Its hunger then became intense—I may say furious. I placed my hands upon it to push it into a chair, when, feeling my touch, it caught me, clasped me around the neck, and would have crushed me to death instantly had I not slipped from its powerful grasp. Thus I always had to be on my guard. I have provided the screw stopper with a spring catch, and . . . usually docile when not hungry; slow and heavy in its movements, which are, of course, purely unconscious; any apparent excitement in movement being due to local irregularities in the blood-supply of the cerebellum, which, if I did not have it enclosed in a silver case that is immovable, I should expose and . . .

The captain looked at the detective with a puzzled air.

"I don't understand it at all," said he.

"Nor I," agreed the detective.

"What do you propose to do?"

"Make a raid."

"Do you want a man?"

"Three. The strongest men in your district."

"Why, the surgeon is old and weak!"

"Nevertheless, I want three strong men; and for that matter, prudence really advises me to take twenty."

★★★★★★

At one o'clock the next morning a cautious, scratching sound might have been heard in the ceiling of the surgeon's operating-room. Shortly afterwards the skylight sash was carefully raised and laid aside. A man peered into the opening. Nothing could be heard.

"That is singular," thought the detective.

He cautiously lowered himself to the floor by a rope, and then stood for some moments listening intently. There was a dead silence. He shot the slide of a dark-lantern, and rapidly swept the room with the light. It was bare, with the exception of a strong iron staple and ring, screwed to the floor in the centre of the room, with a heavy chain attached. The detective then turned his attention to the outer room; it was perfectly bare. He was deeply perplexed. Returning to the inner room, he called softly to the men to descend. While they were thus occupied he re-entered the outer room and examined the door. A glance sufficed. It was kept closed by a spring attachment, and was locked with a strong spring-lock that could be drawn from the inside.

"The bird has just flown," mused the detective. "A singular accident! The discovery and proper use of this thumb-bolt might not have happened once in fifty years, if my theory is correct."

By this time the men were behind him. He noiselessly drew the spring-bolt, opened the door, and looked out into the hall. He heard a peculiar sound. It was as though a gigantic lobster was floundering and scrambling in some distant part of the old house. Accompanying this sound was a loud, whistling breathing, and frequent rasping gasps.

These sounds were heard by still another person—the surgeon's wife; for they originated very near her rooms, which were a considerable distance from her husband's. She had been sleeping lightly, tortured by fear and harassed by frightful dreams. The conspiracy into which she had recently entered, for the destruction of her husband, was a source of great anxiety. She constantly suffered from the most gloomy forebodings, and lived in an atmosphere of terror. Added to the natural horror of her situation were those countless sources of fear which a fright-shaken mind creates and then magnifies. She was, indeed, in a

143

pitiable state, having been driven first by terror to desperation, and then to madness.

Startled thus out of fitful slumber by the noise at her door, she sprang from her bed to the floor, every terror that lurked in her acutely tense mind and diseased imagination starting up and almost overwhelming her. The idea of flight—one of the strongest of all instincts—seized upon her, and she ran to the door, beyond all control of reason. She drew the bolt and flung the door wide open, and then fled wildly down the passage, the appalling hissing and rasping gurgle ringing in her ears apparently with a thousandfold intensity. But the passage was in absolute darkness, and she had not taken a half-dozen steps when she tripped upon an unseen object on the floor. She fell headlong upon it, encountering in it a large, soft, warm substance that writhed and squirmed, and from which came the sounds that had awakened her. Instantly realizing her situation, she uttered a shriek such as only an unnamable terror can inspire. But hardly had her cry started the echoes in the empty corridor when it was suddenly stifled. Two prodigious arms had closed upon her and crushed the life out of her.

The cry performed the office of directing the detective and his assistants, and it also aroused the old surgeon, who occupied rooms between the officers and the object of their search. The cry of agony pierced him to the marrow, and a realization of the cause of it burst upon him with frightful force.

"It has come at last!" he gasped, springing from his bed.

Snatching from a table a dimly-burning lamp and a long knife which he had kept at hand for three years, he dashed into the corridor. The four officers had already started forward, but when they saw him emerge they halted in silence. In that moment of stillness the surgeon paused to listen. He heard the hissing sound and the clumsy floundering of a bulky, living object in the direction of his wife's apartments. It evidently was advancing towards him. A turn in the corridor shut out the view. He turned up the light, which revealed a ghastly pallor in his face.

"Wife!" he called.

There was no response. He hurriedly advanced, the four men following quietly. He turned the angle of the corridor, and ran so rapidly that by the time the officers had come in sight of him again he was twenty steps away. He ran past a huge, shapeless object, sprawling, crawling, and floundering along, and arrived at the body of his wife.

He gave one horrified glance at her face, and staggered away. Then a fury seized him. Clutching the knife firmly, and holding the lamp aloft, he sprang toward the ungainly object in the corridor. It was then that the officers, still advancing cautiously, saw a little more clearly, though still indistinctly, the object of the surgeon's fury, and the cause of the look of unutterable anguish in his face. The hideous sight caused them to pause. They saw what appeared to be a man, yet evidently was not a man; huge, awkward, shapeless; a squirming, lurching, stumbling mass, completely naked. It raised its broad shoulders. *It had no head*, but instead of it a small metallic ball surmounting its massive neck.

"Devil!" exclaimed the surgeon, raising the knife.

"Hold, there!" commanded a stern voice.

The surgeon quickly raised his eyes and saw the four officers, and for a moment fear paralyzed his arm.

"The police!" he gasped.

Then, with a look of redoubled fury, he sent the knife to the hilt into the squirming mass before him. The wounded monster sprang to its feet and wildly threw its arms about, meanwhile emitting fearful sounds from a silver tube through which it breathed. The surgeon aimed another blow, but never gave it. In his blind fury he lost his caution, and was caught in an iron grasp. The struggling threw the lamp some feet toward the officers, and it fell to the floor, shattered to pieces. Simultaneously with the crash the oil took fire, and the corridor was filled with flame. The officers could not approach. Before them was the spreading blaze, and secure behind it were two forms struggling in a fearful embrace. They heard cries and gasps, and saw the gleaming of a knife.

The wood in the house was old and dry. It took fire at

once, and the flames spread with great rapidity. The four officers turned and fled, barely escaping with their lives. In an hour
nothing remained of the mysterious old house and its inmates
but a blackened ruin.

An Original Revenge

(A story from *The Ape, the Idiot & Other People*)

On a certain day I received a letter from a private soldier, named Gratmar, attached to the garrison of San Francisco. I had known him but slightly, the acquaintance having come about through his interest in some stories which I had published, and which he had a way of calling "psychological studies." He was a dreamy, romantic, fine-grained lad, proud as a tiger-lily and sensitive as a blue-bell. What mad caprice led him to join the army I never knew; but I did know that there he was wretchedly out of place, and I foresaw that his rude and repellant environment would make of him in time a deserter, or a suicide, or a murderer.

The letter at first seemed a wild outpouring of despair, for it informed me that before it should reach me its author would be dead by his own hand. But when I had read farther I understood its spirit, and realized how coolly formed a scheme it disclosed and how terrible its purport was intended to be. The worst of the contents was the information that a certain officer (whom he named) had driven him to the deed, and that *he was committing suicide for the sole purpose of gaining thereby the power to revenge himself upon his enemy*! I learned afterward that the officer had received a similar letter.

This was so puzzling that I sat down to reflect upon the young man's peculiarities. He had always seemed somewhat uncanny, and had I proved more sympathetic he doubtless would have gone farther and told me of certain problems which he professed to have solved concerning the life beyond this. One thing that he had said came back vividly:

> If I could only overcome that purely gross and animal love of life that makes us all shun death, I would kill myself, for I know how far more powerful I could be in spirit than in flesh.

The manner of the suicide was startling, and that was what might have been expected from this odd character. Evidently scorning the flummery of funerals, he had gone into a little canyon near the military reservation and blown himself into a million fragments with dynamite, so that all of him that was ever found was some minute particles of flesh and bone.

I kept the letter a secret, for I desired to observe the officer without rousing his suspicion of my purpose; it would be an admirable test of a dead man's power and deliberate intention to haunt the living, for so I interpreted the letter. The officer thus to be punished was an oldish man, short, apoplectic, overbearing, and irascible. Generally he was kind to most of the men in a way; but he was gross and mean, and that explained sufficiently his harsh treatment of young Gratmar, whom he could not understand, and his efforts to break that flighty young man's spirit.

Not very long after the suicide certain modifications in the officer's conduct became apparent to my watchful oversight. His choler, though none the less sporadic, developed a quality which had some of the characteristics of senility; and yet he was still in his prime, and passed for a sound man. He was a bachelor, and had lived always alone; but presently he began to shirk solitude at night and court it in daylight. His brother-officers chaffed him, and thereupon he would laugh in rather a forced and silly fashion, quite different from the ordinary way with him, and would sometimes, on these occasions, blush so violently that his face would become almost purple.

His soldierly alertness and sternness relaxed surprisingly at some times and at others were exaggerated into unnecessary acerbity, his conduct in this regard suggesting that of a drunken man who knows that he is drunk and who now and then makes a brave effort to appear sober. All these things, and more, indicating some mental strain, or some dreadful apprehension, or perhaps something worse than either, were observed partly by me and partly by an intelligent officer whose watch upon the man had been secured by me.

To be more particular, the afflicted man was observed often to start suddenly and in alarm, look quickly round, and make some unintelligent monosyllabic answer, seemingly to an inaudible question that no visible person had asked. He acquired the reputation, too, of having taken lately to nightmares, for in the middle of the night he would shriek in the most dreadful fashion, alarming his roommates prodigiously. After these attacks he would sit up in bed, his ruddy face devoid of colour, his eyes glassy and shining, his breathing broken with gasps, and his body wet with a cold perspiration.

Knowledge of these developments and transformations spread throughout the garrison; but the few (mostly women) who dared to express sympathy or suggest a tonic encountered so violent rebuffs that they blessed Heaven for escaping alive from his word-volleys. Even the garrison surgeon, who had a kindly manner, and the commanding general, who was constructed on dignified and impressive lines, received little thanks for their solicitude. Clearly the doughty old officer, who had fought like a bulldog in two wars and a hundred battles, was suffering deeply from some undiscoverable malady.

The next extraordinary thing which he did was to visit one evening (not so clandestinely as to escape my watch) a spirit medium—extraordinary, because he always had scoffed at the idea of spirit communications. I saw him as he was leaving the medium's rooms. His face was purple, his eyes were bulging and terrified, and he tottered in his walk. A policeman, seeing his distress, advanced to assist him; whereupon the soldier hoarsely begged,—

"Call a hack."

Into it he fell, and asked to be driven to his quarters. I hastily ascended to the medium's rooms, and found her lying unconscious on the floor. Soon, with my aid, she recalled her wits, but her conscious state was even more alarming than the other. At first she regarded me with terror, and cried,—

"It is horrible for you to hound him so!"

I assured her that I was hounding no one.

"Oh, I thought you were the spir—I mean—I—oh, but it was standing exactly where you are!" she exclaimed.

"I suppose so," I agreed, "but you can see that I am not the young man's spirit. However, I am familiar with this whole case, madam, and if I can be of any service in the matter I should be glad if you would inform me. I am aware that our friend is persecuted by a spirit, which visits him frequently, and I am positive that through you it has informed him that the end is not far away, and that our elderly friend's death will assume some terrible form. Is there anything that I can do to avert the tragedy?"

The woman stared at me in a horrified silence. "How did you know these things?" she gasped.

"That is immaterial. When will the tragedy occur? Can I prevent it?"

"Yes, yes!" she exclaimed. "It will happen this very night! But no earthly power can prevent it!"

She came close to me and looked at me with an expression of the most acute terror.

"Merciful God! what will become of me? He is to be murdered, you understand—murdered in cold blood by a spirit—and he knows it and*I know it*! If he is spared long enough he will tell them at the garrison, and they will all think that I had something to do with it! Oh, this is terrible, terrible, and yet I dare not say a word in advance—nobody there would believe in what the spirits say, and they will think that I had a hand in the murder!" The woman's agony was pitiful.

"Be assured that he will say nothing about it," I said; "and if you keep your tongue from wagging you need fear nothing."

With this and a few other hurried words of comfort, I soothed her and hastened away.

For I had interesting work on hand: it is not often that one may be in at such a murder as that! I ran to a livery stable, secured a swift horse, mounted him, and spurred furiously for the reservation. The hack, with its generous start, had gone far on its way, but my horse was nimble, and his legs felt the pricking of my eagerness. A few miles of this furious pursuit brought me within sight of the hack just as it was crossing a dark ravine near the reservation. As I came nearer I imagined that the hack swayed somewhat, and that a fleeing shadow escaped from it into the tree-banked further wall of the ravine. I certainly was not in error with regard to the swaying, for it had roused the dull notice of the driver. I saw him turn, with an air of alarm in his action, and then pull up with a heavy swing upon the reins. At this moment I dashed up and halted.

"Anything the matter?" I asked.

"I don't know," he answered, getting down. "I felt the carriage sway, and I see that the door's wide open. Guess my load thought he'd sobered up enough to get out and walk, without troubling me or his pocket-book."

Meanwhile I too had alighted; then struck a match, and by its light we discovered, through the open door, the "load" huddled confusedly on the floor of the hack, face upward, his chin compressed upon his breast by his leaning against the further door, and looking altogether vulgar, misshapen, and miserably unlike a soldier. He neither moved nor spoke when we called. We hastily clambered within and lifted him upon the seat, but his head rolled about with an awful looseness and freedom, and another match disclosed a ghastly dead face and wide eyes that stared horribly at nothing.

"You would better drive the body to headquarters," I said.

Instead of following, I cantered back to town, housed my horse, and went straightway to bed; and this will prove to be the first information that I was the "mysterious man on a horse," whom the coroner could never find.

About a year afterwards I received the following letter (which is observed to be in fair English) from Stockholm, Sweden:

151

Dear Sir,—For some years I have been reading your remarkable psychological studies with great interest, and I take the liberty to suggest a theme for your able pen. I have just found in a library here a newspaper, dated about a year ago, in which is an account of the mysterious death of a military officer in a hack.

Then followed the particulars, as I have already detailed them, and the very theme of post-mortem revenge which I have adopted in this setting out of facts. Some persons may regard the coincidence between my correspondent's suggestion and my private and exclusive knowledge as being a very remarkable thing; but there are likely even more wonderful things in the world, and at none of them do I longer marvel. More extraordinary still is his suggestion that in the dynamite explosion a dog or a quarter of beef might as well have been employed as a suicide-minded man; that, in short, the man may not have killed himself at all, but might have employed a presumption of such an occurrence to render more effective a physical persecution ending in murder by the living man who had posed as a spirit. The letter even suggested an arrangement with a spirit medium, and I regard that also as a queer thing.

The declared purpose of this letter was to suggest material for another of my "psychological studies;" but I submit that the whole affair is of too grave a character for treatment in the levity of fiction. And if the facts and coincidences should prove less puzzling to others than to me, a praiseworthy service might be done to humanity by the presentation of whatever solution a better understanding than mine might evolve.

The only remaining disclosure which I am prepared now to make is that my correspondent signed himself "Ramtarg,"—an odd-sounding name, but for all I know it may be respectable in Sweden. And yet there is something about the name that haunts me unceasingly, much as does some strange dream which we know we have dreamt and yet which it is impossible to remember.

Two Singular Men

(A story from *The Ape, the Idiot & Other People*)

The first of these was a powerful Italian, topped with a dense brush of rebellious black hair. The circumstances leading up to his employment in the Great Oriental Dime Museum as the "Marvellous Tuft-nosed Wild Man, Hoolagaloo, captured on the Island of Milo, in the Ægean Sea, after a desperate struggle," were these:

He had been a wood-chopper, possessed of prodigious strength and a violent temper. One day he and a companion in the mountains fell out and fought. The Italian then had to walk twenty miles to find a surgeon, being in great need of his services. When he presented himself to the surgeon his face was heavily bandaged with blood-soaked cloths. He began to fumble in his pockets, and his face betrayed deep anxiety when he failed to find what he sought.

"What is the matter?" asked the surgeon, "and what are you seeking?"

The man uncovered his mouth and in a voice like the sound of an ophicleide, answered:

"Mina nosa."

"Your nose!"

"Aha. T'ought I bring 'im, butta no find."

"Brought your nose in your pocket!"

"Dunno—may be losta. Fella fighta me; cut offa da nose."

The surgeon assured him that the severed nose would have been useless.

"But I wanta da nose!" exclaimed the man, in despair.

The surgeon said that he could make a new one, and the man appeared greatly relieved in mind. A removal of the bandages disclosed the fact that a considerable part of the nose was gone. The surgeon then proceeded to perform the familiar rhinoplastic operation, which consists in making a V-shaped incision through the skin of the forehead immediately above the nose, loosening it, and bringing it down with a half-turn, to keep the cuticle outward, and covering the nose-stump with it. In preparing for this he made an interesting discovery. The place for the man's nose was long and his forehead low, so that in order to secure sufficient length for the flap he had to encroach on the hair-covered scalp. There was no help for it. With some misgivings the surgeon shaved the hair and then performed the operation with admirable success.

His fears, however, in time were realized. All around the end of the nose there appeared a broad line of black hair. When the skin was in its normal position above the forehead the hair on the upper edge of it had grown downward; but as the skin was inverted in its new position the hair, of course, grew upward, curving towards the eyes. It gave the man a grotesque and hideous appearance, and this made him furious. The surgeon, having a quick wit and a regard for the integrity of his bones, introduced him to Signor Castellani, proprietor of the Great Oriental Dime Museum, and that enterprising worthy immediately engaged him. And thus it was that the man became the greatest curiosity in the world.

Among his companions in the museum were the Severed Lady, who apparently was nonexistent below the waist; the Remarkable Tattooed Lady, who had been rescued from Chinese pirates in the Coral Sea, and some others. To them the tuft-nosed man was known as Bat—surmised to be a contraction of Bartolommeo.

The other singular man with which this narrative is concerned was a small, delicate, mild-mannered, impecunious fellow, who made a living by writing for the press. He and Castellani were friends, and he was on excellent terms with the "freaks." But as this narrative is to tell the little secrets of the museum, it should be explained that the real object of the young man's deepest admiration was Mademoiselle Zoë, the Severed Lady, billed also as the Wonderful French Phenomenon. She was known in private life as Muggie (formerly Muggy, and probably originally Margaret), and she was the only daughter and special pride of Castellani. Zoë was rosy-cheeked, pretty, and had a freckled nose. The impecunious writer was named Sampey. Sampey secretly loved Zoë.

As the Severed Lady, Mademoiselle Zoë's professional duties were monotonous. They gave her abundant opportunities for observation and reflection, and, being young and of the feminine sex, she dreamed.

What she observed most was eyes. These were the eyes that looked at her as she rested in her little swing when on exhibition. Her gilt booth was very popular, for she was pretty, and some kind-hearted visitors at the show pitied the poor thing because she ended at the waist! But far from being depressed by the apparent absence of all below the lower edge of her gold belt with its glittering diamond buckle, she was cheerful, and now and then would sing a little song. Her sweetness of manner and voice and the plumpness of her rounded arms and shoulders were what had won Sampey's heart and made him all the more zealous in his useful occupation of devising the names which Castellani bestowed on his freaks.

Hoolagaloo had suffered a turning of the head by his good fortune. He imagined that because he was monstrous he was great. That made him arrogant and presumptuous. He, too, loved Zoë. Thus it came about that a rivalry was established between Sampey and the Wild Man of Milo. How was it with Zoë? Which loved she?—or loved she either? Observing and reflecting, she dreamed. As it was eyes only that she saw, it was of eyes only that she dreamed.

"Ah," sighed this innocent girl, "that I could see in reality the eyes of my dreams! So many, many eyes stare at me in my booth, and yet the eyes of my dreams come not! Blue eyes, brown eyes, black eyes, hazel eyes, gray eyes, all of every shade, but not yet have come the eyes I so long to see! Those which do come are commonplace; their owners are commonplace—just ordinary mortals. I'm sure that princes, knights, and heroes *must* have the eyes that beam on me as I sleep. I'm sure, indeed, that such eyes will come in time, and that by such a sign I shall know my hero, my master, my love!"

She cautiously asked the Wild Man of Milo about it one day, but his answer was a coarse guffaw; then, seeing that he had made a mistake, he kissed her. The hair of his tufted nose thus got into her pretty blue eyes, and she shuddered.

Then she went to Sampey, who was wise, cool, and politic. He listened, amazed, but attentive. The opportunity of his life had come. When he had gathered up his dismayed and scattered wits, he gravely answered:

"Muggie, these eyes that appear in your dreams—is it a particular color or a certain expression which they have?"

"Colour," she answered.

"What colour?"

"A soft, pale, limpid amber."

She said it so innocently, so earnestly, so sweetly, that he could doubt neither her sincerity nor her sanity. Thus the crisis had fallen upon him and had nearly crushed him.

Nevertheless, he set his wits at work. Pondering, analyzing, ransacking every nook in the warehouse of his mental resources, he fought bravely with despair. Presently a bright ray of intelligence, descended Heaven knows whence, swept across his thought-pinched face. This bright beam, growing more and more effulgent, mounting higher and higher till it illuminated all his faculties, finally lighted up his way to become one of the two singular men of this narrative.

"I see," he said, trying to veil the glow of triumph in his face, "that you have not wholly mastered the problem of the eyes. True, it is only heroes that have amber eyes. But such eyes are a badge of heroism sent by heaven; and, though a man may not have been heroic in any outward sense, when the essence of true heroism is breathed into him his eyes, without his knowledge of the fact, may assume the amber hue of your dreams. Sometimes, in the development of the spirit of heroism, this colour is only transient; in time it may become permanent. Muggie, these dreams indicate your destiny. You should marry none but a hero, and when he comes you will know him by his amber eyes." With this Sampey sighed, for Muggie was looking earnestly into his gray eyes.

Had he thus, in blind self-sacrifice to the whim of a foolish girl, cast himself into a pit? If so, what meant his light step and cheerful smile as soon as she was out of sight?

Mademoiselle Zoë, the Severed Lady, swung in half-person and sang her little song on a night a week or two afterwards, just as she had sung and swung many a night before. Wondering eyes of every kind were staring at her, and presently her foolish little heart gave a great bound. There before her, regarding her with infinite tenderness, was a divine pair of soft, pale, limpid amber eyes! (A woman in the audience happened also to see this extraordinary spectacle, and it frightened her so badly that she fainted, thinking she had seen a corpse.)

The amber eyes instantly disappeared, along with their owner, one Sampey. A thumpy little heart in a round, plump body knew that it was he; knew, therefore, that her destiny was come, and, most extraordinary of all, in the shape of her good father's literary bureau! Yet what shock there was next day, when the hero of her dreams came to her with his ordinary pale-gray eyes, blurred somewhat and inclined to humidity!

"Sampey!" she exclaimed in dismay, tumbled thus rudely from the clouds.

"Muggie!"

"Your eyes last night—then you were a hero; but to-day——"

"A hero!" innocently echoed Sampey.

"Why, yes! Last night you had amber eyes—such beautiful eyes—the hero-eyes of my dreams!"

"My dear child, you certainly were dreaming."

"Oh, no! I saw them! My heart jumped so! I knew you—I knew you—and your eyes were amber!"

Sampey smiled sadly and a little complacently, and with great modesty said:

"I can't doubt you, my dear child, but I assure you that I was unconscious of my amber eyes. I wish that I could feel at liberty to confess to you that lately I have had strange whisperings of heroism in my soul—but that would be boasting, and true heroism is always modest. Still, I ought not to be surprised that you discovered the actual presence before I was aware even of its existence; but such, indeed, my dear, is the peculiarity of the true hero—he is ever unaware of his own heroism." He took her hand languishingly and squeezed it. She blushed and fled.

Signor Castellani, besides being wealthy, was a man of business. His daughter should marry a man who had money sufficient to insure his worth. With perspicacity rare in a man, he had observed that the two singular men of this narrative admired his daughter. Now, Bat, being a freak, was making money rapidly, while Sampey was only a poor literary bureau! Castellani felt the need of a partner. Why should not a partner be a son-in-law? Surely Bat was much more desirable than Sampey!

Sampey was wise and Bat was foolish. On the other hand, Bat was courageous and Sampey was timid. Bat had the courage of a brute. Sampey knew that there were certain ways of frightening brave brutes—he had even seen a prize-fighter join a church. He prepared for Bat.

One day he entered the museum between exhibitions and sought the Wild Man of Milo. That worthy was leisurely smoking a cigarette in a quiet corner, and was making the smoke curl up gracefully over the hairy tuft on his nose. Sampey was paler than usual and a little nervous, for the business of his visit was tinged with hazard. Bat, who happened to feel good-natured, gave the first greeting.

"Hey!" he called out.

Sampey went straight to him.

"You lika da show, ha, Samp? You come effery day. Gooda place, ha, Samp?"

"A very good place, Bat," quietly answered Sampey, who tried hard to appear indifferent as he fumbled nervously in his pocket.

"Signor Castellani, he biga mon, reecha mon, gooda mon. You like 'im?"

"Very much." Sampey was acting strangely.

Bat's eyes twinkled a little dangerously.

"You lika da gal, too, ha, Samp?"

"The—ah—the tattooed woman? Yes, very well, indeed."

"Ha, you sly Samp! I spik about da leetle ploompa gal—da Mug."

"Oh! Muggie? Castellani's daughter?"

"Ha."

"Well, I don't know her so very well."

"You don' know da Mugga?" Bat's look was becoming dangerously fierce. He straightened himself up from his lounging posture, and his big muscles swelled. "You don' know da Mugga! You tink I no see. You loafa da Mugga! You wanta marry her! You tink 'er reecha, pooty. You miseraba sneaka!" Here Bat, who had worked himself into a fury, swore an eloquent Italian oath.

Sampey's time had come. The two men were alone,—Bat furious and desperate with jealousy; Sampey fearful, but determined; brutality against wit, strength against cunning, fury against patience, a bulldog matched with a mink, a game-cock pitted against an owl.

Sampey pretended to have dropped something accidentally. He stooped to pick it up, and some seconds elapsed before he pretended to have found it. While he was searching for it he approached nearer to Bat, and when he straightened up he brought his face very close to Bat's, and suddenly raised his eyes and stared steadily into those of the Wild Man of Milo.

Bat meanwhile had kept up an insulting tirade, his evident purpose being to force the gentle writer into a fight. But when Sampey raised his eyes and fixed them in a peculiar stare, Bat regarded him a moment in speechless wonder, and then sprang back with a livid face, and in terror cried out:

"Santa Maria!"

For half a minute he gazed, horrified, at the sight which confronted him, his mouth open, his eyes staring—fascinated, terror-stricken, and aghast. Sampey, the gentle, usually dove-eyed, was now transformed. Those were not the accustomed gray eyes with which Bat was familiar, nor yet the limpid, amber eyes which had set poor Zoë's heart bounding; Sampey gazed upon his victim with eyes that were a fierce and insurrectionary scarlet!

Bat, contumelious now no longer, dashed wildly away. He spread his wonderful tale. Castellani, whom it finally reached, frowned, thinking that Bat was drunk. The Tattooed Lady laughed outright. Zoë wondered and was troubled; but that night, just before the curtain of her gilt booth was drawn at the close of the exhibition, there stood her hero Sampey, gazing tenderly at her with eyes of a soft, pale, limpid amber. And she slept soundly after that.

When Sampey visited the museum next day, he was eyed with considerable curiosity by the freaks. Castellani asked him directly what Bat meant by his stories. Sampey had expected this question, and was ready for it. After binding the showman to everlasting secrecy, he said:

"I have made a great discovery, but it is impossible for me to go into all its details. It must be sufficient at present for me to say that after many years of scientific experiment I have learned the secret of changing the colour of my eyes at will."

He said this very simply, as though unconscious of announcing one of the most extraordinary things to which the ages have given birth.

But Castellani was a study. Some great shock, resembling apoplexy, seemed to have invaded his system. Being a shrewd business man, he presently recovered his composure, and then in the most indifferent manner remarked that a person who could change the colour of his eyes at will ought to be able, perhaps, if he should get started right, to make a little money, possibly, out of the accomplishment; and then he offered Sampey forty dollars a week to pose as a freak in the Great Oriental Dime Museum. Sampey, who knew that the Wild Man of Milo's salary was two hundred dollars a week (which, although large, was well earned, seeing that everybody had to pull the tuft on his nose to be sure that it grew there), asked time to consider the splendid offer, which to him was a fortune.

There was the certainty of losing Zoë when she should learn that his amber eyes were not really heroic. He went to a retired showman and asked him what salaries might be commanded by a man with a hair-tufted nose and a man who could change the colour of his eyes to any other colour at will. This showman answered:

"I've seen Castellani's man with the tuft. He gets two hundred dollars a week. That is pretty high. If you can bring me a man who can change the colour of his eyes at will to any other colour, I will pay him a thousand dollars a week and start in the business again."

Sampey slept not a wink that night.

Meanwhile a change had taken place in Zoë: she had suddenly become more charming than ever. Her gentleness and sweetness had become conspicuously augmented, and she was so kind and sweet-mannered to all, including the Wild Man of Milo (whom she had formerly avoided through instinctive fear), that Bat took greater heart and swore to win her, though he might have to wade through oceans of Sampey blood. Mark this: Stake not too much on a woman's condescension to *you*; it may come through love for another.

Zoë was innocent, honest, and confiding. Innocence measures the strength of faith. The charm of faith is its absurdity. Zoë believed in Sampey.

Sampey, grown surprisingly bold and self-reliant, named his terms to Castellani—a half-interest in the business—and Castellani, swear and bully and bluster as he might, must accept. This made Sampey a rich man at once. Castellani, exceedingly gracious and friendly after the signing of the compact, proposed a quiet supper in his private apartments in celebration of the new arrangement, and presently he and Zoë and Sampey were enjoying a very choice meal. Zoë was dazzlingly radiant and pretty, but a certain strange constraint sat between her and Sampey. Once, when she dropped her napkin and Sampey picked it up, his hand accidentally touched one of her daintily slippered feet, and his blushes were painful to see.

While they were thus engaged, Bat, without ceremony, burst in upon them, his face aglow and his eyes flashing triumph. He carried in his hand a small box, which he rudely thrust under their noses. When Sampey saw it he turned deathly pale and shrank back, powerless to move or speak.

"I ketcha da scound!" exclaimed Bat, shaking his finger in the cowering Sampey's face. "I watch 'im; I ketcha da scound! He play you da dirtee tr-r-icks!"

The Wild Man of Milo placed the box on the table and raised the lid. Within appeared a number of curious, small, cup-shaped trinkets of opaque white glass, each marked in the centre with an annular band of colour surrounding a centre of clear glass, the range of colours being great, and the trinkets arranged in pairs according to colour. There were also a vial labelled "cocaine" and a small camel's-hair brush.

"You looka me," resumed Hoolagaloo, greatly excited. "I maka mine eye changa colah, lika da scounda Samp."

With that he dipped the brush into the vial and applied it to his eyes. Then he picked up two of the curious little glass cups, and slipped them, one at a time, over his eyeballs and under his eyelids, where they fitted snugly. They were artificial eyes which Sampey had had made to cover his natural eyeballs on occasion. Bat struck a mock-tragic attitude and hissed:

"*Diavolo!*"

By a strange accident he had picked out two which were not mates. One of his eyes was a soft, pale, limpid amber and the other a fierce and insurrectionary red. These, with his tufted nose and his tragic attitude, gave him an appearance so grotesque and hideous that Zoë, after springing to her feet and throwing her arms wildly aloft, fell in a dead faint into Sampey's arms.

Bat gloated over his rival; Castellani was dumfounded. Presently Sampey's nerve returned with his wits.

"Well," he remarked, contemptuously, drawing Zoë closer and holding her with a tender solicitude—"well, what of it?"

His insolence enraged Hoolagaloo. "H—hwat of eet! Santa Maria! Da scound! Ha, ha! Da gal no marry you now!"

Sampey deliberately moved Zoë so that he might reach his watch, and after looking calmly at it a moment he said:

"Muggie and I have been married just thirty hours."

The announcement stunned the Wild Man. Castellani himself had a hard mental struggle to realize the situation, and then, with his accustomed equanimity and his old-time air of authority, he said:

"Well, phat is oll the row aboot, annyhow? D'ye want to shpile th' mon's thrick, Misther Bat? An' thin, Misther Bat, it's a domned gude wan, it is; an' more'n thot, me gintlemanly son-in-law is me partner, too, Misther Bat, I'd have ye know, an' he's got aut'ority in this show."

That finished the Wild Man of Milo. He staggered out, shaved his nose, bought an axe, and fled to the mountains to chop wood again, leaving the Mysterious Man with the Spectre Eyes to become the happiest husband and the most prosperous freak and showman in the world.

The Faithful Amulet

(A story from *The Ape, the Idiot & Other People*)

A quaint old rogue, who called himself Rabaya, the Mystic, was one of the many extraordinary characters of that odd corner of San Francisco known as the Latin Quarter. His business was the selling of charms and amulets, and his generally harmless practices received an impressive aspect from his Hindu parentage, his great age, his small, wizened frame, his deeply wrinkled face, his outlandish dress, and the barbaric fittings of his den.

One of his most constant customers was James Freeman, the half-piratical owner and skipper of the *Blue Crane*. This queer little *barkentine*, of light tonnage but wonderful sailing qualities, is remembered in every port between Sitka and Callao. All sorts of strange stories are told of her exploits, but these mostly were manufactured by superstitious and highly imaginative sailors, who commonly demonstrate the natural affinity existing between idleness and lying. It has been said not only that she engaged in smuggling, piracy, and "blackbirding" (which is kidnapping Gilbert Islanders and selling them to the coffee-planters of Central America), but that she maintained special relations with Satan, founded on the power of mysterious charms which her skipper was supposed to have procured from some mysterious source and was known to employ on occasion.

Beyond the information which his manifests and clearance papers divulged, nothing of his supposed shady operations could be learned either from him or his crew; for his sailors, like him, were a strangely silent lot—all sharp, keen-eyed young fellows who never drank and who kept to themselves when in port. An uncommon circumstance was that there were never any vacancies in the crew, except one that happened as the result of Freeman's last visit to Rabaya, and it came about in the following remarkable manner:

Freeman, like most other men who follow the sea, was superstitious, and he ascribed his fair luck to the charms which he secretly procured from Rabaya. It is now known that he visited the mystic whenever he came to the port of San Francisco, and there are some today who believe that Rabaya had an interest in the supposed buccaneering enterprises of the *Blue Crane*.

Among the most intelligent and active of the *Blue Crane*'s crew was a Malay known to his mates as the Flying Devil. This had come to him by reason of his extraordinary agility. No monkey could have been more active than he in the rigging; he could make flying leaps with astonishing ease. He could not have been more than twenty-five years old, but he had the shrivelled appearance of an old man, and was small and lean. His face was smooth-shaved and wrinkled, his eyes deep-set and intensely black and brilliant. His mouth was his most forbidding feature. It was large, and the thin lips were drawn tightly over large and protruding teeth, its aspect being prognathous and menacing. Although quiet and not given to laughter, at times he would smile, and then the expression of his face was such as to give even Freeman a sensation of impending danger.

It was never clearly known what was the real mission of the *Blue Crane* when she sailed the last time from San Francisco. Some supposed that she intended to loot a sunken vessel of her treasure; others that the enterprise was one of simple piracy, involving the killing of the crew and the scuttling of the ship in mid-ocean; others that a certain large consignment of opium, for which the customs authorities were on the lookout, was likely about to be smuggled into some port of Puget Sound. In any event, the business ahead must have been important, for it is now known that in order to ensure its success Freeman bought an uncommonly expensive and potent charm from Rabaya.

When Freeman went to buy this charm he failed to notice that the Flying Devil was slyly following him; neither he nor the half-blind charm-seller observed the Malay slip into Rabaya's den and witness the matter that there went forward. The intruder must have heard something that stirred every evil instinct in him. Rabaya (whom I could hardly be persuaded to believe under oath) years afterwards told me that the charm which he sold to Freeman was one of extraordinary virtue.

For many generations it had been in the family of one of India's proudest *rajahs*, and until it was stolen the arms of England could not prevail over that part of the far East. If borne by a person of lofty character (as he solemnly informed me he believed Freeman to be) it would never fail to bring the highest good fortune; for, although the amulet was laden with evil powers as well as good, a worthy person could resist the evil and employ only the good. Contrariwise, the amulet in the hands of an evil person would be a most potent and dangerous engine of harm.

It was a small and very old trinket, made of copper and representing a serpent twined grotesquely about a human heart; through the heart a dagger was thrust, and the loop for holding the suspending string was formed by one of the coils of the snake. The charm had a wonderful history, which must be reserved for a future story; the sum of it being that as it had been as often in the hands of bad men as of good, it had wrought as many calamities as blessings. It was perfectly safe and useful—so Rabaya soberly told me—in the hands of such a man as Freeman.

Now, as no one knows the soundings and breadth of his own wickedness, the Flying Devil (who, Rabaya explained, must have overheard the conversation attending its transference to Freeman) reflected only that if he could secure possession of the charm his fortune would be made; as he could not procure it by other means, he must steal it. Moreover, he must have seen the price—five thousand dollars in gold—which Freeman paid for the trinket; and that alone was sufficient to move the Malay's cupidity. At all events, it is known that he set himself to steal the charm and desert from the *barkentine*.

From this point on to the catastrophe my information is somewhat hazy. I cannot say, for instance, just how the theft was committed, but it is certain that Freeman was not aware of it until a considerable time had passed. What did concern him particularly was the absence of the Malay when the *barkentine* was weighing anchor and giving a line for a tow out to sea. The Malay was a valuable sailor; to replace him adequately was clearly so impossible a task that Freeman decided, after a profitless and delaying search of hours, to leave port without him or another in his place. It was with a heavy heart, somewhat lightened by a confident assumption that the amulet was safe in his possession, that Freeman headed down the channel for the Golden Gate.

Meanwhile, the Flying Devil was having strange adventures. In a hastily arranged disguise, the principal feature of which was a gentleman's street dress, in which he might pass careless scrutiny as a thrifty Japanese awkwardly trying to adapt himself to the customs of his environment, he emerged from a water-front lodging-house of the poorer sort, and ascended leisurely to the summit of Telegraph Hill, in order to make a careful survey of the city from that prominent height; for it was needful that he know how best to escape. From that alluring eminence he saw not only a great part of the city, but also nearly the whole of the bay of San Francisco and the shores, towns, and mountains lying beyond.

His first particular attention was given to the *Blue Crane*, upon which he looked nearly straight down as she rolled gently at her moorings at the foot of Lombard Street. Two miles to the west he saw the trees which conceal the soldiers' barracks, and the commanding general's residence on the high promontory known as Black Point, and these invited him to seek concealment in their shadows until the advent of night would enable him to work his way down the peninsula of San Francisco to the distant blue mountains of San Mateo. Surmising that Freeman would make a search for him, and that it would be confined to the docks and their near vicinity, he imagined that it would not be a difficult matter to escape.

After getting his bearings the Malay was in the act of descending the hill by its northern flank, when he observed a stranger leaning against the parapet crowning the hill. The man seemed to be watching him. Not reflecting that his somewhat singular appearance might have accounted for the scrutiny, his suspicions were roused; he feared, albeit wrongly, that he was followed, for the stranger had come up soon after him. Assuming an air of indifference, he strolled about until he was very near the stranger, and then with the swiftness and ferocity of a tiger he sprang and slipped a knife-blade between the man's ribs. The stranger sank with a groan, and the Malay fled down the hill.

It was a curious circumstance that the man fell in front of one of the openings which neglect had permitted the rains to wash underneath the parapet. He floundered as some dying men will, and these movements caused him to work his body through the opening. That done, he started rolling down the steep eastern declivity, the speed of his flight increasing with every bound. Many cottages are perched precariously on this precipitous slope.

Mrs. Armour, a resident of one of them, was sitting in a rear room near the window, sewing, when she was amazed to see a man flying through the sash close beside her. He came with so great violence that he tore through a thin partition into an adjoining room and landed in a shapeless heap against the opposite wall. Mrs. Armour screamed for help. A great commotion ensued, but it was some time before the flight of the body was connected with a murder on the parapet. Nevertheless, the police were active, and presently a dozen of them were upon the broad trail which the murderer had left in his flight down the hill.

In a short time the Malay found himself in the lumber-piles of the northern water-front. Thence, after gathering himself together, he walked leisurely westward in the rear of the wire-works, and traversed a little sand-beach where mothers and nurses had children out for an airing. The desperate spirit of perversity which possessed the man (and which Rabaya afterwards explained by the possession of the amulet), made reckless by a belief that the charm which he carried would preserve him from all menaces, led him to steal a small hand-satchel that lay on the beach near a well-dressed woman. He walked away with it, and then opened it and was rejoiced to find that it contained some money and fine jewellery. At this juncture one of the children, who had observed the Malay's theft, called the woman's attention to him. She started in pursuit, raising a loud outcry, which emptied the adjacent drinking-saloons of a pursuing crowd.

The Malay leaped forward with ample ability to outstrip all his pursuers, but just as he arrived in front of a large swimming establishment a bullet from a policeman's pistol brought him to his knees. The crowd quickly pressed around him. The criminal staggered to his feet, made a fierce dash at a man who stood in his way, and sank a good knife into his body. Then he bounded away, fled swiftly past a narrow beach where swimming-clubs have their houses, and disappeared in the ruins of a large old building that lay at the foot of a sandy bluff on the water's edge. He was trailed a short distance within the ruins by a thin stream of blood which he left, and there he was lost. It was supposed that he had escaped to the old woollen-mill on Black Point.

As in all other cases where a mob pursues a fleeing criminal, the search was wild and disorderly, so that if the Malay had left any trail beyond the ruins it would have been obliterated by trampling feet. Only one policeman was in the crowd, but others, summoned by telephone, were rapidly approaching from all directions. Unintelligent and contradictory rumours bewildered the police for a time, but they formed a long picket line covering an arc which stretched from North Beach to the new gasworks far beyond Black Point.

It was about this time that Captain Freeman cast off and started out to sea.

The summit of Black Point is crowned with the tall eucalyptus-trees which the Flying Devil had seen from Telegraph Hill. A high fence, which encloses the general's house, extends along the bluff of Black Point, near the edge. A sentry paced in front of the gate to the grounds, keeping out all who had not provided themselves with a pass. The sentry had seen the crowd gathering towards the east, and in the distance he noticed the brass buttons of the police glistening in the western sunlight. He wondered what could be afoot.

While he was thus engaged he observed a small, dark, wiry man emerging upon the bluff from the direction of the woollen-mill at its eastern base. The stranger made straight for the gate.

"You can't go in there," said the soldier, "unless you have a pass."

"Da w'at?" asked the stranger.

"A pass," repeated the sentry; and then, seeing that the man was a foreigner and imperfectly acquainted with English, he made signs to explain his remark, still carrying his bayonet-tipped rifle at shoulder-arms. The stranger, whose sharp gleam of eye gave the soldier an odd sensation, nodded and smiled.

"Oh!" said he; "I have."

He thrust his hand into his side-pocket, advancing mean-while, and sending a swift glance about. In the next moment the soldier found himself sinking to the ground with an open jugular.

The Malay slipped within the grounds and disappeared in the shrubbery. It was nearly an hour afterwards that the soldier's body was discovered, and, the crowd of police and citizens arriving, it became known to the garrison that the desperate criminal was immediately at hand. The bugle sounded and the soldiers came tumbling out of barracks. Then began a search of every corner of the post.

It is likely that a feeling of relief came to many a stout heart when it was announced that the man had escaped by water, and was now being swiftly carried down the channel towards the Golden Gate by the ebb tide. He was clearly seen in a small boat, keeping such a course as was possible by means of a rude board in place of oars. His escape had occurred thus: Upon entering the grounds he ran along the eastern fence, behind the shrubbery, to a transverse fence separating the garden from the rear premises. He leaped the fence, and then found himself face to face with a large and formidable mastiff. He killed the brute in a strange and bold manner—by choking. There was evidence of a long and fearful struggle between man and brute. The apparent reason for the man's failure to use the knife was the first necessity of choking the dog into silence and the subsequent need of employing both hands to maintain that advantage.

After disposing of the dog the Flying Devil, wounded though he was, performed a feat worthy of his *sobriquet*; he leaped the rear fence. At the foot of the bluff he found a boat chained to a post sunk into the sand. There was no way to release the boat except by digging up the post. This the Malay did with his hands for tools, and then threw the post into the boat, and pushed off with a board that he found on the beach. Then he swung out into the tide, and it was some minutes afterwards that he was discovered from the fort; and then he was so far away, and there was so much doubt of his identity, that the gunners hesitated for a time to fire upon him. Then two dramatic things occurred.

Meeting the drifting boat was a heavy bank of fog which was rolling in through the Golden Gate. The murderer was heading straight for it, paddling vigorously with the tide. If once the fog should enfold him he would be lost in the Pacific or killed on the rocks almost beyond a peradventure, and yet he was heading for such a fate with all the strength that he possessed. This was what first convinced his pursuers that he was the man whom they sought—none other would have pursued so desperate a course. At the same time a marine glass brought conviction, and the order was given to open fire.

A six-pound brass cannon roared, and splinters flew from the boat; but its occupant, with tantalizing bravado, rose and waved his hand defiantly. The six-pounder then sent out a percussion shell, and just as the frail boat was entering the fog it was blown into a thousand fragments. Some of the observers swore positively that they saw the Malay floundering in the water a moment after the boat was destroyed and before he was engulfed by the fog, but this was deemed incredible. In a short time the order of the post had been restored and the police had taken themselves away.

The other dramatic occurrence must remain largely a matter of surmise, but only because the evidence is so strange.

The great steel gun employed at the fort to announce the setting of the sun thrust its black muzzle into the fog. Had it been fired with shot or shell its missile would have struck the hills on the opposite side of the channel. But the gun was never so loaded; blank cartridges were sufficient for its function. The bore of the piece was of so generous a diameter that a child or small man might have crept into it had such a feat ever been thought of or dared.

There are three circumstances indicating that the fleeing man escaped alive from the wreck of his boat, and that he made a safe landing in the fog on the treacherous rocks at the foot of the bluff crowned by the guns. The first of these was suggested by the gunner who fired the piece that day, two or three hours after the destruction of the fleeing man's boat; and even that would have received no attention under ordinary circumstances, and, in fact, did receive none at all until long afterwards, when Rabaya reported that he had been visited by Freeman, who told him of the two other strange circumstances. The gunner related that when he fired the cannon that day he discovered that it recoiled in a most unaccountable manner, as though it had been loaded with something in addition to a blank cartridge. But he had loaded the gun himself, and was positive that he had placed no shot in the barrel. At that time he was utterly unable to account for the recoil.

The second strange occurrence came to my knowledge through Rabaya. Freeman told him that as he was towing out to sea that afternoon he encountered a heavy fog immediately after turning from the bay into the channel. The tow-boat had to proceed very slowly. When his vessel had arrived at a point opposite Black Point he heard the sunset gun, and immediately afterwards strange particles began to fall upon the *barkentine*, which was exactly in the vertical plane of the gun's range. He had sailed many waters and had seen many kinds of showers, but this was different from all others. Fragments of a sticky substance fell all over the deck, and clung to the sails and spars where they touched them. They seemed to be finely shredded flesh, mixed with particles of shattered bone, with a strip of cloth here and there; and the particles that looked like flesh were of a blackish red and smelled of powder. The visitation gave the skipper and his crew a "creepy" sensation, and awed them somewhat—in short, they were depressed by the strange circumstance to such an extent that Captain Freeman had to employ stern measures to keep down a mutiny, so fearful were the men of going to sea under that terrible omen.

The third circumstance is equally singular. As Freeman was pacing the deck and talking reassuringly to his crew his foot struck a small, grimy, metallic object lying on the deck. He picked it up and discovered that it, too, bore the odour of burned powder. When he had cleaned it he was amazed to discover that it was the amulet which he had bought that very day from Rabaya. He could not believe it was the same until he had made a search and found that it had been stolen from his pocket.

It needs only to be added that the Flying Devil was never seen afterwards.

The Gloomy Shadow

(A story from *The Monster Maker and Other Stories*)

My father enjoyed, among his other scientific attainments, a large family and an intimate acquaintance with the mysteries of phrenology. He was likewise an extremely methodical man, which is tantamount to saying that he was a conscientious man. There can be no conception of duty without a matured and coherent plan for its performance.

My father's principal idea of duty to his children found expression in the choice of proper vocations for them, and he based this choice upon careful phrenological analysis of their several heads. It is no small trick to be a good phrenologist. It involves intimate knowledge of cranial anatomy coupled with vast experience and intelligent observation. My father took his children in hand when they were yet of a very tender age and from a survey of their brain conformations he plotted their lives. Thus, to my eldest sister (next to whom I came in the order of introduction to life), he allotted the life pastime of teacher. For the brother who came next to me, both in sex and succession, he chose the distinction of the whistle and billy. To the next, a sister, he assigned the disagreeable task of a dutiful wife, and so on down to the very last chapter of this long reiteration of his personal heredity, with one exception, and that was I.

He had never diagnosticated my particular brain disease.

Why was it? I had asked myself that question a million times. I had asked my mother also, but she was a timid woman and contented herself with putting her arms around me and kissing me, and telling me that my father knew best, that I, being his first male offspring, probably was reserved for some very high walk in life. These puttings-off only half reassured me, for I knew that my father was a hard, though righteous, master in his own house, and that not a member of the family, from my mother down to the little two-year-old, whom my father already had set apart to disgrace the family as a politician, dared question his motives or suggest his policy.

Time passed, and yet my career had not been chosen. Of all the children I was the only one who had not been made up into a firecracker to explode at the proper time. I was becoming a big boy, with a violent tendency to legs. A white down was beginning to form upon my upper lip, and by this and other indications I knew that soon I should be a *man*.

Why had my father neglected me? The more I thought about it the more mysterious his neglect became. I had arrived at an age when the human mind begins to operate of its own volition; when fancy runs riot and imagination is opening its eyes; when collar and cravat are ceasing to be nuisances, and the ripe sunset falls upon the willing eye; when the plaint of the whippoorwill in the twilight sets the soul a-dreaming, and the twinkling firefly kindles a spark of unrest; when Nature, after yawns interminable, rouses at last into wakefulness and folds us lovingly and caressingly in her warm embrace.

With adolescence comes, in a boy, strength; in a girl, tenderness. I feared my father, but I loved him. Did he despise me? I knew an old lighting-blasted tree that always reminded me of my father. Tall and gaunt and thin it stood, and one gnarled branch remained; and if I looked at it from a certain point of view it seemed to be my father standing there in awful solitude, and with uplifted hand calling down the curse of heaven upon me; but if I got on the other side the expression changed entirely, and the tree looked like my father invoking heaven's blessing upon me. Which point of view was it that marked my destiny? With boyish adolescence comes strength, and with strength independence. Why should I fear my father? He was a man—was not I also nearly a man? He had been kind to me all my life. He had laid violent hands upon me only once, and that was a long time ago, when he caught me trying to brain one of the little slaves with a heavy piece of iron; and then he whipped me till I was ill, and my mother cried a whole day because I was delirious and with a fever from the punishment. But I was a small boy then—what had I to fear now? I would go to my father and ask him to do for me what he had done for his other children.

Yet I hesitated. In the sharpened condition of my mental faculties I reflected upon some strange things I had seen and not understood. I had often detected my father watching me closely and with what I believed was a troubled look. When he would find that I had discovered him he would appear ashamed and more troubled yet. What did it mean? Had the gaunt old tree in the meadow cast its shadow upon me? Was it curses, or was it blessings? There must be light in order that shadows may exist. The gnarled branch pointed to heaven, whence light comes—and also curses.

Thus was I torn and racked. Discontent took up its habitation with me. Could not my father see that the flower was fading and the seed-pod ripening? He had dug the ground for the sowing, or would the seed be scattered among brambles and briars and strangled in the germination? I blamed my father—blamed him aloud to my mother; and I wish now that my tongue had been cut out for doing it.

There came the time when I could wait no longer. I went to my father and demanded, firmly but respectfully, as a duty from a father to a son, that he apply science to the laying out of a plan for my future conduct.

I shall never forget the profound astonishment, pain, anxiety and embarrassment that my father manifested when I made my demand. At first he showed anger, impatience and contempt, but these were succeeded by a pity that transfixed me, and then by a horror that drove me mad, my brain awhirl and ugly itching and turmoil rattling through my nerves. Quick and intelligent, he saw my rebellion, my exasperation, my wounded self-esteem, my turbulent blood surging, my jerking biceps, my grinding teeth, my rambling, unconscious and predatory finger-grasp, and then he was frightened and pale. I saw it plainly. Try as much as he would to conceal it, I saw it, I saw it! My father afraid of me! My father cowering before me, white and trembling! My father, a great, strong man, standing aghast before his puny son! My father, who had faced death with Scott in Mexico and who had fought like a tiger by Stonewall Jackson's side—this old soldier of a hundred battles, with a sabre cut across his cheek, a man who could face the levelled pistol of an opposing duellist without the tremor of a nerve—this strong man, towering in manly strength and dignity and pride, stood a-bashed and fear-stricken before a miserable boy, his own son, whom a word or a blow would have sent cowering and howling away like a whipped dog!

What did it mean?

"Father," I demanded, "tell me what you mean.

"My son," said he, weakly and tremulously, "listen to your father. You are my eldest son. The honour of my name will rest upon your shoulders. Be content. Be manly. Respect your mother. Take life as you find it, and do the best you can for yourself and your mother and me. Be just to all. And mark you, my son: If ever temptation should assail you; if ever reason should feel inclined to succumb to passion; if ever the chains of wholesome restraint should be tugged at by the rash hand of Desire, then remember your mother—-a good and gentle mother, who prays for you oftener than you dream of, who watches over you and loves you and imbues your circumstances with the tender essence of her sweet presence. Be her stay and comfort in her declining years. Let your arm gather the strength of trusty manhood, to be expended in shielding her from rough buffetings; and do not thus early in life permit Discontent to whisper in your ear vague longings that, being resonant, are empty, hollow and delusive. Go, my son."

It was the strangest speech I had heard in all my life. I left him, chilled to the marrow, sick at heart, touched by his appeal, but bewildered by the occasion of its delivery, numb of intellect, sore with puzzlings, and above all aching with a terror that, refusing to take shape and be torn out like an affronting eye, worked gnawingly at my vitals and stabbed me with invisible daggers.

What should I do? My mother was left to me—always a good mother, patient, kind and attentive. Did my father regard me as a monster? If so, did my mother also? She had given no sign of it—she had always been the same mother to me. Had she ever stood at the edge of the meadow and seen the riven tree calling down curses upon me, or had she ever gone to the other side where stood the giant old oak with the muscadine vine climbing to its summit and trying to strangle the very angel that bore it heavenward and seen the other and gender aspect?

I sought my mother without delay. Why did I? What was there in common between her sweet gentleness and my tumultuous unrest? Who can measure the strength of that mysterious and invisible cord which binds mother and son, though different as heaven and hell—this attenuated link, invisible as truth, impalpable as purity, inconceivable as right, impotent as strength, unimaginable as eternity? Can you weigh the odour of a rose? Would you measure off into rods, perches or poles the efficacy of a sigh, the aching of unsatisfied desire, the hope that feeds upon faith, the fondness that abides with possession, the longing of love, the grasping of affection, the tenderness born of fear, and, greater and grander than all, the community of hereditary instincts?

Where was my mother? I had lost no time in seeking her. But where was she? She was not where I expected to find her— where I had been sure of finding her. She ought to have been sitting in her low wicker chair in the bay window of the family room, sewing, and now and then looking up at the clock to see if it was time to order dinner. The little table, with innumerable and not understandable compartments, and mysterious nooks and corners, ought to have been just at her right elbow. Her embroidered footstool should have been in front of her chair, and her daintily slippered feet should have been resting upon it.

The old Maltese cat, gray, wise and wicked, should have been curled up on the rug that the ottoman rested upon, utterly unconcerned over the ferocious aspect of the tiger's head on that end of the rug which was nearest the grate.

When I burst into the room my mother was not there!

What is superstition? What mean those whispered and unconscious deductions from the unusual? Snap a single cog in the machinery of life, and there ensue a bursting and a rattling and a banging that wake us up to the realization of living! Enjoyment is disturbance. There is life only in turmoil, in derangement of ordered things, in perversions of law. Hunt no further for the secret of the anarchist's existence, the scrambling of the politician, the source of ambition's whispering and sighing and wrangling down all the life-lighted avenues of human existence.

Where would be the pleasure of living were it not for the novelty of expected death?

She was not there. Then where was she? The old cat, warped with sin, obsequious as a Pharisee, patient as time, blinked at me—and kept a wary eye on my uncertain boot. The tiger's head yawned sleepily and impudently. The clock lacked thirty seconds of the time for ordering dinner.

My mother suddenly emerged from the parlour, the tall form of my father following. I saw the gaunt tree in the meadow calling down curses upon me. My mother was very pale. Her eyes wandered and her lips were white. She walked as in a dream—as in a nightmare, wherein skeletons and bloody flesh were busy disembowelling the repose of wistful sleep. She saw me. Had I gone to her and struck her in the face (God forgive the thought!) or stabbed her to the heart with a knife (Heaven blast me for the sacrilegious imagining!) she could not have been more sorely stricken than she was at beholding me. She looked at me in horror. Her eyes stared wildly.

Her lips, becoming purple, parted in desperate agony and fear; and, with upthrown hands and a cry that rang all the way down from destiny to death, she fell senseless to the floor.

She was my mother, and I loved her; but that unconscious

glance of horror, that look of repulsion—blacker than night and deeper than hell—whence came it? The shadow of the tree had fallen upon her.

In what was I horrible? Was all repulsion centred in me, and did it blaze from my eyes, dribble from my finger-tips and exude from the pores of my skin? The tree came from the meadow into the room. With outstretched arm it pointed to the door and said:

"You have frightened your mother; go!"

The cat leered at me as I slunk away, and the tiger's head yawned with ineffable relief.

This mystery, this awful shadow, this impenetrable darkness, this enshrouding mist that enveloped me—whence came it? Whither would it lead me? Into what devious paths should I wander in its enfolding obscurity?

Science remained. Through the mist it beckoned dimly, beyond the darkness it faintly shone, above the shadow it loomed grim and immovable. Faith is the perverted longing for knowledge.

Learning is the cradle of despair. I would be rocked to sleep.

I knew a phrenologist who, like my father, was an able man. He did not know me—so much the better. I sought that man. It is a strange tale, my friends.

He was a professional phrenologist, and kept a shop where he examined heads for a moderate charge. He glanced at me only casually when I entered the room, because I was only a boy. (I have since learned that his principal business was the determination of occupations for those who already had chosen the course of their lives.) He was quite indifferent to me, but I am certain he was polite when he asked me to be seated.

I told him what I wanted. He laid his hands carelessly upon my head, but he had hardly done more than that when he sprang back and his face was livid with terror.

Here we were—we two—I a youth, he a man. It was not a large room. I was a strong lad. I walked to the door, locked it and put the key into my pocket.

There were only two of us—he and I. The blinding mist had come with me into the room, the shadow also was there and the darkness. I believe that through it all I saw the tall, lightning-blasted tree in the meadow. Only two of us and a mystery between us, the truth in his consciousness. I had strong arms. My fingers had a firm grasp and, no doubt, they could span the neck of an ordinary man. In my time I had squeezed the juice out of grapes and from the juice I had made wine and upon drinking the wine I had seen marvellous and enchanting visions that were sweeter than my hope of heaven.

I was calm about it at first, but I was bound to know what he knew—determined he should tell me what horrible thing my cranium revealed. I once had strangled a vicious dog—choked him till his tongue hung out and his eyes were ready to burst from their sockets, and then threw his carcass aside. I repeat that I was calm at first; but when he flatly refused to tell me, there came a strange kind of creeping into my arms—an intense accumulation of nervous force that clamoured for exercise.

"Tell me!" I demanded, softly it is true, but the tone made him cower.

"I cannot," he cried.

"Tell me!" That creeping feeling in my arms was getting beyond control.

"Impossible!" he implored.

"It is too horrible!"

"Tell me!"

My hands had a peculiar way of opening and closing, and they felt desperate, hungry, empty.

"What do you wish to know?" asked the man, trying to put me off.

"I wish to know," I answered, still calmly, "what vocation I am suited for."

The creeping feeling in my arms was steadily assuming the more decided form of outreaching, and my fingers itched amazingly. He saw it.

"There is only one thing in life that you are fitted to be," he finally said, "and it pains me infinitely to add that it is the only thing which Nature in her inscrutable wisdom has decided that you cannot avoid being."

"And what is that?"

"A murderer!"

★★★★★★

My friends, what is destiny? For one, honour; for another, a rope. I do not complain. I love and respect Nature too much to whimper at her decrees. A gaunt lightning-stripped tree in a meadow, the plaint of a whippoorwill in the twilight, a Maltese cat sodden with crime, a sweet face blanched with horror—these are the microscopes with which gentle Nature provides us. (My dear sir, you are pulling that strap too hard—it hurts.) I am not talking for mercy or pity. Behold in me the infinite faith of one who loves Nature and bows to her law. (Keep the cap a moment longer, and then you may put it on me.) She marked out my life; I followed her inclination.

Farewell; may you all be happy as I am now in having fulfilled the destiny under which I was born! (Will that knot slip easily? There—but don't draw it too tight; my head won't slip through!)

The Haunted Automaton

(A story from *The Monster Maker and other Stories*)

Old man Erkins had three principal faults: he was rich, stingy, and a hard drinker. For the first of these he was to blame; for the second, pitied; for the third—but wait and read further before you express an opinion. At all events, by reason of these things and of others that I shall now write concerning him, I say and you will say that he should have been killed; which I am restrained from doing in this very line by the necessities of this story and not at all by fear either of the law or of punishment in the world to come.

Upon recovering from a hard spree, toward the end of which he would begin to see strange things, Erkins would not touch a drop for several days; then, recovering his nerve, he would laugh at his past timidity and—take a drink; the next day one, the next three, the next four, and so on, until snakes and other queer things would creep out of dark places.

There was an old servant, named Sarah, that kept his large prison (for such was his house) in order; and the one green spot in her shaky old life was a pretty girl, old Erkins' niece, ward and prisoner combined—Alice by name, and the prettiest girl in all the country thereabout, though a very unhappy one, to be sure. Alice had inherited Sarah, who was Alice's mother's trusted servant, and who vowed that she never, never would leave the poor young orphan, though the old house should swarm with snakes and things.

Now, the old miser loved his niece in a certain way. There are persons who love others so deeply that they murder them. There are various ways of committing murder, and one of the cruellest is to shut up a pretty girl in a big house and never let a young fellow even look at her.

Merely because she accidentally—entirely accidentally—fell in love with a poor but good-looking young machinist whom she met at church, her old guardian, in a spirit of mean tyranny, forbade her ever going out again, and in a most insulting and over-bearing manner told this young man, Howard Rankin, that the girl should never see him again, and that any mendicant fortune-hunter who should ever present himself at the house or seek to capture her for her quarter of a million would be riddled with buckshot.

Old Erkins had a mania for curious mechanisms. He had clocks that did all manner of wonderful things, and hundreds of other ingenious contrivances of various kinds. Whenever he read of some curious invention he would have it. He never tired of amusing himself with these things. There was one thing that Erkins needed to complete his happiness as well as his collection, and that was an automaton—a working counterfeit man. He had read everything that had ever been written on the subject of such automata. He had visited museums and waxworks shows, and had seen gladiators and *Zouaves* dying their several deaths again and again; but they were all too suggestive, for there were times when old Erkins' nerves were weak. Once he did buy a dying gladiator at enormous expense, but on the occasion of his next bad spell that gladiator's departing life seemed to take the form of numberless snakes and monkeys; and, frantic with fright, its owner chopped it to pieces with a hatchet.

Howard Rankin had a certain inventive genius. Knowing the old man's weakness, he conceived the idea of constructing an automaton, with which he hoped, he told a friend, to reinstate himself in the old man's good graces. However, this was a secret. All that he gave out was that he was going to construct an automaton—he knew what would result. He really did think that he loved Alice very, very deeply. Why shouldn't he? He promptly began to put his idea into execution, and selected the back room of his work-shop.

Very soon the project caused such talk that old Erkins heard of it. As the work progressed and favoured friends were permitted to see the wonderful automaton as it grew under its author's hands, old Erkins, hearing the stories, became more and more interested. When a few months had passed he heard that the automaton was nearly finished.

Erkins could restrain himself no longer—he must see that automaton and must secure it. But how should he proceed? He had grossly insulted the inventor. This was a serious difficulty. He pondered over it a few days, and then boldly sent a polite note, asking permission to see the automaton. A formal note, granting the request, came in reply. The old man went at once.

The young man received him with polite condescension. Erkins' keen old eyes glittered eagerly; and Howard, noticing it, was secretly elated accordingly. Outwardly he was stiff and cold.

"And so you are at work on an automaton?" Erkins asked, as he was ushered into the back room.

"Yes," deliberately responded the young mechanic, as he quietly proceeded with his work.

"Cheerful one?"

"What?"

"Cheerful?"

"What do you mean?"

"It doesn't die, or anything of that sort, does it?"

"Oh, no!"

"'Cause I had a dying gladiator once, and it died so hard that sna—that—that it was unpleasant."

He stepped closer to the half finished automaton. It sat in an easy-chair. "So I killed it," he said.

"Killed what?"

"Gladiator."

He was devoured with curiosity concerning Howard's automaton, and yet felt such timidity that he hesitated about asking questions. Howard, volunteering no information, continued his work. Presently Erkins mustered up courage.

"I see you haven't put on its head yet," he essayed.

"No."

"Haven't got it ready?"

"No."

There was a pause.

"What will it do?"

"A good many things."

The old man went round it and examined it narrowly. It was the figure of a fop, dressed in the extreme of fashion, sitting in an indolent posture.

"Everything finished except the head, eh?"

"Yes," answered Howard; who seeing that he had carried his indifference far enough, left off his work, and said: "The head is to be the main part, because the more important work is to be done by it, and great care is required in making its wax face, its eyes, and so forth. Here is the block of it, with the machinery inside. That blonde wig will be its hair. As the automaton now is, however, it can give all the limb motions, though they are comparatively insignificant." Howard inserted a key in a hole in the back of the chair and wound up the automaton. The slight clicking of machinery was audible. Old Erkins trembled with excitement as he saw the automaton begin to move. It brought its right hand to the place where its mouth would be, then lowered it; brought up its left hand, and then crossed its legs.

"The right hand," explained Howard, "will carry a cigar, for the automaton will smoke. See—it will take a few puffs and then withdraw the cigar. The other hand is now taking up an eyeglass. I must now stop the machinery, as other attachments, not yet supplied, will have to be added, and still other machinery, the most intricate of all, is contained within the head."

"What will you do with the automaton?" asked Erkins, feeling his way.

"Don't know—probably keep it for my own amusement."

"Wouldn't you sell it?"

"Sell it! why, who is rich enough to buy it!"

Erkins' heart sank.

"What shall you ask for it?" he inquired in sheer desperation.

"A thousand dollars."

Erkins' heart leaped with joy.

"I'll take it," he eagerly said. He had expected to hear five-thousand.

"It's a go," quietly responded Howard.

Then Erkins began to reflect that possibly he had been too hasty.

"I may be giving you too much," he said.

"Don't take it if you don't want it," coolly answered the young man.

"Will you give me a written guaranty of what it will do?" he asked.

Howard pondered a moment. "I will do not only that," he said, "but more; for I have great confidence in the automaton. Let me see. This is the 12th of November. I will be married on Wednesday, the 24th of next month, the day before Christmas. I shall want eight hundred dollars for my wedding and to start in life. I—"

"Married!" exclaimed old Erkins in astonishment.

"Yes. I will take eight hundred dollars down. If the automaton please you, you are to pay the balance; if in any particular it fall below your expectations, you may keep the two hundred. I will give you a written guaranty that the automaton shall cross and uncross its legs, smoke cigars, adjust its eye-glass, incline its head, open and close its eyes, wink and talk—speak two or three words."

"Good!" cried the old man. "It's a bargain." Erkins was very happy when he left. He had had two triumphs—secured the automaton and learned that Alice and her fortune were no longer in danger.

According to agreement the automaton was delivered on Saturday, December 20th, by a friend of Howard's, the inventor sending word that under the circumstances he had no desire to enter Mr. Erkins' house. The automaton was encased in a large box provided with handles, and four men were brought to carry it into the house. Old Erkins danced about in great excitement and high glee. It was a time of such rejoicing with him that he called Alice and Old Sarah to share his happiness and see the wonderful automaton. Much of his exhilaration was due to drink, for the old man was rapidly reaching the limit, and in two or three days his old wriggling friends would surely be upon him.

"How's Rankin getting along with his wedding?" asked Erkins of the friend.

The latter gave some offhand reply, and as he did so he saw Alice stagger backward to the wall and her face blanch.."By the way, Alice," said wicked old Erkins, delighting in the cruel stab he was giving, "Howard Rankin is to be married next Wednesday."

The poor girl could say nothing, for her heart was broken; but old Erkins did not notice her strange conduct nor see the agony of shame, humiliation and despair she suffered. Sarah saw it all, and it wrung her faithful old heart. She slipped her arm around the young girl's waist and would have led her away; but Erkins commanded them to remain, and Erkins' word was law.

The men set down the big box in the hall.

"Mr. Erkins," said the friend, "here are certain instructions that Howard sent for the management of the automaton. He insists that they be carried out to the letter, or he will not be responsible for failure."

The old man hastily read the instructions. Among them there was this one:

"The automaton must be kept in a room with a temperature not below 65 degrees Fahrenheit nor above 75 degrees, otherwise the springs, catgut strings, the wax of the face and of the head, and the glue of the various parts will be ruined."

Here was another:

"There must be little light in the room, or the delicate colours in the face and hands will fade; and the automaton must not be placed with its face to the light"

Another instruction made careful provision for ventilation, thus:

"Exterior air, which at this time of year is either damp or frosty, must be excluded, and hence the window should never be opened; but as fresh air is necessary, the door must always be left slightly ajar—say six inches—and it must not open into any other room, but into a hall."

Winding at night or more than once a day was forbidden. There were also minute instructions for preparing and lighting the cigars that the automaton should smoke.

Erkins reflected. There was only one room in the house which permitted of compliance with these instructions, and that was upstairs. He slept downstairs, and he had intended to place it in a room adjoining his bedroom; but as he used that one for an office and kept a hot fire in it, the automaton would be ruined there. The only objection he had to its going upstairs was upon account of his fear that Sarah or Alice, who occupied rooms near the one that must receive the automaton, would surreptitiously wind up the treasure at unseasonable times and thus ruin it. But had he been shrewd enough to guess at the loathing they had for a thing that came from Howard's hands, he would have felt no uneasiness.

"Sarah," he sternly said, "I must put the automaton in the southwest room upstairs; but if either you or Alice dare to touch it or enter the room where it is, I'll murder you. Do you understand that? I'll murder you both."

The four men carried the big box to the southwest room upstairs and set it just where it should be, according to the instructions. Old Erkins, gleeful and brutal, forced Sarah and Alice to accompany it, and compelled them to stand and see it uncovered. This was done by removing the top, ends, and sides of the box and lifting a cloth that covered the figure. The wonderful automaton sat revealed.

Alice had secretly hoped that Howard had made the automaton to resemble himself, though ever so slightly; but when she saw the figure, with flaxen hair and moustache, so different from his, which were black; and the broad black eyebrows; and the painted cheeks, so different from his own pale face; and the foppish costume; and the effeminately curled hair; and the general air of impudence that pervaded the whole figure, her last hope departed. There was not a shadow of Howard's quiet manliness in anything about this mimic man.

Old Erkins regarded it otherwise. He saw only a wonderful mechanism, finished and decked out with fine art; and that was all he cared for. The artificial fop reclined indolently in an easy-. chair. Its head hung upon its breast and its eyes were closed, its appearance being that of a slumbering man.

The four carriers were dismissed, and the friend produced a key, inserted it in a hole in the back of the chair, and wound up the automaton. It raised its head, opened its eyes sleepily, and with the greatest dignity it slowly turned its head as though regarding each member of the company, and then it smiled and very graciously bowed. Howard's friend produced a cigar and carefully prepared it, as a lesson to Erkins, the automaton meanwhile continuing to bow and smile. Following the instructions, the friend laid the cigar on a little stand convenient to the automaton's right hand, and the automaton with absolutely accurate movement brought the cigar to its mouth and with great deliberation took several puffs. Then it removed the cigar, and with its left hand adjusted an eyeglass, with which it gravely regarded the company; then puffed at the cigar again, and then crossed its legs.

"I must go now," said the friend. "The automaton will keep this up thirty minutes longer, and then it will have run down; but it must not be wound again till tomorrow. Remember the instructions;" and he left.

Alice then begged to be allowed to go, as she was dying with a headache, she said, and had seen enough of the automaton; and so old Erkins, deeply disgusted, dismissed them.

He remained alone with the automaton, sitting directly in front of it and eagerly drinking with his eyes every one of the slow, dignified, accurate motions that it made. The only sound audible was a faint ticking, a very soft creaking, of the intricate machinery. This comparative silence, and the subtle wisdom that the automaton seemed to have and its deliberate manner, and its impudence, began to work upon Erkins' diseased imagination. As the thing continued to smoke, and adjust its eyeglass, and cross its legs, and open and close its eyes and bow so gravely, it took on, in Erkins' opinion, a kind of uncanny, supernatural air that disturbed its owner. Erkins' mind was not exactly right, and he knew it; but even making due allowance for it he was positive the thing was acting strangely. It seemed to be trying to exasperate him.

This feeling was steadily growing upon Erkins; so that when there came a sharp little click in the machinery and the automaton dropped the cigar to the floor and boldly winked at Erkins, the old man began to experience downright fright. Yet he reflected that the guaranty called for winks. Still, this wink was too knowing. It was an insidious, wise, searching wink, that seemed to show cognizance of every sin that Erkins had ever committed. It was a leering, impudent wink; such a wink as innocence would be incapable of; a dangerous, mocking wink. It winked not only once, but twice, thrice, four times; taking a long time between winks, and accompanying each with a sinister leer. It did nothing but wink. Everything about it was perfectly still with the exception of that one eye-lid, and the stare that it kept fastened upon Erkins was a cold and deadly stare; a stare that saw through and through him, he thought, and that acted upon him with such strange effect that it held him bound, cold with terror, to his seat.

It was also in the guaranty that the automaton should speak. As yet it had not spoken. When it had winked several times there came another sharp little click, which startled Erkins. The old man had forgotten all about the speaking, but that little click warned him that something else was coming. What would it be? Something awful, he instinctively felt.

The automaton sat still for five long seconds, and then very slowly, very cautiously, very mysteriously, it leaned forward and said in a hollow, ghostly voice, that seemed to come up from the bowels of the earth:

"I'm haunted!".Erkins shivered, and he thought his heart had ceased beating. The automaton slowly resumed its former posture and fixed its dead stare upon its owner. It sat thus for what seemed to Erkins an age, and then again as before it leaned forward and in sepulchral tones it said:

"I'm haunted!"

Erkins could hear it no longer. White and trembling with fright, he backed out of the room, carefully left the door as the specifications required, and went out into the garden and shook himself like a dog.

"That thing," he muttered, "is worse than a sna—than the dying gladiator. But it's a beautiful piece of work," he presently added, when he had somewhat recovered his nerve; "and of course I shall get used to it. Of course."

Nevertheless, he needed something to help him in this and he sought it in his liquor. He drank frightfully all that day, and toward evening his old unwelcome visitors began to show themselves. And they were unusually bold. He went early to bed, and actually one hideous old monkey had the effrontery to pretend he was a dying gladiator. A young monkey assumed all the airs of a fop, and smoked a cigar, adjusted an eye-glass, crossed its legs, smiled and bowed, and then winked at the miserable old man in the most impudent and insulting manner; and, not satisfied with that, it leaned forward mysteriously from its perch on the footboard of the bed, and in a rasping, sepulchral whisper, said:

"I'm haunted!"

Thus passed this hideous night—one of snakes, monkeys, dying gladiators, fops who declared they were haunted, and horrible nightmares.

But Sunday morning came at last, and old Erkins ushered in the new day with deep draughts of brandy. He was trying to steady himself for a second interview with the automaton.

At last he entered the automaton's room. There sat the ingeniously constructed thing, sound asleep in its chair. Erkins approached it gingerly, but it sat so quiet and harmless, and looked so weak and effeminate, and so unlike the ghostly thing that leered and winked at him the day before, declaring it was haunted, that his courage revived and he laughed at his fright. The old fellow was badly shattered from drinking, and his old knees tottered and his bony hands trembled as he went to the mantel and returned with the key to wind the automaton. He was very nervous and jerky about the winding; but he managed to get through with it in a fashion, and then he sat down in front of the automaton and awaited developments.

The same old motions were exactly repeated, although the automaton had to puff an imaginary cigar, as Erkins was too badly shaken up to remember it. But the oversight soon began to trouble him. In his befogged condition of mind he imagined that the automaton laid it up against him. He was positive that under the smile lurked a wicked look, and he was thoroughly convinced of this when the first click came and the winking and leering commenced. There was then exhibited by that soft-appearing automaton a diabolical deviltry and a deeply mysterious cunning that no mechanical thing—so Erkins thought—could show; and when it came to the second click, and began slowly to lean forward, the horrible thought stole into the old man's mind that the devil himself sat before him.

"I'm haunted!"

Erkins' blood ran cold. He suffered an agony of fright. Every nerve quivered, and he gasped for breath. A deathly perspiration exuded from his face and trickled down his cheeks. With hands upraised and fingers outspread, with gaping mouth and wide-staring eyes, he gazed with a terrible, tragic fascination at the awful thing before him.

"I'm haunted!". The blind yet ever-watchful instinct of self-preservation dragged the old man tottering from his seat and thrust him out. Stumbling, staggering, mumbling, he found his way to his own room, and fell headlong upon the floor, and passed into grateful unconsciousness.

He lay thus an hour or more, and recovering, crawled to his bed. There he remained all day, discussing in his mind the ways and means for executing a design that he had conceived.

"He didn't exactly say it would be a cheerful one," he mused. "He said merely that it wouldn't die. But it does worse than that. The gladiator wasn't haunted. It was simply dying—dying all the time. Well, I put it out of its misery. I'll have to do another thing like that. I'm going to kill that haunted automaton if I die in the attempt."

Such was his design. But he was not yet able to put it into execution. He tried his strength; he could hardly stand. The day wore away, and still he was too weak. He drank more brandy. Night finally came, and then he dreaded the undertaking in the dark.

Finally twelve o'clock struck; then one o'clock. The frightful visitors had quit creeping about the halls, and all had congregated in his room. He drank more. He became stronger, and there came to him a boldness born of desperation. Not another minute would he delay the annihilation of the haunted automaton. He got out of bed and lighted a candle. He knew where to find the hatchet with which he had put a stop to the sufferings of the dying gladiator, and he desired to use that particular hatchet in the deadly work that lay before him. It was in the rear part of the house. He found it. He went cautiously upstairs and approached the room of the haunted automaton. As he drew near to it he became more and more violently agitated—so much so, in fact, that when he pushed the door to enter the room the candle fell from his trembling hand and was instantly extinguished. He nerved himself with all his might, for he was determined to accomplish the work.

As he approached stealthily, step by step, he imagined he felt that maddening wink, and momentarily he expected to hear that unearthly voice declare, "I'm haunted." So, he decided to strike from the rear. He crept around and got behind the chair. He took one step forward, and that brought him just close enough. He raised the heavy hatchet in both hands, and with all the strength of a madman brought down its keen edge upon the head of his unconscious victim.

The automaton must have turned to air, for the blow fell upon empty space; and the strength that he had thrown into it precipitated him headlong into the automatons chair. But the haunted automaton was gone!

The old man, mad with terror and raving in delirium tremens, ran from the room, shrieking for help. He burst into Sarah's room. She was gone. He tore into Alice's room. She too was gone.

Yelling, screaming, raving, pursued by a thousand demons, desperately mad, he flew out of the house and down the street, shrieking "I'm haunted! I'm haunted! Help! Help!"

A policeman caught him and took him to prison. On Wednesday he was calm and rational, though somewhat ill and weak. A lawyer visited him at the hospital, whither he had been taken from jail, and handed him the following note, which the old man read several times before he could fully grasp its meaning:

My Dear Sir: I told you a few weeks ago that I should be married today, Wednesday, the 24th December. I have kept my word, as I was married an hour ago. If you want an automaton you may have that dummy that you saw in the back room of my workshop; for in reality that was the one you bought, and it has never left my shop. The money you paid me on account was just what I wanted to marry on. It is a little singular that when I told you I should marry today I had not even asked the girl! She never dreamed that such was my intention until last Saturday night, when I presented myself to her old servant, whose scream when she discovered me I greatly feared would betray my presence to a certain person who did not want me there. But the girl I wanted was sensible, and we made all necessary preparations and left the house Sunday. I feared that a certain person would hear our foot-falls, though we went on tiptoes and as softly as possible.

That certain person was the girl's uncle. He had done me

a bad turn, and I am now even with him; for not only did I frighten him out of his wits but I stole his niece from under his very nose and made him pay all the expenses of the wedding.

She is an excellent girl and is rich besides. By the way, her name is Alice and she is your niece; and as I am now her legal guardian, I desire that you should make to Mr——, the bearer of this, my attorney, a full accounting of all her property.

And by the way, further, we are to have a little dinner at our hotel this evening, at which our friends are expected. Can't you come? Do so, and let's be friends; for Christmas is a time when we should all make up. Hope you are better.

Howard Rankin, *alias* The Haunted Automaton.

The old man thought it all over—and went; and I am happy to add that he never drank another drop.

The Haunted Burglar

(A story from The Monster Maker and Other Stories)

Anthony Ross doubtless had the oddest and most complex temperament that ever assured the success of burglary as a business. This fact is mentioned in order that those who choose may employ it as an explanation of the extraordinary ideas that entered his head and gave a strangely tragic character to his career.

Though ignorant, the man had an uncommonly fine mind in certain aspect. Thus it happened that, while lacking moral perception, he cherished an artistic pride in the smooth, elegant, and finished conduct of his work. Hence a blunder on his part invariably filled him with grief and humiliation; and it was the steadily increasing recurrence of these errors that finally impelled him to make a deliberate analysis of his case.

Among the stupid acts with which he charged himself was the murder of the banker Uriah Mattson, a feeble old man whom a simple choking or a sufficient tap on the skull would have rendered helpless. Instead of that, he had choked his victim to death in the most brutal and unnecessary manner, and in doing so had used the fingers of his left hand in a singularly sprawled and awkward fashion. The whole act was utterly unlike him; it appalled and horrified him,—not for the sin of taking human life, but because it was unnecessary, dangerous, subversive of the principles of skilled burglary, and monstrously inartistic.

A similar mishap had occurred in the case of Miss Jellison, a wealthy spinster, merely because she was in the act of waking, which meant an ensuing scream. In this case, as in the other, he was unspeakably shocked to discover that the fatal choking had been done by the left hand, with sprawled and awkward fingers, and with a savage ferocity entirely uncalled for by his peril.

In setting himself to analyze these incongruous and revolting things he dragged forth from his memory numerous other acts, unlike those two in detail, but similar to them in spirit. Thus, in a fit of passionate anger at the whimpering of an infant, he had flung it brutally against the wall.

Another time he was nearly discovered through the needless torturing of a cat, whose cries set pursuers at his heels. These and other insane, inartistic, and ferocious acts he arrayed for serious analysis.

Finally the realization burst upon him that all his aberrations of conduct had proceeded from his left hand and arm. Search his recollection ever so diligently, he could not recall a single instance wherein his right hand had failed to proceed on perfectly fine, sure, and artistic lines.

When he made this discovery he realized that he had brought himself face to face with a terrifying mystery; and its horrors were increased when he reflected that while his left hand had committed acts of stupid atrocity in the pursuit of his burglarious enterprises, on many occasions when he was not so engaged it had acted with a less harmful but none the less coarse, irrational, and inartistic purpose.

It was not difficult for such a man to arrive at strange conclusions. The explanation that promptly suggested itself, and that his coolest and shrewdest wisdom could not shake, was that his left arm was under the dominion of a perverse and malicious spirit, that it was an entity apart from his own spirit, and that it had fastened itself upon that part of his body to produce his ruin.

It were useless, however inviting, to speculate upon the order of mind capable of arriving at such a conclusion; it is more to the point to narrate the terrible happenings to which it gave rise.

About a month after the burglar's mental struggle a strange-looking man applied for a situation at a saw-mill a hundred miles away. His appearance was exceedingly distressing. Either a grievous bodily illness or fearful mental anguish had made his face wan and haggard and filled his eyes with the light of a hard desperation that gave promise of dire results. There were no marks of a vagabond on his clothing or in his manner. He did not seem to be suffering for physical necessities. He held his head aloft and walked like a man, and an understanding glance would have seen that his look of determination meant something profounder and more far-reaching than the ordinary business concerns of life.

He gave the name of Hope. His manner was so engaging, yet withal so firm and abstracted, that he secured a position without difficulty; and so faithfully did he work, and so quick was his intelligence, that in good time his request to be given the management of a saw was granted. It might have been noticed that his face thereupon wore a deeper and more haggard look, but that its rigors were softened by a light of happy expectancy. As he cultivated no friendships among the men, he had no confidants; he went his dark way alone to the end.

He seemed to take more than the pleasure of an efficient workman in observing the products of his skill. He would stealthily hug the big brown logs as they approached the saw, and his eyes would blaze when the great tool went singing and roaring at its work. The foreman, mistaking this eagerness for carelessness, quietly cautioned him to beware; but when the next log was mounted for the saw the stranger appeared to slip and fall. He clasped the moving log in his arms, and the next moment the insatiable teeth had severed his left arm near the shoulder, and the stranger sank with a groan into the soft sawdust that filled the pit.

There was the usual commotion attending such accidents, for the faces of the workmen turn white when they see one of their number thus maimed for life. But Hope received good surgical care, and in due time was able to be abroad. Then the men observed that a remarkable change had come over him. His moroseness had disappeared, and in its stead was a hearty cheer of manner that amazed them. Was the losing of a precious arm a thing to make a wretched man happy? Hope was given light work in the office, and might have remained to the end of his days a competent and prosperous man; but one day he left, and was never seen thereabout again.

Then Anthony Ross, the burglar, reappeared upon the scenes of his former exploits. The police were dismayed to note the arrival of a man whom all their skill had been unable to convict of terrible crimes which they were certain he had committed, and they questioned him about the loss of his arm; but he laughed them away with the fine old sangfroid with which they were familiar, and soon his handiwork appeared in reports of daring burglaries.

A watch of extraordinary care and minuteness was set upon him, but that availed nothing until a singular thing occurred to baffle the officers beyond measure: Ross had suddenly become wildly reckless and walked red-handed into the mouth of the law. By evidence that seemed indisputable a burglary and atrocious murder were traced to him. Stranger than all else, he made no effort to escape, though leaving a hanging trail behind him. When the officers overhauled him, they found him in a state of utter dejection, wholly different from the light-hearted bearing that had characterized him ever since he had returned without his left arm. Neither admitting nor denying his guilt, he bore himself with the hopelessness of a man already condemned to the gallows.

Even when he was brought before a jury and placed on trial, he made no fight for his life.

Although possessed of abundant means, he refused to employ an attorney, and treated with scant courtesy the one assigned him by the judge. He betrayed irritation at the slow dragging of the case as the prosecution piled up its evidence against him. His whole manner indicated that he wished the trial to end as soon as possible and hoped for a verdict of guilty.

This incomprehensible behaviour placed the voting and ambitious attorney on his mettle. He realized that some inexplicable mystery lay behind the matter, and this sharpened his zeal to find it. He plied his client with all manner of questions, and tried in all way to secure his confidence:

Ross remained sullen, morose, and wholly given over to despairing resignation. The young lawyer had made a wonderful discovery, which he at first felt confident would clear the prisoner, but any mention of it to Ross would only throw him into a violent passion and cause him to tremble as with a palsy. His conduct on such occasions was terrible beyond measure. He seemed utterly beside himself, and thus his attorney had become convinced of the man's insanity. The trouble in proving it was that he dared not mention his discovery to others, and that Ross exhibited no signs of mania unless that one subject was broached.

The prosecution made out a case that looked impregnable, and this fact seemed to fill the prisoner with peace. The young lawyer for the defence had summoned a number of witnesses, but in the end he used only one. His opening statement to the jury was merely that it was a physical impossibility for the prisoner to have committed the murder,—which was done by choking. Ross made a frantic attempt to stop him from putting forth that defence, and from the dock wildly denounced it as a lie.

The young lawyer nevertheless proceeded with what he deemed his duty to his unwilling client. He called a photographer and had him produce a large picture of the murdered man's face and neck. He proved that the portrait was that of the person whom Ross was charged with having killed. As he approached the climax of the scene, Ross became entirety ungovernable in his frantic efforts to stop the introduction of the evidence, and so it became necessary to bind and gag him and strap him to the chair.

When quiet was restored, the lawyer handed the photograph to the jury and quietly remarked:

"You may see for yourselves that the choking was done with

the left hand, and you have observed that my client has no such member."

He was unmistakably right. The imprint of the thumb and fingers, forced into the flesh in a singularly ferocious, sprawling, and awkward manner, was shown in the photograph with absolute clearness. The prosecution, taken wholly by surprise, blustered and made attempts to assail the evidence, but without success. The jury returned a verdict of not guilty.

Meanwhile the prisoner had fainted, and his gag and bonds had been removed; but he recovered at the moment when the verdict was announced. He staggered to his feet, and his eyes rolled; then with a thick tongue he exclaimed:

"It was the left arm that did it! This one"—holding his right arm as high as he could reach—"never made a mistake. It was always the left one. A spirit of mischief and murder was in it. I cut it off in a saw-mill, but the spirit stayed where the arm used to be, and it choked this man to death. I didn't want you to acquit me. I wanted you to hang me. I can't go through life having this thing haunting me and spoiling my business and making a murderer of me. It tries to choke me while I sleep. There it is! Can't you see it?" And he looked with wide-staring eyes at his left side.

"Mr. Sheriff," gravely said the judge, "take this man before the Commissioners of Lunacy tomorrow."

The Woman of the Inner Room

(A story from The Monster Maker and Other Stories)

Dr. Osborne, hastily summoned to the receiving hospital, found there a handsome, well-dressed young man with an ugly hole in his skull about an inch and a half above the left ear. The injured man evidently was not suffering, but the desperate nature of his hurt was seen in the deep pallor of his face. His expression was placid, unintelligent, and absolutely silly. Yet he was freely alive—his breathing was good, his heart observed its functions, his temperature was normal, and his skin was warm and moist. Dr. Osborne cleared the wound with a sponge.

"How was the lad hurt?" he asked of the officers who were standing about.

No one could tell. A few minutes ago someone had seen him staggering along the street, clinging to the house-walls to keep from falling, a thin stream of blood trickling down his face, and had pointed him out to a policeman.

Dr. Osborne looked closely at the wound. Then he tried to insert a finger in the opening, but failed. He looked around upon the men, and asked them to show him their hands.

"No," he said, after examining them; "your fingers are all too blunt Farley, go and call my daughter—she is sitting in my buggy at the door."

Before she came, Dr. Osborne asked:

"Do you know who he is?"

None could inform him. Not a scrap of paper by which he might be identified could be found upon him.

The surgeon's daughter entered. She was an attractive girl—rather tall and slight, had brown eyes and hair, and carried herself with a fine unconscious grace. She glanced at the man lying on the operating-table, suddenly checked her advance, and became pale. Her father, with a reassuring manner, took her by the arm, and led her forward.

"Don't be alarmed, Agnes," he said; "I have tested your nerve before, and have never seen it fail. Let me see your hand." He took it in his and examined it closely. "That is just what I need," he resumed; "long, slender fingers—you have a beautiful hand, Agnes."

This embarrassed her, but she became stronger.

"Now, my child, I must learn the nature of the wound in this young man's head. Come a little closer, my dear; he does not know what is going on. Have you ever seen him before?"

"No," she replied, approaching nearer and regarding his face steadily; "but he appears to be a man of means and refinement."

"Yes; that is clear. But come closer, Agnes. Why, you are all right! You see, it is a small hole, and that probably accounts for the fact that he is still alive; but it has penetrated the skull, and that makes the case a very serious one. It is necessary that I know what made the wound, in order to determine what to do; and the quickest way in the world is to let the wound tell its own story. My fingers are so thick that I can do nothing. Yours are exactly suited."

"My fingers? What do you want me to do, father?"

"I want you to insert a finger in the wound and tell me what you find, after a careful examination of the edges of the bone."

The girl hesitated. "But—why?" she asked.

"So that I may know what instrument was employed, if the hole is round and has rather clean edges, it was made by a bullet—in which event, there is no reasonable hope of recovery, If, however, it is three-cornered, or otherwise angular, or in any great degree ragged, then something else made it—a pick-axe or some other instrument; and in that case there is a bare chance of saving his life. Besides, the knowledge will be very useful to the officers in digging up what appears to be a mysterious crime. You can ascertain that, can't you?"

"I will try."

Under her father's direction, but in a gingerly manner, she stood behind the young man's head, her face close above his, and put the fine, long forefinger of her left hand into the wound. As she did so, her eyes met the empty stare of his. Very slowly and carefully, watching his face all the time, she felt the edges of the bone and then withdrew her finger.

"It is smooth and round," she said.

"Ah!" exclaimed her father; "then there is no hope, poor fellow! But let us try a little further Agnes, my dear, you did that bravely, as I knew you would: but now I want you to put your finger in again, and push it very slowly and carefully as far as you can. The bullet may not have gone far."

The girl, again looking down upon the calm, peaceful face, with its blank stare and senseless smile, explored the wound with her finger. Her touch was sure and gentle, but as her finger came in contact with the brain, and she felt its warmth and the regular and smooth pressure of the pulsations, her nerves went upon a strain. Still she looked down into the handsome young face, but she was growing pale. All of a sudden, for some wholly unaccountable reason, the young man's blank expression and silly smile passed away, and a certain intelligence sat upon his face.

The surgeon saw this, and it appeared to him to be a matter of uncommon importance. At the same moment, a peculiar look came into his daughter's face. She had begun to relax in the course of fainting, but instantly she swung back upon a nervous balance which was so prominent as to suggest a strong stimulation. The young man looked up into her eyes with a vague interest; she looked down into his with fear and horror. Then she suddenly withdrew her finger and stepped back beyond the range of his vision. The look of vacuity again took a hold upon him.

The girl, without addressing anyone particularly, said, nervously and hurriedly; "You had better send to the bank and tell his father."

"What bank?" asked her father, in surprise.

"The Citizens' Bank."

"Who is his father?"

"Mr. Blanchard, the president of the bank. This is his son, Charles."

Her father regarded her with amazement, but he refrained from asking her questions. He merely remarked; "But you said just now that you did not know him."

The girl looked confused and made no reply.

The surgeon sent an officer to the bank. His attention returned to the patient, and as his daughter had not made as thorough an examination as he desired, he asked her if she felt strong enough to make another attempt. She complied, but with much hesitation. Again did a sickness and weakness assail her as her finger slipped into the wound, and again did the young man's face brighten. He fixed his eyes on her face, seemingly in recognition, and in a thick, stammering voice, he said:

"Why, Agnes, is it you? So, you are the one—this is what jealousy has done. This is what I get for being his friend."

"Do you blame me, Charles?"

"Why should I? It is too late for that now."

"Does Frank know?"

"He does not; but she is madly in love with him."

"And she is a stranger to you?"

"Absolutely. I never saw her before. I believe he has her in hiding, and that he will shield her."

"But he is not a traitor."

"She may have some unaccountable hold upon him."

"He would not deceive me so."

"Who can tell?"

The excitement which had kept back the encroachment of weakness now failed of purpose.

The girl withdrew her finger, and the young man sank back into his former lethargic condition.

All color fled the girl's face; her eyes were fixed vacantly in a stare of horror.

"Agnes," said her father, approaching her hastily, "what is the matter? Are you faint?"

"I—I don't know, father." She trembled, as though with apoplexy.

"What is all this he has been telling you?" he asked.

She was too far gone to reply, but her father mistook her weakness for hesitation.

"Come into the open air, my child. This repulsive ordeal and the ravings of that delirious man have borne too heavily upon your nerves. Come, my daughter."

Those were his words, but a great dread had arisen within him. As soon as they had stepped without, he pressed the question upon her with a certain hardness which came from his anxiety:

"What does all this mean? What do you know about the shooting?"

Her voice was kept back by a gasp, and with a lurch she slipped from her father's grasp and went all disorganized down to the ground before he could save her. He picked her up, placed her in the buggy, and drove rapidly to his home. When she recovered she found her mother in anxious watch upon her, for her father had gone to see what could be done for the wounded man.

Mrs. Osborne had been informed by her husband of the singular occurrence at the receiving hospital, and the good woman was unhappy over it. But with her usual fair tact she asked no questions, believing that the close understanding between her and her daughter would bring forth an explanation in safe time. She was disappointed, therefore, when Agnes, upon coming into consciousness, spoke no word of the most important matter. More than that, she said she had a grievous headache and desired to be left alone, that she might sleep. Mrs. Osborne withdrew, and immediately the girl went about the task of slipping away from the house unseen. She did this with whole success. In a few minutes she was in the office of a young physician named

Frank Armour.

There was nothing commonplace in this young man's appearance. He was tall, slender, and pale, and to the manifest effects of rigorous study were added evidences of some kind of trouble that was wearing him out. He occupied two rooms—a reception-room and, behind it, a consultation-room. She found him sitting in the front room; the door leading into the other was closed. His face brightened greatly when he saw her standing before him.

"Agnes" he cried; "I am very glad to see you. All loads drop from my shoulders when your sweet face appears. You said the other day that you were not coming to the office any more, for fear people would talk about you—as though that should make any difference, seeing that we are soon to be married!"

His manner was so gentle, so full of evidences of genuine affection, that her suspicions concerning him were much weakened. But she had come to make sure of her position, and the mysteries of the wounded man's speech had to be cleared up.

"Frank," she asked, "have you seen your friend Charles Blanchard today?"

"No; I haven't seen him since last night. By the way, he scolded me again for not taking him around to your house and introducing him to you. Now, really, Agnes, I don't think you ought to keep putting me off about bringing him, as he is really a very delightful man, and I am sure you will like him."

"We will talk about that some other time, Frank. There is something else I want to ask you now. Do you really think you love me and me alone?"

"I am very certain of it, Agnes; but I don't see any reason for such a question."

"I know that you never go into society, and you have told me that you pay attentions to no one except me."

"That is the truth, Agnes; but to save my life I don't understand you. You are pale and ill. Something has happened to give you trouble and you have suddenly become suspicious of me."

Should she tell him of the fatal wounding of his best friend?

Was it not possible first to extort from him some explanation of that friend's singular disclosures? The fact that she had received this knowledge from him—if, indeed, knowledge it was—troubled her greatly. The man had sown distrust in her mind, and it was like poison.

"Frank," she said, presently, unable to see him longer in ignorance of his friend's condition, "Charles Blanchard has been seriously hurt, and I came to tell you so."

"Seriously hurt?" asked Armour, in alarm; "when and how?"

"He was found less than two hours ago and taken to the receiving hospital, where my father is attending him now."

The young physician was now upon his feet, nervous and excited.

"How was he hurt, Agnes? Tell me all about it."

"Nothing is known except that he was found staggering along the street with a pistol wound in the head."

Armour's face was livid, and his trembling legs nearly failed to support his weight.

"He was not killed instantly?" he asked.

"No; but he is unconscious."

"Certainly."

"The bullet must have been a small one."

"No doubt, no doubt!" cried the unhappy man; "I must go to see him at once."

He picked up his hat and was starting away, expecting her to leave the room with him. But she sat still, remarking:

"I will wait until you return, if you promise to come back soon."

Armour's disappointment and annoyance were visibly manifest. He shot a quick glance toward the door of the adjoining room, and then walked over to it and cautiously tried the knob. The door was locked. He made a show of feeling in his pocket for the key, but his whole manner was so openly embarrassed that the sharp-sighted girl noticed it.

"Agnes," said he, turning upon her somewhat impatiently, "there is no doubt I shall be gone a long time, and it would be unreasonable for me to ask you to wait."

"Nevertheless," she said, in rather a hard tone, looking him steadily in the eyes, "I will stay here and wait for you. If you stay away long I will turn on the spring-latch and thus lock the door when I leave."

An evident fear seized upon the young physician. He was anxious to go to his suffering friend, and was unwilling to leave Agnes in his office. She saw all this very plainly.

"And, by the way, Frank," she resumed, "as I am very tired, I will go into the back room and rest on the lounge." She started toward the door, pretending not to have noticed that it was locked, and tried to open it.

"Why, it is locked!" she exclaimed.

Armour's uneasiness had increased to positive suffering.

"Yes—he stammered.

"Is anyone in there?"

"Agnes—Well?"

"You are acting in a strange and unaccountable way today."

"I?" she asked, in great astonishment; "I don't understand you, Frank." Then she walked straight up to him, and, placing her hands on his shoulders, said, with dignity and tenderness: "I merely asked you if there was anyone in the room, and you are offended. Let us be candid with each other, Frank. What does it mean?"

"I may have a patient in that room, and—A low moaning in a woman's voice, indistinctly heard from the inner room, interrupted him. His faced turned scarlet and then pale, and all the time the steady gaze of the surgeon's daughter was upon him. She took her hands from his shoulders, looking much humiliated; and, with a painful sadness which he had never before seen in her conduct, she simply said:

"I don't think it is customary for physicians to lock their patients up; but if I have been rude I beg you to forgive me. I will not annoy you by staying. Goodbye, Frank."

She extended her hand, which he seized eagerly; but she quickly withdrew it and left the room.

He followed her into the passage-way.

"Agnes," he said "you surely don't suspect that"—but she was fleeing down the stairs so rapidly that he could not finish the foolish sentence.

The girl went so quickly along the crowded street that people turned in wonder to look at her.

Her eyes were filled with tears, her face was very pale, and her lips were tightly caught between her teeth. "I never would have dreamed it," she said to herself, over and over; "never, never, never! Oh, it will kill me, it will kill me!" She re-entered her home as secretly as she had left it, flung herself wearily upon her bed, and cried as though her heart was broken.

The police had gone intelligently to work upon the mystery of the shooting. Mr. Blanchard, the father of the wounded man, had arrived, overcome with grief and horror. Dr. Armour, he said, was the only intimate friend his son had. He was entirely unable to suggest any cause for the shooting, which undoubtedly had not been done with a suicidal hand. The police repeated to him all that they could remember of the disjointed and unintelligible conversation between his son and Agnes Osborne, and this account puzzled him sorely. What mysterious blind was there between his son and this young woman? She had denied all knowledge of him, and yet she gave the information of his identity.

When and how had he been her friend, not knowing her? Why had she discovered an anxiety that he should not blame her for the deed that would cost him his life? Why was she desirous of learning from him whether Frank Armour knew anything about the tragedy? Who was this that was madly in love with Armour, and what possible connection could there be between this fact and that of the shooting? Who was the woman referred to in their conversation, and why should Armour keep her in hiding? How could her jealousy of young Blanchard be the moving cause of the desperate assault?

Mr. Blanchard was not the only one who tried to bring some light out of the darkness of all this singular and deplorable transaction. A broken-hearted girl, tossing and weeping on her bed, asked herself these questions, or some of them, many times, and the police were weighing them with all the care and precision of trained hunters of crime, With Dr. Osborne the matter was far more serious than with the police. Lacking his knowledge that the young man's temporary restoration to a state of consciousness was not explainable on ordinary grounds, they did not see the true value of the fact Dr. Osborne reasoned that a wound of that character must necessarily produce a disorganization of the mental functions and present a condition of unconsciousness This had been the case until his daughter had inserted her finger far into the wound, when at once the sufferer's face brightened and a condition resembling consciousness ensued.

Dr. Osborne was too wise to assume that young Blanchard's ability to speak and apparently carry forward a conversation was positive evidence of consciousness, for he knew that the vagaries of a disorganized mind are of unimaginable variety. But this case was unique—nothing in the books or his experience had a suggestion of its form or colour. The whole case was this: His daughter had betrayed fright upon seeing the wounded man at the station, but had recovered from that; and, indeed, her condition might have been construed as one of natural repugnance, overcome by an intelligent direction of the will. It was clear enough so far. When she placed her finger in the edge of the wound there was sign neither of recognition on her part nor consciousness on his; it was only when she had pushed her finger into the brain that those two facts came into existence.

This appeared to the surgeon to be a very strange coincidence. Not only was the young man apparently restored to consciousness, but the two, supposed to have been strangers, recognized each other, and, worse than all else, betrayed a certain ill-defined common knowledge of the crime. All these things threw Dr. Osborne into the most conflicting surmises and brought him into a condition of positive unhappiness. The extraordinary scientific features of the case were overshadowed by his anxieties, His daughter had engaged herself, with his assent, to marry Dr.

Armour, and yet this young physician had been placed in a peculiar light by the words of the dying man. Prolonged thinking brought only wider distraction, and the unhappy father determined to question his daughter, depending on the close sympathy between them to bring the whole truth from her.

It was some time, however, before he could find the opportunity. Mr. Blanchard had removed his son to his home and had retained Dr. Osborne to attend him. When the surgeon had done all that was possible, he went to his home and sought his daughter. But she could not be found.

After nearly crying her heart out upon her return from Armour's office, she got up, brought herself under control, and then realized that she had been treated shamefully by the man whom she loved above all others in the world. It was easy for her grief to become shame and her shame anger. It was not possible for her yet to think seriously upon any plan that might bring suffering or ruin to her lover; but it was within her power to work serious mischief to some mysterious woman who had come between her and him, and this was a matter to be attended to. Accordingly she cleared up her face, made herself very bright and pretty, and went at once to consult the chief of police.

That functionary was vastly surprised to see her. He had been given a full report of the scene at the receiving hospital, and when he saw the girl enter his office looking so bright, confident, and handsome, and announce her name and mission, he was sorely perplexed. In truth, Chief Holloway had certain ideas which would have given Miss Agnes discomfort if she had known of their existence.

"I have come to ask you, Mr. Holloway," she said, "if you have made any discoveries concerning the shooting of Mr. Blanchard."

The officer, somewhat taken aback by her directness, tried, after a heavy fashion, to cover his position under some remarks in which discretion was outlined as a duty. "But this is rather a singular question from you, Miss Osborne, considering that you yourself are supposed to know all about the matter."

The very boldness and brutality of the assault served an excellent purpose; for the girl, not dreaming that her talk with young Blanchard had taken wings, or that anyone suspected her of knowledge, was shocked with surprise.

"What makes you think that?" she quickly asked.

This put him in command of the situation, for he felt his power.

"Your conversation with young Blanchard showed that both you and he know all about it, and then, after you left him you went to see Dr. Armour, who also appears to be pretty badly mixed up in the whole affair."

All this came like a whirlwind, and badly frightened the girl.

"Now," resumed Holloway, "although you have come ostensibly to make inquiries, I think your ultimate purpose was to give some very important information. I should be pleased to hear it."

Agnes caught her breath. "How can I know anything?" she asked, realizing that her time had come, but with a rush that unnerved her; "Mr. Blanchard spoke in a rambling way."

"But he was not as evasive as you are at this moment."

"Evasive? Really, sir——"

"This is no time for by-play." sternly interrupted the officer; "no doubt you understand that you yourself are in a very peculiar position. If what you know would endanger your own safety by your telling it, I can easily understand your feelings."

The sting was felt, but the girl rallied and gave this opinion:

"You said something just now that makes me think you suspect Dr. Armour of having a guilty knowledge of the affair. If you mean by that to charge him with the crime, you are entirely in error."

"But you are careful not to deny that he knows something of importance. Why do you not say openly that you and Armour know who fired the shot, and that you two, possibly for prudential reasons, are doing all you can to conceal your knowledge and shield the criminal?"

The very brutality and directness of the question roused the inmost nature of the girl. With scarlet face and flashing eyes she said:

"If you will come with me, I will show you the murderer."

This was a windfall that Holloway had not dared to hope for. He promptly followed Agnes.

When they had reached the street, she said:

"It will be necessary to see Dr. Armour first, and I think he is at Mr. Blanchard's. We will go there first."

"As you please."

They found both Dr. Amour and Dr. Osborne at the young man's house. The two physicians—-the father and the lover— were vastly surprised so see Agnes and the chief of police walk in together. For her part, Agnes felt so guilty that she could not bear to look Armour full in the face.

She felt that a wild jealousy had led her so take a desperate and dangerous step, the end of which she could not foresee. But did her lover really deserve to be spared? Had he not deceived her shamefully? The young man felt that a high barrier had come between him and Agnes, and hence he had nothing to say to her. Holloway readily saw that a heavy constraint rested upon them both, and it appeared, in his eyes, an important affair.

"Agnes," said her father, taking her by the hand, and looking her anxiously in the eyes, "where have you been?"

"To see Mr. Holloway, father."

"For what purpose?"

"To learn if he had discovered anything."

This was not the place for pressing the matter, and so her father asked her no more questions.

There was a moment of general embarrassment among the four persons in the room, and it was broken by the chief, who asked that in the cause of justice Miss Osborne be permitted to repeat the experiment of inserting her finger in the wound. With surprising alacrity both the physicians objected, saying that the wound had been dressed, that the sufferer was then very low from shock, and that such an experiment would likely have a fatal issue. Holloway smiled in a peculiar manner, and, looking steadily at Armour, added:

"I hardly expected that you would consent."

This thrust cut the young man to the quick, and he shot a look at Agnes that revealed his suspicion of her hand in the policy of the officer.

"Of course I have no desire to increase the young man's danger," remarked Holloway; "but the result of the former experiment was so important that I deemed it advisable to repeat it if possible. However, I think it is hardly necessary. As soon as I had learned all the particulars of that experiment, I laid them before a prominent physician of this city, and requested his written opinion concerning them. I think this is the proper time to inform you concerning it, for several reasons, which will appear later."

Thereupon Holloway read an ingenious paper, only a short extract from which can be set forth here. It is as follows:

Admitting a wide latitude for deception on the part of the young woman, and the possibility of error in your account, the whole affair seems preposterous and not worthy of serious attention. But we shall treat it, not as a fact, but as a hypothetical case." (The hypothesis was here stated in agreement with the reported facts, and this explanation followed:) "The bullet was small, and hence the laceration of the brain matter was not extensive nor the primary shock very great. The unconsciousness observed apparently resulted from the severing of the nerves ramifying throughout the brain and from the rupturing of the innumerable chains of brain-cells in the path of the bullet. These lacerations, by destroying the continuity of the brain texture, disorganized the mind by interrupting the coordination of its functions.

If, now, some plan could have been devised for bringing together the severed ends of tissue in such a manner as would permit of their resuming theft normal occupation of transmitting molecular activity, there is a rare possibility that its employment would have restored consciousness.

216

By a very singular accident, the young woman may have performed that service when she inserted her finger deep into the brain; but, in order for this result to have been accomplished, a most extraordinary series of events must have occurred."

The finger is a sensitive member, from the fact that it contains so large a number of nerves."

These nerves, called peripheral, terminate under a thin cuticle, through which sensation is easily experienced. When her finger was inserted in the brain tissue, her nerve-ends came approximately in contact with the severed nerves of the brain over the entire field of laceration."

Thus the mechanical condition of nerve-continuity was restored in the brain of the wounded man, and consciousness was the result."

But it is evident that the molecular transmission did not occur directly through her finger."

That was not possible, for the reason that her nerves do not run straight through her finger from one side to the other. If we should trace one of these nerves, we should find that, starting at the termination in the finger, it runs up the arm into the brain. A sensation, starting from the end and going to the brain, would there meet and be assimilated by a large number of other sensations, this being the result of coordination. The brain would then decide what action to take, and then would direct the efferent, or outrunning, nerves to move the muscles with a definite purpose. It is clear, then, that the movement of sensation through the wounded man's brain tissue, after the restoration of continuity, must have become communicated to the nervous system of the woman."

In other words, no sensation could pass through his brain without passing through hers also. In this way, their two brains would act largely as one, and the active thoughts of one would be known to the other. By this sort of reasoning we may account for the fact that, although the two persons were strangers to each other, mutual recognition came when the knowledge of both became the possession of each. Hence we must infer that the young woman knows as much concerning the person who did the shooting as does the wounded man himself?

The effect of this extraordinary document can hardly be imagined. From Dr. Osborne it lifted a load that was likely to crush him. But why had not his daughter been candid with him? Now that there no longer could be a fair suspicion that she had any criminal association with the crime, why had she acted in so strange a manner?

Armour's thoughts took a very different turn. His pallor increased until it became alarming, and his knees were unsteady from weakness. The man's agony was so painfully visible that Agnes felt a fearful dread for the end that must come.

The immediate result of all this was that the three men fixed a steady gaze upon her, in which was a commingling of peculiar motives and sensations.

"Miss Osborne," finally said Holloway, "this scientific report leads us to believe that you are fully aware of the identity of the one who fired the shot. In corroboration of these conclusions, you have confessed your knowledge by offering your services to point out the murderer to me. Will you be so kind as to keep your promise?"

All that was womanly in the girl found cause both for alarm and encouragement in this situation. Against her sense of wrong weighed that of tenderness and affection. She found courage to look Armour squarely in the face, hoping to receive some sign that might guide her; but she found—as she read his expression—only contempt and defiance struggling through the cloud of anguish which sat upon him.

"I will keep my promise," she said, with much firmness; "we will now go to Dr. Armour's office."

Besides becoming somewhat more rigid, as though bracing himself to meet some fearful ordeal, Armour betrayed no emotion. Dr. Osborne appeared to be overcome with astonishment and anxiety. Chief Holloway only smiled.

These four went at once to Armour's office in utter silence, each feeling the imminence of a catastrophe. The young physician admitted them into the outer room, and then closed the door.

With great abruptness, he then asked this question:

"Will someone be kind enough to explain the object of this visitation?"

Holloway was on the point of speaking, but Agnes stepped before him, and, looking Armour firmly in the face, said:

"I believe that the person who committed this crime is concealed in your consultation-room. If I am wrong, heaven will punish me as I deserve. So far as I am able to discover, no reason exists why I should pretend to deny the knowledge which I have. The murderer is a woman, and you are concealing and shielding her in that room."

Armour, though pale as death, did not flinch before this accusation. On the contrary, his chest expanded, his eyes flashed, and, with head thrown back, he said: "It was a woman who did the shooting, as I now believe, and it is true that she at this moment is kept in concealment by me in my inner office. I had hoped to be able to conceal her act from the world, for if ever there was an occasion for the exercise of the noblest human traits, it is in the case before us. Let me tell you something—you who mistake suspicion for skill in unearthing crime, and you who are moved by even less worthy motives—crime cannot exist in the absence of accountability. Has it occurred to you to imagine that this woman may not have been responsible for her act?

"Do you know what an epileptic fit is? Surely you do, Dr. Osborne. You are familiar with the strange forms which this disease may take. You know that the sweetest natures are at times wholly perverted by it; that its manifestations are complex and obscure; that sometimes, instead of the violent spasms with which we are all familiar the malady takes the form of mental and physical activity, in which we find an impulse to commit extraordinary acts as the result of monstrous misconceptions. When this condition occurs, all the principles of the victim's nature may be wholly eclipsed, conscience entirely suppressed, and the power to discriminate between right and wrong completely lost. After the attack has passed, there remains no recollection of what was done during its continuance.

"I inform you—and I am able to prove my assertion—that the woman who shot my dearest friend is now in my inner office; that she came to me from a distant city only yesterday to be treated for this very malady; that very soon after her arrival, I informed her, as was my duty and pleasure, that I was engaged to marry a very charming and kind-hearted young lady. It is a breach of delicate confidence on my part to inform you that, in spite of a brave effort to appear glad for my good fortune, she could not conceal a certain unhappiness which I know was perfectly natural, but it is my duty now to tell you everything.

"I now know that the sorrow which my news caused her brought on an attack of what is known as masked epilepsy, to which she is subject. The thing uppermost in her mind was that someone was dearer to me than she was; although normally a woman of unexampled sweetness and goodness, she determined, in her condition of temporary insanity, to kill that person. I need not inform you that she most have started out with the clear purpose of killing the young lady to whom I was affianced. But she knew, also, that young Blanchard was my dearest friend, and, in her wild mental condition, she happened to find him fast, and she fired into his brain the bullet that was intended for another."

The young man paused awhile, but he did not cast a glance at Agnes, who, feeling unaccountably faint as these strange revelations were made, had sunk helpless upon a chair "Mr. Holloway," resumed Armour, "I ask your promise that you will not arrest this woman now, but that you take proper steps to verify my assertions; and as she has recovered from her attack, and has no recollection whatever of the tragedy, you say nothing to her about it now, and that you never mention it to a soul if you find that what I have told you is true.

"I cheerfully give those two promises," said Holloway.

"Then," said Armour, "I will present the lady to you."

With that he went to the door of the inner room, unlocked it, and stepped within. In the next moment he returned, supporting on his arm a pale, sweet-faced, beautiful woman of fifty, in whose sad and gentle face was no trace of the fearful thing she had done. Armour, with his head thrown hack and glowing with all the pride of a gentleman, thus presented her:

"Miss Osborne and gentlemen, I have the honour to make you acquainted with my mother."

LEONAUR

ALSO FROM LEONAUR
AVAILABLE IN SOFTCOVER OR HARDCOVER WITH DUST JACKET

MR MUKERJI'S GHOSTS *by S. Mukerji*—Supernatural tales from the British Raj period by India's Ghost story collector.

KIPLINGS GHOSTS *by Rudyard Kipling*—Twelve stories of Ghosts, Hauntings, Curses, Werewolves & Magic.

THE COLLECTED SUPERNATURAL AND WEIRD FICTION OF WASHINGTON IRVING: VOLUME 1 *by Washington Irving*—Including one novel 'A History of New York', and nine short stories of the Strange and Unusual.

THE COLLECTED SUPERNATURAL AND WEIRD FICTION OF WASHINGTON IRVING: VOLUME 2 *by Washington Irving*—Including three novelettes 'The Legend of the Sleepy Hollow', 'Dolph Heyliger', 'The Adventure of the Black Fisherman' and thirty-two short stories of the Strange and Unusual.

THE COLLECTED SUPERNATURAL AND WEIRD FICTION OF JOHN KENDRICK BANGS: VOLUME 1 *by John Kendrick Bangs*—Including one novel 'Toppleton's Client or A Spirit in Exile', and ten short stories of the Strange and Unusual.

THE COLLECTED SUPERNATURAL AND WEIRD FICTION OF JOHN KENDRICK BANGS: VOLUME 2 *by John Kendrick Bangs*—Including four novellas 'A House-Boat on the Styx', 'The Pursuit of the House-Boat', 'The Enchanted Typewriter' and 'Mr. Munchausen' of the Strange and Unusual.

THE COLLECTED SUPERNATURAL AND WEIRD FICTION OF JOHN KENDRICK BANGS: VOLUME 3 *by John Kendrick Bangs*—Including twor novellas 'Olympian Nights', 'Roger Camerden: A Strange Story', and ten short stories of the Strange and Unusual.

THE COLLECTED SUPERNATURAL AND WEIRD FICTION OF MARY SHELLEY: VOLUME 1 *by Mary Shelley*—Including one novel 'Frankenstein or the Modern Prometheus', and fourteen short stories of the Strange and Unusual.

THE COLLECTED SUPERNATURAL AND WEIRD FICTION OF MARY SHELLEY: VOLUME 2 *by Mary Shelley*—Including one novel 'The Last Man', and three short stories of the Strange and Unusual.

THE COLLECTED SUPERNATURAL AND WEIRD FICTION OF AMELIA B. EDWARDS *by Amelia B. Edwards*—Contains two novelettes 'Monsieur Maurice', and 'The Discovery of the Treasure Isles', one ballad 'A Legend of Boisguilbert' and seventeen short stories to cill the blood.